P9-CDJ-455

WINTER DOOR

Book Two

THE GATEWAY TRILOGY

WINTER DOOR

ISOBELLE CARMODY

RANDOM HOUSE NEW YORK

Copyright © 2003, 2006 by Isobelle Carmody
Jacket art copyright © 2006 by Greg Spalenka

All rights reserved.
Published in the United States by Random House Children's Books,
a division of Random House, Inc., New York. Originally published in Australia
as *The Winter Door* by Penguin Books Australia, Camberwell, in 2003.

RANDOM HOUSE and colophon are registered trademarks of Random House, Inc.

www.randomhouse.com/kids
www.randomhouse.com/teens

Educators and librarians, for a variety of teaching tools, visit us at
www.randomhouse.com/teachers

Library of Congress Cataloging-in-Publication Data
Carmody, Isobelle.
Winter door / Isobelle Carmody.
p. cm. — (The gateway trilogy ; bk. 2)
Originally published: Camberwell, Australia: Penguin Books Australia, 2003.
SUMMARY: When her own world and Valley are threatened with an endless
winter, Rage and her friends seek to stop the powerful Stormlord from using the
despair of others to create the bleak weather.
ISBN 0-375-83018-9 (trade) — ISBN 0-375-93018-3 (lib. bdg.) —
ISBN 0-375-83019-7 (pbk.)
[1. Despair—Fiction. 2. Winter—Fiction.
3. Magic—Fiction. 4. Fantasy.] I. Title.
PZ7.C2176Win 2005 [Fic]—dc22 2005012518

Printed in the United States of America
10 9 8 7 6 5 4 3 2 1
First American Edition

For my nephew John,
brave enough to be gentle

If human lives be, for their very brevity,

sweet, then beast lives are sweeter still.

But sweetest of all is the Mayfly day.

That life, between sunrise and set, is

pure ecstasy.

1

There was a rattle of hailstones against the window.

Rage looked up, startled, but there was nothing to see. Her own reflection got in the way. She went close to the glass, looking through her shadow. Even the gnarled lemon tree that grew right outside the window was invisible. It was so dark that the glass might have been painted black.

The window shuddered under another onslaught, and the lights dimmed for a moment. Rage reached up to pull the curtain closed, wishing her uncle were home. He had left a note saying that he had gone out to check the fences and would not be back until late. That meant he had gone to the far paddocks, where the snow had pulled the fences down. Rage shivered. It wasn't that she was afraid of being alone, but tonight the darkness was so thick that it might have been a black fog or some huge, dark animal prowling the night.

Rage turned the radio on as she set about washing the dishes. The radio announcer said that it was right on five-thirty p.m. and that the news would be coming up after the next song. Then a singer began to wail about being lonely to the sound of a twanging guitar. Rage dried a plate, thinking wistfully of the dishes she had washed whenever Mam cooked up one of her experimental seven-course meals. She thought of the night at the beginning of last spring when Mam had failed to come and get her from school. The way the headmaster's shoulders hunched during the call to check with the police. She had wanted to run away from the room and not hear what he would tell her. But there was no use in running away from bad news.

The news had been of her mother's car accident.

Mam was still in Hopeton General Hospital all these months later. When she had awakened from her long and dangerous coma to the amazement of the doctors and nurses, Rage had thought that it would be a matter of weeks before she would come home. But her mother had continued to grow paler and weaker, and now there was talk about moving her to Leary, where the hospital had better facilities and all sorts of important specialists.

Overhead, thunder cracked and echoed and the music fused into screeching and hissing. Then the radio went dead and the lights went out. Rage groped for the candle and matches that were on the sill in every room, but even as she took them up, the lights came back on. She set the candle in a bottle just the same and laid the matches by it in readiness. This was by far the worst winter since she and her mother had come to Winnoway Farm. In fact, it was the worst winter anyone could *remember*, according to the radio. Mam loved unpredictable, difficult weather. The only thing she didn't care for were the sorts of perfect sunny days that most people seemed to spend their lives wishing for. She said there was no mystery in such days. But after *this* winter,

Rage thought that even Mam might yearn for a simple warm day with a bright, clean sky. Rage wouldn't have bet her life on it, though, because her mother was as unpredictable as the weather she loved.

The radio gave an asthmatic wheeze and came back to life. The announcer spoke in a fuzzy but serious voice about the dangers of black ice on the roads. Then he quoted statistics about how many car accidents had happened since the winter had begun. As he came to the end of the news, the radio screamed and died again.

Rage wiped the sink down, wondering if her mother was watching the storm and longing to be out in it. She had a bed by a window in Hopeton General, but the nurses said that she slept most of the time. Last weekend when Rage had visited the hospital, Mam had been half-dazed. Rage had asked the nurse what was wrong with her. The nurse explained gravely that her mother needed lots of quiet and calm, so they had given her medication to make her sleepy and relaxed.

As usual, Uncle Samuel hadn't been in to see Mam; he just talked to her doctors. In the car on the way home, Rage had told Uncle Samuel what the nurse had said. That was when he had told her about the possibility of moving Mam to the Leary hospital. He said that there were two more serious operations that Mam had to undergo, one on her spine and one on her neck. But first the doctors needed to know why she wasn't getting stronger, and they thought it would be better done at the bigger hospital.

Rage had wanted desperately to tell Uncle Samuel to go in and see Mam. She was sure that if her mother saw her long-lost beloved brother, it would be better for her than a hundred medicines. But the doctors had forbidden any shocks, and Uncle Samuel had told Rage that seeing him would be a shock to her mother, even if it was a good one. After that, there was no point in arguing because Uncle Samuel had spent his whole life rebelling against the things he had been told to do, and he blamed himself for what had happened to Mam. He was now so determined to do what was right, Rage knew she would never be able to convince him that in this case, the right thing might be *not* following the rules. If only there were someone to advise her. In stories there was always a true friend or an old, wise mentor who told you what to do.

Rage glanced over her shoulder at Billy Thunder sprawled on the mat in front of the potbelly stove and wished she could ask him for advice. But there was no telling what the big toffee-colored dog thought now. He seemed content to lie by the fire and to tag along after her or Uncle Samuel. There was nothing to show that he remembered the journey to the magical land of Valley, or that he missed his friends who had stayed there. But how could he have forgotten them? The little syrup-colored Chihuahua, Mr. Walker; the tan-and-white bull terrier, Elle; the neighbor's goat, Goaty; and Billy's own mother, the enormous Bear? She had thought she knew the dogs well before the firecat had lured them all through the enchanted bramble gate, but only after the dogs' trans-formations into part-humans, when they had been able to speak with her, had she understood their true natures. Billy had become the most human, a boy of bright, com-plicated thoughts and clever ideas. Could he really have forgotten how much he had loved to think?

Rage got up and went over to sit beside the dog, angling her back to soak up the warmth radiating from the stove. Billy sighed and laid his head against her. Like all dogs, he knew when someone was unhappy, but how much more than that did he understand? She gently scratched between his shoulder blades. He had told her when he was a boy that it was the place a dog most wanted to be scratched because no matter how he contorted himself, he could not reach it.

"Dogs spend their whole lives with that spot driving them crazy. And humans wonder why they howl at the moon and try to bite the wheels of cars," he had said.

Now he gave an ecstatic yawn and sort of melted sideways onto her knee, one big paw winding slowly in the air. Rage smiled and thought she might be happier if she could just forget all that had happened in Valley, too. Sometimes it felt like she had dreamed it all—her journey in search of a wizard who could give her magic to waken her mother. Except that it *had* happened, because Billy was the only dog left. He might have stayed in Valley with the others, but at the last minute he had jumped through the world gate after Rage, becoming a dog again. For a while after that, he had been a strangely alert and intelligent dog, and she had thought that he remembered everything and was his new self inside the old shape. But as the months passed, he had gone back to being a simple, sweet-natured, boisterous young dog. Rage had discovered that much as she loved Billy as a dog, she missed the keen mind of his human self.

A flash of lightning lit the kitchen through the open curtains. Rage counted. It was not long before the thunder crashed, which meant that the storm was approaching rapidly. It was almost seven now, according to the mantel clock. Rage chided herself for wasting so much time daydreaming. Fortunately, her only homework was to read part of a play called *A Midsummer Night's*

Dream. A troupe of real actors was coming to her school to rehearse and then perform the play. There was an exciting but unconfirmed rumor that some students were going to be invited to perform in it as well.

Rage got up and found her copy of the play in her schoolbag. She had tried to read it on the bus, but it was written in strange old English, with lots of words she didn't understand and had to look up. The bus had jolted so much through the snow that she had put the play aside. Instead, she drifted into a daydream of Valley and the little winged man she had met there named Puck, just like the fairy man in the play.

Now Rage noticed that the playbook was slightly torn. The new librarian would scold her for that. No use saying that Logan Ryder had done it, snatching the book and tossing it into the air. Logan was the school bad boy, but no one would do anything because, short of expelling him, everything that could be done had been done to him, with no effect. Unfortunately, he never did anything bad enough to warrant being expelled. Rage had overheard the music teacher say wearily to another teacher that Logan Ryder was on his fifth family and maybe with luck the next would be in another school district. Rage could not imagine why Logan had been in so many families, but she could well imagine that he wore them out.

He had never bothered with her until the last two months, when he had taken to hanging around and jeering at her. He was always borrowing the books she returned to the library and then telling her the next day how pathetic they had been. Rage was confounded by the purpose of his bullying. She didn't mouth at him or sneer at him. She was neither an A student nor dull-witted, and she was no show-off. And yet the way he had looked, she had felt that for some unknown reason he hated her. The memory of his glittering green gaze made her shiver. She glanced out the small side window at the dark, swirling night, wishing again that she could ask someone's advice. But Mam was too ill, Uncle Samuel too distant, and Billy could no longer talk to her. Then Rage sat up straight and returned to her reading because, after all, wasn't that one of the lessons that she had learned from Valley: that sometimes *no one* could help you?

She had reached a slightly confusing part in the play where everyone was chasing everyone else around in the forest when she heard the front door bang open and shut.

"A bad night," Uncle Samuel said in his deep, scratchy voice when he entered the kitchen. He had already taken off his long oilskin coat and boots, and now he unwound the layers of sweaters and shirts. He set them down along the back of the couch as methodically as Rage always pictured him setting up a solitary camp in the jungle all those years he had been missing. He lowered himself into the deep chair by the fire with a sigh. Rage could almost imagine that, hunched in the seat and turned away, he was her sour, silent grandfather.

"The fences are worse than I thought," he said. "Can't wait until spring or there will be nothing left to repair. I'll start tomorrow if it's not snowing." He fiddled with the radio dial.

Rage put the kettle on and made a pot of very strong, very hot tea. Then she sat down to her homework because she had the feeling that it would annoy him if she scuttled out of his sight every time he appeared. She stayed there for another ten minutes, pretended to yawn, then got up. She poured a mug of the tea and pushed sugar and milk close to the big hand resting on the snowy tablecloth, wishing that she could sit at her uncle's feet and ask if he had seen storms like this in the jungles.

As she gathered her books, the radio announcer began to talk about the roads again, speculating about the cause for the extreme weather. Rage murmured that she was going to bed and stood up. From the doorway, she cast one last glance back at Uncle Samuel hunched in the chair, then closed the door quietly between them.

Billy Thunder had risen with her, and now he nudged at her leg as she set the bag of schoolbooks on the hall sideboard. Rage slipped her feet into her gum boots before opening the outside door to let him out. Standing on the step with her arms wrapped around her, she watched Billy disappear into the dense darkness. Teeth chattering, she opened her mouth to call him back, but a buffeting surge of wind sucked the breath out of her. A few flakes of half-formed snow whirled out of the blackness to land against her cheeks, and suddenly she had the eerie feeling that she was being watched.

She told herself it was ridiculous to imagine someone peering at her from the darkness, for who on earth could be out in weather like this? Even so, she wanted to go back in, but where was Billy now?

Suddenly he bounded out of the night, and Rage gave a squeal of fright. The dog gave her a puzzled look as he slipped past her, but she was too shaky to do more than turn and fumble the door open and stagger inside. She leaned back against the closed door and gave an unsteady laugh. When her heartbeat had returned to normal, she checked her books for the next day, and she polished the white salt maps off the toes of her school boots.

In the bathroom, her eyes in the mirror were still big and dark from the fright she had given herself, but she ignored them as she washed her face and brushed her teeth. On impulse, she opened the other side of the bathroom cabinet and took out a slim bottle of Mam's homemade violet-petal perfume and sprayed it over her arms.

In her bedroom, Rage switched on the lilac lamp at her bedside and put on her pajamas. Leaving Billy to arrange himself on the rug, Rage climbed into bed and snuggled down under the covers with a sigh. To her surprise, Billy padded over to the bed and rested his head on the coverlets. His eyes glowed darkly in the light of the lamp as he looked at her. She reached out and patted his silky ears with a feeling of terrible sadness.

The smell of violets rose from her skin and she blinked back tears. "I love you, Billy Thunder. No matter what form you are in," she whispered.

Just for a second, the sharp intelligence was there again. *What is wrong?* he seemed to be asking.

She wished that she could tell him and that he could answer her. *Oh, no you don't,* she commanded herself, realizing she had almost slipped back into her memories again. She patted Billy and told him firmly to lie down. She closed her eyes and slept, dimly aware of the storm battering the house.

Rage gazed over the long dam. It had once been a magnificent wilderness owned by Grandfather's brother, her great-uncle Peter, before he had become a wizard and abandoned their world for one of his own making. She had been to the dam a few times since returning from Valley. She had tried to imagine it as green and vibrant as it must have been before the government flooded it. It was impossible to believe that only a thin curtain of magic separated the dam from Valley. The water shimmered like pale pink satin in the afternoon light. Long, narrow shadows of the drowned trees that poked out of the water lay in charcoal slashes across it. Perhaps in the parallel magical world of Valley, these very trees were flourishing.

Beside her, Billy growled, and Rage automatically dropped her hand to his collar. In the same moment, she realized that the dam ought to have been frozen and bordered by snowy hills. Then she saw what Billy was growling at, and her mouth fell open in surprise. For sitting on a bare, flat stone right at the edge of the water was a tiny hourglass, the very same hourglass that Rage had carried during her whole perilous journey through Valley. But this could not be *that* hourglass, no matter how much it looked like it, because that hourglass had shattered on the shore of the Endless Sea.

This is just a dream, she thought.

"Jusst a dream," sneered the slinky, sulfurous voice of the firecat.

"If *you're* in my dream, then it must be a nightmare," Rage said coldly.

"Nassty ragewinnoway," the voice accused.

"Go away," Rage said crossly. No wonder that Billy was growling. None of the animals had ever trusted the wretched creature, and their instincts had been right.

"Sstupid ragewinnoway," the firecat said.

"I thought I told you to go away," Rage snapped.

The air by the dam shimmered and distorted, and Rage squinted her eyes against the hot brightness as the firecat appeared. It was impossible to look at it properly. All Rage could make out was a suggestion of slitted red cat's eyes, radiant with fury above needle-sharp teeth.

"Firecat bringing warning!" it sizzled at her.

"You ought to warn me about yourself," Rage retorted, turning away with deliberate rudeness, though she was careful to keep the firecat in the edge of her sight. No telling what it was capable of doing. Billy was still growling and his hackles were up, so Rage kept a firm grip on his collar. He might get burned if he attacked.

"Sstupid dogboy," the firecat hissed. "Why sstaying him in that sstupid shape?"

"He can't be a boy in my world," Rage said coldly. "Go away, or I will let him bite you."

"Wizard needing ragewinnoway," the firecat snarled urgently.

Rage pointed at the hourglass. "Have you managed to trap him again? How clever of you! Where am I supposed to take him this time? Not to the shore of the Endless Sea again? Maybe to the bottom of the bottomless ocean? Or to the next-to-last star?"

There was a long silence. Long enough for Rage to reflect that she was silly for getting mad with a dream.

"Firecat . . . needing wizard," the firecat spat with such furious anguish that in spite of herself, Rage was touched. "Can bringing you to him!" it added eagerly, as if it felt her weakening.

Her heart hardened at this familiar offer. "I know this is a dream, but even in a dream I'm not going anywhere with you. And I honestly don't care enough about your master to want to help him if he has gone and got himself into trouble again." Rage was startled to hear the strength of her dislike of the wizard in her words.

The firecat made a sound of spitting fury and frustration. "If not caring for wizard, maybe caring for your sstupid world, sstupid ragewinnoway."

A bell began to ring insistently and the dream slipped away. "I am waking . . . ," she murmured.

"Yesss! Waking to nightmare, sstupid ragewinnoway," the firecat snarled after her.

Rage groped to silence the clamoring alarm clock and sat up, blinking into the darkness. She had left the lamp on and she needed it. Daylight in midwinter usually lasted no more than three or four hours, but lately even that had been hidden behind storm clouds. Rage could not remember the last time she had seen a blue sky. She resisted the temptation to snuggle back down under the covers, knowing that she had no time to dawdle.

The school bus that usually picked up the remote farm students had been unable to come for the last month because of the snowy roads. Mrs. Marren from a few farms over had been taking Rage to town with her own children. Mrs. Marren always honked even as she was braking to a halt at the bottom of Winnoway drive, and she was cross if Rage did not come out immediately. Rage could hardly blame her because the minute the car stopped, the twins would be out of their seat belts and trying to kill one another. The only person who had any influence over them was their sister, Anabel, a scary fourteen-year-old who painted her nails and lips black and wrote bad, flowery poems full of death and violence.

Rage had set her alarm an hour earlier than usual

because the day before, Mrs. Marren had told her that she would no longer bring the car up the hill road to the gate of Winnoway farm. It was too steep and slippery. Rage dressed and washed quickly. She took money to buy lunch and grabbed a banana instead of banging around in the kitchen. Switching off her bedroom heater and giving Billy a hug goodbye, she pulled on her coat and scarf in the hall, slung her schoolbag over her shoulder, and stepped into her boots before slipping outside. It was so dark that she stopped on the step for a moment, wondering if she was imagining that it was darker than the day before.

Pulling up the hood on her coat and sinking her mouth in her scarf to cut the icy bite of the air in her throat, Rage made her way along the snowy path. Even before she reached the gate, the soles of her feet began to feel numb. She had grown so much the last couple of months that she didn't fit into her good hiking boots or her thick coat anymore.

Opening and closing the farm gate behind her carefully, Rage picked her way cautiously down the steepest part of the road. The sky was just beginning to lighten to blue-black at the horizon when she reached the main road. Pushing her gloved hands inside her coat and under her armpits, she stomped back and forth, hoping that Mrs. Marren would be her usual punctual self.

A wolf howled.

Startled and incredulous, Rage stopped and listened until the sound faded. Everyone knew there were wolves in the high mountains of the range that ended in the hills above Hopeton, but they never came down so low. She squinted into the gritty dimness, trying to spot any movement. Wolves didn't often attack humans, preferring to target sheep and goats and domestic pets, but who knew what this long, bitter winter might drive them to do?

The wolf howled again, and this time others answered. Rage felt the hair on her neck prickle. It sounded as if the wolves, if they really were wolves and not stray dogs, were some distance away, but snow could distort sound, making faraway things sound close and close things sound far.

"When in danger, have courage and do what you can," she remembered the stern, husky voice of the witch Mother from Valley saying. The voice didn't summon up any courage, but it did provoke the stubborn part of herself that Rage had discovered in Valley. Floundering awkwardly through the deep snow to a small stand of trees, she hung her schoolbag on a knot alongside the lowest branch of the nearest tree, then turned to face the road. If Mrs. Marren came, she could quickly run back to the signpost marking the hill road, and if wolves did appear, she could climb the tree.

She heard the howling again, but all at once the arc of car headlights dipped over the curve of the road. With a yelp of relief, she grabbed her bag and hurried back to the gate. Until she climbed into the warm, messy interior of the Marrens' Range Rover, she did not realize how cold she was. The warmth of the car made her feel slightly sick, though she was glad of it. She felt the bright, unfriendly gaze of Anabel Marren.

"What were you doing over by the trees?" she demanded.

"Sometimes I put crusts in a holder we hung on that tree for the birds and squirrels," Rage said truthfully enough.

"Put your seat belt back on properly, Anabel dear," Mrs. Marren admonished as they pulled away from the curb.

"You're weird," Hugh Marren announced, leaning forward to look past his twin brother at Rage. The twins' faces were puffy and greenish in the dash light, and the fact that they were identical made Rage feel that she had stepped into a science fiction movie about cloning.

"And your uncle is weird," Isaac added. The twins watched with interest to see how Rage would react to the jibes.

"Boys!" Mrs. Marren said, glancing backward. The car swerved dangerously.

"It's okay, Mrs. Marren," Rage said. "I guess anyone who explores jungles is bound to seem a bit strange to people."

"Your whole family is strange, my dad says," Hugh reiterated.

"*Hugh-ey!*" Mrs. Marren shrieked and aimed a wild slap backward toward her son. It missed Hugh but got Isaac, who began to shriek as his mother fought to bring the car out of a fishtail skid. "Don't mind them, Rebecca Jane," Mrs. Marren added when she had the car back on the correct side of the road.

"Jesus, Mum, don't call her Rebecca Jane," Anabel said. "It's so lame. It makes you sound like one of the Waltons. Good night, Rebecca Jane! Good night, Jim Bob!"

"Anabel, please don't swear, darling," Mrs. Marren said. "Rebecca Jane, you don't mind me calling you that, do you? After all, it *is* your real name."

Rage made an anonymous sound and tensed up, knowing that the next inevitable step in the conversation would be for Mrs. Marren to say something about her mother using such a horrible nickname instead of her real name. Then she would ask about Mam's health. Rage felt that she truly could not bear to talk about her mother to Mrs. Marren just now. Help came from an unexpected quarter as Anabel said accusingly to her mother, "You don't believe in God and neither do I, so how could it be swearing to say *Jesus?*"

"It's disrespectful, darling," Mrs. Marren said primly, diverted from her interrogation of Rage.

"Disrespectful to what? Someone's imaginary friend?"

"Anabel! I hate to hear you talk in this dreadful, cynical way."

Isaac's yowls were tapering off, now that his mother was ignoring him. Suddenly he gave his twin a look of spiteful inspiration and reached out to drag savagely on his tow-colored hair. Hugh screamed and the pair began to kick and pummel one another. Laying her cheek against the freezing glass, Rage watched her pale image run unevenly across the undulating ice blue of the snowy, deserted fields and half-obscured stands of trees they passed, wondering again why the winter should be so long and savage this year. Could it really have something to do with the world's weather changing, as the geography teacher claimed?

"If this keeps up, there will be *no* videos tonight," Mrs. Marren threatened. "So tell me, Rebecca Jane, how is your uncle's book coming along?"

"Fine, I guess," Rage said, not liking this subject, either. Why did adults think it was their right to ask you about everything? Except Uncle Samuel, who didn't ask her anything at all. On their first night together at Winnoway, her uncle had begun to open mysterious-looking crates and sewn-up packages. He had shown her a whole pile of stained and battered leather-bound notepads held together by rubber bands, saying they were notes for a book about rare plants. But Uncle Samuel had barely touched Mam's battered portable typewriter since his return. After the doctor had told him it would be better if he did not see Mam yet, he had thrown himself into the farm maintenance. "Catching up" he called it. But somehow he had never got to his own work, and that seemed a bad sign to Rage.

"Rage?"

There was an irritated note in Mrs. Marren's voice. To Rage's relief, the twins began to exchange crude words before she could be reproached for her inattention. The lecture on bad language lasted noisily all the way to the outskirts of town, where she and Anabel got out.

"She won't punish them," Anabel sneered, twisting up a black lipstick and smoothing it onto her lips. "Not getting videos would mean she'd have to entertain them. She'd rather have two little television zombies."

Rage felt acutely uncomfortable. When she had first started getting rides with the Marrens, she and Anabel had not spoken to one another at all. But lately Anabel had taken to talking whenever they were alone. Like her mother, Anabel made conversation consisting of questions, and Rage's every instinct was to say as little as she could.

On impulse, when she heard Anabel draw breath to speak again, Rage suddenly launched into a long and intentionally dull retelling of a story told by a girl at school. She went on as long as she could, praying that someone else would turn up, but she couldn't see even one soul in either direction in the street. It would have been easy to imagine that they were the only two people in all the world. Finally, she came to an abrupt halt, aware that she did not even know what her last words had been.

Anabel was staring at her. "Your uncle is not the only weird one," she said, but in a less nasty voice than usual.

"Weird," Rage echoed, having lately discovered that saying the other girl's words back to her was the quickest way to end a conversation.

"You wouldn't see it because you're weird, too," Anabel continued, the edge back in her voice.

Without thinking it through, Rage turned to the older girl. "What do you want from me, Anabel?"

The older girl actually looked comically startled, her mouth making a black, moist O. Her tongue looked very red inside that black circle. Then her eyes narrowed to slits. "What makes you think *I* want anything from *you*, Miss think-yourself-better-than-everyone-else? You're not, you know. Being weird is *not* being better. My mother takes you to town because she pities you!"

"I don't think I'm better than anyone," Rage said indignantly.

"Yes you do. You act so perfect, but everyone knows you did something to those dogs of yours that disappeared," Anabel accused.

Rage said nothing. This was not the first time Anabel had made sinister references to the disappearance of Bear, Elle, and Mr. Walker. Rage knew that there were horrible rumors at the school, and she suspected that Anabel had begun them. Several times the older girl had gotten other school kids to offer suggestions about what Rage might have done with the dogs.

The bus groaned around the corner, and instead of

standing back to let Anabel enter first as she usually did, Rage climbed into the warmth and took the seat right behind the bus driver. It was against Anabel's cool creed to sit anywhere near the front of the bus. Usually Rage sat three or four rows back, but she felt too tired to care where she sat.

It took just over an hour to get to school in normal weather by bus, but today it had taken almost two hours and they were yet to arrive. It felt to Rage as if she had already lived through a long, hard day, and it had not even properly begun. "And there'll probably be another storm tonight," she muttered to herself. Recognizing Goaty's doom-mongering voice, she grinned and corrected herself. Not *Goaty*. *Gilbert*. Elle had given Goaty his longed-for real name shortly before they had all parted. How Rage missed them: Elle's bright, strong courage, Mr. Walker's odd combination of sharpness and dreaminess, Gilbert's exaggerated gloominess, Bear's powerful presence. She wondered if they had stayed the same or if Valley had further changed them. Except for Bear, who had already changed beyond belief.

Sighing, Rage pushed Valley from her mind yet again as the bus lurched to a stop in front of the school.

Despite everything, the morning went quickly with classes she liked, then there was lunchtime, and she spent it in the library reading *A Midsummer Night's Dream*. For once, it neither snowed nor rained, but she overheard one of the teachers saying the worst so far was coming on the weekend.

When she went to her final class of the day, English, she was relieved to find Logan Ryder was absent. Mrs. Gosford told them to take out their copies of

A Midsummer Night's Dream and led them swiftly into a discussion. The kids were soon complaining about the language.

"It's too hard," one of the boys said.

Another boy said, "It's how they talk. By the time you figure out what they're saying, you forget what the last person said. Why can't they just say things straight out?"

Mrs. Gosford sighed. "Look, let's just read a little aloud, and I'm sure you'll find it less complex than you think. I assume you all read through at least some of the play as I asked?" Her brown eyes passed skeptically around the roomful of nodding kids, and Rage tried to hide a smile. Unfortunately, the teacher caught it. "Rage? Perhaps you would start? Don't worry too much about meaning at this point. Just try to savor the words. See how they feel in your mouth."

Feeling hot with embarrassment, Rage flicked through the pages. The book fell open at some of Puck's lines, which she had been reading at lunchtime. She thought she had a reasonable grasp of what they meant, and so she said softly, "This is from one of Puck's speeches."

"Stand up and read," Mrs. Gosford suggested with an encouraging smile. "Remember, Puck is a powerful though comic figure. He is one of the fairy folk, but he aligns with humans. He is *touched* by them. Go on, Rage." She was one of the few teachers who had liked Rage's mother and hence called Rage by the name Mam had used.

Rage stood, and at that moment the door banged open and Logan Ryder entered.

"Sit down, Logan," the teacher said.

"Don't you want to hear my excuse?" Logan asked insolently. He towered over the teacher, and he was close enough that she had to look up at him.

"No, Logan. Not now. I will hear anything you want to say after the class. We are looking at *A Midsummer Night's Dream.*"

"Sure, ma'am, but I dunno 'bout this fairy book you got us reading," Logan said loudly in a mock southern accent as he slouched into his seat.

Rage was relieved to be waved down.

Mrs. Gosford said, "Look, perhaps some of you feel that Shakespeare has nothing to offer because it was written and is set in another age and because there are, at least in this play, elements of fantasy. But the reason Shakespeare's writing is classic is precisely because it rises above the time for which and in which it was written. It transcends. *Transcends!*" she repeated exultantly. "It speaks so deeply about its subjects that it goes beyond the present and the past and even the future to speak to all ages. Shakespeare wrote about love and jealousy and fear and anger and worship and betrayal. Those are universal human concerns, things we will all have to face in our lifetime, and entering these plays and words gives us ways to think about them as issues."

"But what about the fairies?" Logan asked very seriously.

That made a lot of the kids laugh, and even Mrs. Gosford smiled a bit, but she didn't let it go too far. "I can see you have a problem with fairies, Logan, and maybe you and I can discuss that after class. All I will say is that fairy tales and myths in certain works represent deep philosophical truths, or they are at least an attempt to grapple with such truths. They represent things that we can think and talk about, but not see and touch and hear and smell. Puck and the other fairy folk represent another way of seeing the world and how it works."

Rage crossed her fingers, but the teacher's eyes only turned back to her. "One of Puck's speeches, you said, Rage?" Mrs. Gosford prompted.

Rage stood again slowly and prayed that the bell would go, or that there would be some announcements that would take them through to the end of the period. Or that there would be a fire drill. Or a bomb scare. Or maybe she could just have a heart attack.

"Go on, Rage," the teacher said.

Rage began. She had planned to stumble and mumble so badly that Mrs. Gosford would get impatient and take over reading herself. Instead, once she started reading the words aloud, she was struck by how much easier it was to understand them when you did that. She imagined that she was the Puck she knew from Valley, with his devotion to the witch Mother, declaiming in the grove in the Place of Shining Waters.

"Bravo!" the teacher cried when Rage came to the end of the speech, and applauded rapturously. The other kids clapped, too, and Rage felt the blood rise to her cheeks, realizing that she had made a spectacle of herself—and in front of Logan Ryder. She did not need even to look at him to feel his hatred.

There was a knock at the door and Rage was infinitely relieved—until she saw with dismay that the longed-for visitor was awful Mrs. Somersby. She had disliked the woman since she had tried to bully the Johnsons into putting Rage into a state children's home after Mam's accident. Rage sank deep into her seat, hiding herself behind Harry Galloway.

"Class," Mrs. Gosford said after a quiet word with Mrs. Somersby, "I am afraid we have to end the session a fraction early. I'd like you now to give your attention to Mrs. Somersby, who is the community liaison with the child welfare agency for Hopeton."

Mrs. Somersby began to speak in her commanding voice about, of all things, the weather. "Class, I do not need to tell you that the dreadful weather this winter has brought this part of the country to its knees. Many of the public bus routes are out of use, and several school buses have been cancelled. Parents have been keeping their children home several days each week, or driving them in the most hazardous conditions. The council, the school committee, and the child welfare organization for our region have sought other means of enabling children from remote parts to attend school."

Mrs. Somersby held up a piece of green paper. "This sheet is to be taken home by students who live outside the town limits. It explains that a program is being set up to allow these children to live in town during the week and, in some cases, for the remainder of the winter. All other students should take home the pink sheet, which explains the aims of the program in the hope that parents in town will consider offering space in their homes to rural students. The forms on the bottom of both notes should be returned tomorrow. I know it is short notice, but the situation is grave. If there are any questions, your parents or guardians"—her eyes touched on Rage and her mouth twitched in distaste—"can call me using the number at the bottom of the sheet. I will be home this evening and tomorrow morning, and there will be a parents' meeting before the weekend."

Mrs. Somersby nodded to Mrs. Gosford, who began

to distribute green and pink sheets. As Rage ran her eyes over her own green sheet, she could feel Mrs. Somersby's eyes boring into her. Of course, there was no way that she would show the notice to her uncle, because he might be glad of the chance to hand responsibility for her over to someone else.

After everything that had happened in English, Mrs. Marren's news that Anabel was staying in town that night was such a relief that Rage had to fight not to smile as she climbed into the car. It meant a peaceful trip home and again the next morning. Or as peaceful as a trip could be with the twins at one another's throats.

Only when she was inside did she see that Mrs. Johnson was in the front seat. The old woman greeted Rage fondly and explained that Mrs. Marren was giving her a lift home to save Mr. Johnson the trip down to town when he was feeling poorly. Rage was delighted. Not only would Mrs. Marren be too busy gossiping to ask her usual questions, but she would be bound to take them right up to the top of the hill road.

Tuning out the bickering of the twins, Rage gazed out the window. Her ears pricked up when Mrs. Marren said that if the roads got any worse, she would keep the twins home the next day. Rage hoped the weather would be bad because Uncle Samuel would surely let her stay home if Mrs. Marren was keeping the twins home. She liked school usually, but the thought of not having to see Anabel, Mrs. Marren, the twins, or Logan Ryder and curling up all day by the fire reading, cuddled up with Billy, made her hope for a blizzard. Then she thought that if the weather really turned worse, she and her uncle might be unable to see Mam on the weekend.

Rage crossed her fingers hastily to cancel out the previous wish and substituted one for clear, perfect weather for the next four days.

Rage helped Mrs. Johnson from the car when they arrived. She thanked Mrs. Marren, hoping that she would offer to come up to the top of the road in the morning, but Mrs. Marren merely reminded Rage to make sure she was down in time. "I'll call your uncle if the weather is too bad to go in," she added.

The wind had dropped, and on their way up the Johnsons' path, Mrs. Johnson said, "I visited your mam this morning, Rage. Poor thing looks so weak even after all this time." The wind gave a shriek as they came onto the verandah, and Mrs. Johnson shuddered. "It fair chills my blood to hear the wind moan like that. Sometimes you could swear it was something alive."

She opened the door and held it ajar for Rage, who was carrying Mrs. Johnson's overnight case and grocery bags as well as her own schoolbag. Entering the familiar, dim-lit hallway with its faded cherry carpet and striped wallpaper, Rage was startled how small and shabby it looked. Nevertheless, she had a strong impulse to turn up the hall and go into the little bedroom she had stayed in when Mam had first been in hospital. Instead, she set down the case and her schoolbag and took the shopping bag into the kitchen, where she began automatically to unpack it.

"No need to do that, dear," Mrs. Johnson said, looking pleased and plugging in the teakettle. "Oh well, you do that for me, and I'll make us a nice cup of tea and butter some scones. I don't suppose your house will be warm with your poor uncle out mending the fences. Mr. Johnson said on the phone that he went out this morning, even though the weather was so bad."

"He puts the oil heater in my bedroom on, and the fire will be ready to light," Rage assured her.

"Oh, I know your uncle takes fine care of you, no matter what anybody says to the contrary. But I just want to remind you that you are welcome here any time. Truth to tell, I missed you something awful when you left, though you only went back next door. The house felt a mite emptier. Even Mr. Johnson said so."

Rage was touched by the thought that the bad-tempered old farmer might have missed her. On the other hand, his missing her could just as easily be something that Mrs. Johnson had dreamed up. Smiling a little, Rage put the milk in the fridge and the apples in a bowl, just as she had done in the past. Then she sat down and gladly wrapped her cold hands around a mug of tea as Mrs. Johnson carried a tray to Mr. Johnson, who was sick in bed.

Left alone, Rage dug into her pocket and took out Mrs. Somersby's green form. If she didn't take it back tomorrow, signed by Uncle Samuel, Mrs. Somersby would telephone. That was the sort of woman she was. If *Rage* signed it for her uncle, saying they were not interested, there was still a possibility that Mrs. Somersby would ring to argue. Uncle Samuel almost never answered the telephone, but if he was in the kitchen when the call came, it might be awkward saying he wasn't around.

Her head began to ache as it always did when her thoughts went in circles for too long. She was glad to have them interrupted by Mrs. Johnson returning and preparing a plate of scones and jam. "It just came to me, Rage, dear. Why don't you stay for dinner tonight if your uncle is out? I have a nice pie from the bakery in town, and it will be more than enough since poor Henry says he doesn't feel up to more than broth."

Rage hesitated, then shook her head. "I had better not tonight, Mrs. Johnson. I have a lot of homework to do, and Uncle Samuel said he would leave something out for me."

"You are a good girl, Rage," Mrs. Johnson said, passing the scones. "So mature and considerate of other people. You've grown up such a lot since you stayed with us. Of course, kiddies do grow up fast when they have to cope with such awful things as you have had to bear, and you *were* very young for your age." She blinked and dabbed at the corner of her eyes with her apron. "Let me wrap up some of those scones for your uncle, then. Skin and bone is all he is and that's a shame in a man. Of course, he would be better fed with a wife, but I suppose he didn't meet many likely young ladies in the jungle?"

Rage smiled at Mrs. Johnson's old-fashioned ideas about men and women and shrugged.

"You'll be going down to see poor Mary this weekend as usual?" Mrs. Johnson asked.

Mary was Mam's name, and Rage had to swallow a hard lump before she could speak. "It will depend on the weather."

"How terrible to have to deal with this winter on top of all of your troubles, my dear!" Mrs. Johnson crooned. "I really thought that poor Mary would heal once she woke from that coma, but they do say these things take time."

Rage rose to go home, thanking the older woman for her hospitality. She pulled on her thin coat and collected her bag before slipping out into a cold, dark night. It was swirling with wind and wet snow, but Rage was too busy thinking about Mrs. Johnson's observation that she had grown up a lot to notice.

Rage opened the door of Winnoway homestead to find Billy waiting inside the door. She knelt and put her arms around him, hugging him for a long moment and nuzzling her cold face into his silky fur. Then she stood and flicked on the hall light. Billy followed closely when she padded along to the door leading to the kitchen and sitting room. It was freezing cold in the kitchen, but the fire was set up and it caught at once when she put a match to it. She watched the flame lick along the edges of the crumpled newspapers as she sank to the floor and pulled an old shawl of Grandmother Reny's around her shoulders. Billy came and sat beside her, radiating his usual warmth. She thought of Anabel Marren and Logan Ryder and wondered what it was about her that so provoked them. Mrs. Somersby seemed to dislike her, too. Was she really so weird?

A picture came into her mind of Mam, who had never fitted anyone's idea of a mother. Very slight, and younger than most of the other mothers, she had seemed more like an older sister. She wore her glossy black hair short and spiky, and she dressed in dark clothes and flat shoes. People could never imagine that Rage was her daughter because Rage was so blond. The only thing they had in common was their amber-colored eyes. Winnoway eyes—the same color as Uncle Samuel's eyes and the wizard's.

Billy licked her, dragging her out of her memories. Then he trotted to the door and gave her a meaningful look over his shoulder. She laughed shakily, remembering that he needed to go out after being locked inside for half the day. Once she opened the back door and Billy trotted out, Rage went back to the kitchen. Her uncle had left a casserole out on the sideboard. One prod at it told her that it was still more than half frozen. Shrugging, she put the casserole into the oven on a low temperature. Then she switched on the radio and set about ironing her shirt for school the next day.

The wind was howling again, and snow flew hard against the window glass by the time she sat down to eat. Despite the delicious smell, she found that she had little hunger. In the end, she scraped most of the food into Billy's dish. She switched the radio off while she did math homework, and then on again as she washed the dishes. Rage barely heard what was being said until someone began to speak about the death of an expensive stud mare on a farm in the next valley.

". . . Initial reports suggest a wolf pack is responsible, but there are some inconsistencies . . . police are investigating a number of . . ." The voice crackled into gibberish and Rage threw down the tea towel and hurried to adjust the antenna. ". . . the weather conditions . . . ," an older man said suddenly. *An expert*, Rage supposed. A long crackle of static smothered his voice, and then another man's voice came on, slow and uncertain. *A farmer*, Rage thought. ". . . telling you them things I saw warn't no wolves . . . never seen no wolf with . . . have you, mister?"

The announcer came back. "That was Mr. Edmund Brewster from Brewster Fresh Eggs, who claims that . . ." Again the crackle drowned his voice, and then the radio fell silent. Seconds later the phone rang. Rage answered, one hand pressed against her chest to feel her heart knocking against her ribs. It was Mrs. Marren ringing to confirm that she would be driving in the morning, as she had just heard that the weather would clear the next day. Rage thanked her and rang off. She had barely replaced the receiver when it rang again.

"Mrs. Marren?" she asked.

The voice that answered was a male voice. "Can I speak to Rebecca Jane Winnoway?"

"I'm Rebecca Jane," Rage said, mystified. "Who is this?"

"Ah'm Rebeccah-jay-ne?" A voice echoed her words and puzzled tone, but the mockery underneath was familiar.

"Logan?" Rage asked incredulously.

"Ah well, that would be telling. But let me give you a warning. Watch your back." She almost laughed, hearing such stupid gangster movie dialogue in Logan Ryder's voice, except there was nothing funny about being hated.

"What is the matter with you?" she whispered.

"*Me?*" Logan snarled, going back to his own voice. "There's nothing wrong with me. *I'm* normal. You're the one! Never talking to anyone and reading Shakespeare in your prissy little voice. What a suck! Making that stupid fat cow of an English teacher clap. Making me look like an idiot. You think you're so special!"

Rage was astounded both by the viciousness in his voice and upon hearing again that she thought herself better than other people. "I don't—" she began, but the phone on the other end of the line slammed down. As she replaced the receiver, she noticed that her hands were shaking. "I *don't* think I'm special!" she said aloud.

But the words of the witch Mother floated through her mind. "*There is one here among us. . . . Child you are, Rage Winnoway, and more than that, too . . . I did not speak idly before when I said that upon you rests our only hope."*

Rage frowned and wondered if that was it. What had happened in Valley *had* made her feel different from other people; how could it not? And maybe it was her awareness of being different that Logan and Anabel saw as pride and conceit. Neither of them had paid any attention to her before she had gone to Valley. But knowing the reason for a problem, and solving it, were not the same thing.

Rage felt tired and lonely and close to tears again.

She had tried so hard not to lose herself in memories of Valley, but not thinking about it was like constantly holding something in one hand and trying to do everything with the other. And it was all the harder because the sicker Mam became, the more Rage's thoughts escaped there. Going to Valley hadn't saved Mam before. But so many important things had happened there to change Rage, and turn her into the person who had been able to wake Mam, that part of her insisted that if she could only go back, maybe she would figure out another way to help Mam. But the wizard had closed the gate as he had promised to do.

"You can't go back," she told herself aloud.

2

Rage was standing by the dam, only now it was winter, and snow was flying. She half expected to dream of the firecat, but instead, she heard the sound of howling in the high, distant hills.

"That doesn't sound like a wolf," she murmured.

"It doesn't smell like one, either," Billy said, and Rage whirled to find him standing beside her in his human form, frowning and staring up at the hills.

"Billy!" she cried, hurling herself at him.

He gave a laugh and his arms went around her as they stumbled backward and went sprawling in the snow. Rage hugged him and kissed him, delirious with joy. She noticed with a little shock that he looked older—more young man than boy now, but was that possible when less than a year had passed?

Suddenly shy, she pulled away from him and got up, brushing off her clothes.

But as they stood up, a wave of joy flowed through her again and she caught his hands in hers. "Oh, Billy, you can't imagine how glad I am to be able to talk with you again!"

"I have tried to come to you in this form, but you would never let me come except as a dog."

Rage gaped at him. "What do you mean I wouldn't let you come? Isn't this a dream?" she asked.

"Oh yes," Billy said easily. "Dreams are dreams, and you can't mistake them for anything else."

"But then what do you mean by saying I wouldn't let you come?"

Billy didn't answer. He was looking around at the frozen hills under their snowy pelt and at the dam. He lifted his chin and gave the air a serious sniff. "The cold smells wrong," he murmured.

"Wrong?" Rage echoed stupidly.

"*You* couldn't smell it. Humans can't smell wrongness," Billy said.

Rage woke.

As soon as Rage stepped out the front door, it began snowing heavily, as if it had been waiting for her. The snow fell more and more thickly as she walked, so that by the time she reached the front gate of Winnoway, she could see nothing in front of her. The flashlight she carried almost made it worse, but she couldn't bring herself to stumble along in the darkness and snow. She trudged down to the main road, telling herself that snow was a lot better than ice. It was deathly quiet except for the loud sound of her breathing and her boots crunching into the snow crust. If there were wolves howling now, she would not have heard them, but no animal would be out hunting in such a snowfall. Only humans tried to go against nature.

Rage was relieved to see the Marrens' Range Rover loom out of the whiteness just as she reached the road.

She could hear the twins screaming at one another even before she opened the door. She climbed into the noisy warmth with gratitude, barely hearing Mrs. Marren complaining bitterly about the unreliability of weather forecasters.

It turned out to be a strange sort of day at school. A lot of kids from outlying farms had not come in, and many other children were absent as well. A lot of teachers were away, too, so year-levels were combined under the watchful eye of substitute teachers, or of teachers of other classes. Most students were instructed to read texts for the next term in whatever subject they would normally be in, or do homework based on old test questions for that subject.

At the end of fourth period, Rage made her way to her homeroom. There was a note on the board saying that afternoon classes were suspended. All students except those with specific permission to be elsewhere were directed to the central hall after lunch, where a movie would be shown. Since this could be anything from one she would like to see to a movie on dental hygiene, Rage didn't know whether to be glad or not. She wouldn't mind seeing a real movie. She noticed a smaller note on the board announcing that pink and green forms for the new program were to be left in a tray on the reception desk in the main office. Her hand crept to the pocket where she still had the form. She was trying to decide whether to sign it in her uncle's name and turn it in, when lunchtime was announced. The bell sounded eerily loud in the white and silent day. Relieved, Rage decided to decide after lunch.

Snow had ceased to fall at some point in the morning, and teachers shooed students outside for what they called "a gasp of fresh air." Rage noted that none of the teachers felt the need of fresh air. The strangeness was even more pronounced outside because everyone was so subdued and well-behaved. Instead of the rowdy school ground full of laughter and shrieks, there was silence as unnatural as the winter. Rage sat on a seat under a little stand of pine trees that offered a view from the rooftops of the school buildings to the hills clumped at the edge of town.

Unwrapping her lunch, she noted how many students were sitting alone to eat because their friends were absent. This reminded her of the dream of Billy in his human shape. It had been so wonderful to see him and to hear him talk again. She wondered what it had meant that he was older. Was it because animals aged more quickly than humans?

Rage threw her crusts under the tree for the birds before making her way back to the library. She needed to get some material about the Antarctic for a geography project. She was still photocopying when the bell rang for the end of lunch. She quickly finished, then hurried through the empty passages to the darkened auditorium and slid into a seat right at the end of a row and near the exit door, hoping there had not been a roll call. The movie turned out to be something that she had already seen, but at least it was a real movie.

The end-of-day bell sounded louder than usual, waking her from a light drowse. The small number of students quickly left school as Rage collected her coat and bag from her locker without hurrying. It took Mrs. Marren at least half an hour to get across town to the bus stop where she picked Rage and Anabel up, and Rage saw no point in catching the early bus and freezing for twenty minutes. There was no sign of Anabel when the late bus trundled up, but that was not unusual. Anabel often took the first bus so that she and her friends could stand and talk. Rage always wondered what they could find to talk about after spending lunchtime, class time, and even recess gossiping.

When Rage climbed out of the bus, she found that she was alone at the bus stop. Either Anabel had missed both buses, or she was staying in town another night. The latter was more likely, and Rage's heart lifted. She turned to wave to the friendly bus driver, who frowned at her as if she were a stranger. Disconcerted, she dropped her hand. She stared after the bus, wondering if it was possible that he hadn't recognized her.

She had been at the stop for a good fifteen minutes longer than usual, and the cold had begun digging its claws into her when it occurred to her that maybe Mrs. Marren had picked Anabel up right from school. Mrs. Marren might have called the school to say that she would pick them both up there because of the weather, and in retaliation for the previous morning, Anabel had neglected to tell her. Rage's heart sank at the thought of having to call Uncle Samuel to come and get her. She waited another fifteen minutes, then, teeth chattering like castanets, began to walk back to the school. It was only about six blocks if she cut through two lanes, but the heavy snowdrifts made it hard work. The first phone booth she saw, she stopped and called the Marrens' number. There was no answer. She tried to call home and got the answering machine, with her own voice inviting her to leave a message or call back later. She left a message telling Uncle Samuel that Mrs. Marren had not come and that she would be in the school library. The only problem was that it might be hours before he came.

Rage considered going to the office, but the staff were sure to contact Mrs. Somersby. It was beginning to snow very lightly again, and it had grown darker by the time the school came in sight. It was deserted, all the classrooms dark and the street empty, but the library lights were on.

She had gone only a few steps along the school street when she saw someone standing by the gate leading to the school's second bike shed. Rage would have to walk right by him, and her steps slowed at the realization that there were no houses on the other side of the street: only a white wasteland that in any season but winter was a park with clumps of trees and swings and a climbing frame.

Rage felt ridiculous imagining that she might need to scream for help. "Whoever it is must be waiting for someone," she murmured to herself.

Who would be waiting outside for someone in weather like this? Mr. Walker's sharp little voice demanded inside her mind.

Rage was unable to bring herself to turn back or to cross the road because it would be too obvious why she had done it. She was so nervous that she thought if the person sneezed, she would probably have a heart attack. The idea made her want to laugh, and all at once the clouds let through more light. Then she did laugh because now she could see that the person was just Logan Ryder.

"What are you doing here?" she asked, too relieved that it was someone she knew to worry that it was some-one who disliked her.

"Waiting for you," Logan said.

Rage's heart skipped a beat. Logan's green eyes flared at her like neon lights as he straightened up.

"Why did you call me last night?" she asked. To her surprise, it was Elle's voice that came out, light and strong and challenging.

"Call you?" Logan sounded puzzled enough that Rage wondered if she had dreamed it after all. Then he gave a snarling laugh. "Yeah, I gave you a wake-up call."

"I *don't* think I'm better than anyone else," Rage said quietly, hitching her schoolbag onto her shoulder so that she could run if she needed to.

"You think you're special because your mum is in hospital. A lot of kids have dead mothers and fathers," Logan growled.

"I told you I don't think I'm special," Rage said. "But even if I did, why do you care?"

Confusion passed fleetingly over his face. Then Logan glowered at her. "Tough talk for a little girl out all alone in the night."

"It's not night and I'm not a little girl," Rage said evenly. She forced herself to start walking toward him again. He stepped into the middle of the path, blocking her way.

"I have a message for you," he said in a sinister voice.

Rage was surprised to hear him use exactly the same words as the firecat in her dream. She gave a startled laugh.

Anger distorted Logan's features and he lunged, grabbing the handles of her bag and wrenching it off her shoulder. Rage clung to the bag, and to her belief that this was just a school-ground scuffle.

"Leave me alone. I don't want to hear any message from you," she shouted.

"So you don't want to hear about what happened?" Logan jerked the bag lightly and Rage stumbled closer. She let the handles slide down to her fingers so that she could step back, and she glared at him.

"I don't want to hear anything you have to say, Logan Ryder, now let go of my bag!"

"You don't want to know what happened to Mrs. Marren?" Logan taunted, giving the bag another light tug that unbalanced her and further loosened her grip.

Rage felt a hot little dart of shock. "Mrs. Marren? What are you talking about?"

"So you *do* want the message?"

Rage's fear melted into an intense weariness and she stopped struggling. "If you have a message from Mrs. Marren, Logan, then just tell it to me instead of acting like some stupid gangster in a movie."

Logan's expression grew uglier. "You think you can give me orders?" He wrenched the bag out of her hand, unzipped it, and emptied it onto the snow, then threw it down.

Rage gave a cry of dismay. "You rotten pig," she yelled. She would have flown at him despite the disparity in their sizes, but suddenly there was a sound that made them both freeze.

It was a deep, savage growling.

Rage turned toward the sound. She saw with dreamy horror that three enormous wolves with pale, silver-tipped pelts and flaring green eyes were hurtling across the football oval beyond the park on the other side of the road. All at once she registered that the wolves were running *toward them*.

"Oh my God! Run!" she screamed. She grabbed hold of Logan's parka, breaking his paralyzed stance as she pulled him toward the school gate. She let go then and ran for the bike shed, praying it would be open. She did not have the slightest doubt that if the nightmarish beasts caught them, they would be killed. Logan passed Rage and slammed his bulk into the shed door so hard that if it had not swung open on impact, he would surely have broken something. The door gave a great metallic clang as it rebounded off the inner wall. They hurled themselves inside and turned to slam the door shut.

"The bar," Rage gasped, and Logan was beside her, their breaths rasping in unison as they lifted it into place.

A second later the wolves were at the metal door, smashing and snarling as if there were a whole pack of them instead of only three. Fortunately, the door was heavy metal, as were the shed walls and floor. The bluish security light above the door made Logan look pale and ill, and Rage supposed that she looked the same.

"The roof," Logan hissed, jerking his chin upward.

Rage looked up to see that there was a section of transparent Perspex. She shook her head. "They couldn't possibly climb—" She stopped because all of a sudden the animals outside had fallen silent. She made a move toward the door, and Logan grabbed convulsively at her arm. She shook him off and pressed her ear against the metal by the crack between door and jamb. The hair on her arms rose as she heard the sound of ragged breathing. A picture came into her mind of a wolf pressing its ear to the door on the other side. She drew back sharply, terror and helplessness rushing through her veins.

"What did—" Logan began, then something landed heavily on the roof. This time it was Logan who moved first, turning and literally dragging Rage after him to the bathroom in the back of the shed. He pushed her in first and shot the bolt behind himself just as the Perspex in the roof cracked with a violent report. Of one accord, they pressed themselves against the wall on either side of the malodorous toilet bowl, as far from the door as possible.

Rage listened so hard her head ached, but she couldn't hear any movement. Time passed. It grew colder, and the silence went on and on until Rage finally pushed her fear aside and gathered her wits. She knew that wolves were stealthy, clever hunters, but they would not wait long if there was other prey out there, easier to catch. It might even be that she had imagined the cracking sound of the roof giving way. How on earth could wolves leap onto the roof, after all, even if they had been as gigantic as she had imagined? Glancing at Logan's pale, set face, it occurred to her with a faint sense of hysteria that they were waiting for the surprise terror that always happened in the movies when you thought the characters were safe. The body you thought was dead that leapt up and grabbed the hero. The dragon that had been killed, then opened its maddened eye. The face that suddenly appeared at the window.

The wind moaned. It wasn't as cold in the shed bathroom as it had been outside, but it was cold enough, and they must have been standing there for an hour. Rage couldn't feel her toes. She forced herself to stand up.

"What are you doing?" Logan whispered. The white showed all around his green irises.

"We can't stay in here forever," Rage whispered. Her voice sounded strange and husky, as if she had screamed for hours.

"What if one of those things is waiting inside?" Logan whispered. He was sweating. Oddly, knowing that Logan was so frightened made Rage feel less so. After all, she had faced some pretty terrifying things in her life already, hadn't she?

"I'd rather get eaten than freeze to death slowly in a smelly bathroom," she said in Rue's stern, no-nonsense voice.

Another silence.

"All right," Logan said at last. "But don't blame me if we get eaten."

This was so completely absurd that, incredibly, Rage started to laugh. It was more than half hysteria, and she was shivering so hard that her laughter sounded like some sort of convulsion. She tried to stifle the sound, but this only made her laugh the harder. She doubled over and tears leaked from her eyes. She saw that after his first look of astonishment, Logan was laughing, too. *Logan Ryder and me are laughing together,* she thought incredulously, which made her laugh even more. They were both hanging on to the cistern, leaning over the pee-smelling toilet, and this seemed the funniest thing of all.

When they managed to gain some measure of control, Logan gasped, "Well, if anything *was* out there, that would have convinced them a couple of maniacs were in here, and they would've taken off."

That broke them both up again, but after a bit, Rage's stomach hurt so much from laughing that she had to make herself stop. And suddenly she was quite certain that they were safe. She reached for the door and then hesitated and looked at Logan. He sobered and nodded, and they left the bathroom.

Rage's heart sped up again at the sight of drifts of snow in the shed and great, jagged pieces of shattered Perspex. The skylight had broken but there were no beasts. The Perspex must have collapsed under a load of snow. Most likely the thump they had heard hadn't been a wolf landing on the roof but the roof buckling a little under its weight of snow. She went to the door and rested her hands on the crossbar. The feel of the chill metal under her fingers was like an icy burn, reminding her of the sheer black malevolence she had felt when she had put her face against the jamb earlier. All her fear flowed back. She might have drawn away, but Logan reached out and put his hands on the bar beside hers. "Okay, let's do it, then," he rasped. They lifted the bar smoothly, hooked it back in place, and heaved open the door.

A blast of icy wind clawed at their faces, snatching Rage's breath away, but there were no growls. No giant wolves leaping at them.

"Gone," Rage said shakily, pulling her coat around her, half convinced that she had imagined the wolves. Maybe they hadn't even been anything more than a pack of feral dogs turned vicious by the weather. The door jerked violently and Logan caught hold of it. "We better shut it or the wind will break it right off."

Rage nodded and they fought to close it. Then they leaned into the wind and went along the track to the outer fence. At the fence gate, Logan pointed to an enormous, smudged footprint. They stared at it in horror for a full three minutes, Rage thinking it looked more like a bear track than a wolf print.

"We better get to the school in case they come back," she said shakily.

On the other side of the gate, her books and notes lay scattered in a pile, pages fluttering in the wind where the snow had not buried them. Several loose sheets had blown against the fence. Rage stared at them in wonder, feeling as if the tug-of-war with her bag had happened in another life. She noticed absently that Logan's battered backpack lay beside the fence, where he must have put it to free his hands.

"Blast!" Logan muttered, his voice slurred with cold. He knelt down and began shoveling everything back into her schoolbag.

"Forget them," Rage said, glancing around.

"You go ahead and I'll catch up," he said determinedly.

"You're mad!" Rage said, falling onto her knees and helping him.

The job was done quickly. Logan zipped the bag and handed it to Rage. He threw his backpack over his shoulder and, side by side, they hurried along the footpath toward the oasis of light ahead that was the school. They did not speak until the doors had hissed shut. Rage turned to see them both reflected in the sheets of glass. Beyond was only the darkness and the flying snow.

"Those things could be through that glass in about a second," Logan murmured, voicing her own thought.

"We ought to call someone," Rage said.

"Look," Logan said in a peculiar voice. She looked at him. "I'm sorry about the books," he went on. "I'll tell the library I did it and pay for the ones that are wrecked."

She shrugged, and her mind stuttered sideways to the call he had made. "I don't think I'm better than anyone else, Logan. I really don't. If I seem different sometimes, it's because of some things that happened to me last summer. Not just my mam being in an accident."

He gave her a look she could not quite read, and she thought he might ask *What things?* but instead he said, "Maybe we better make it an anonymous call to the cops. We ought to let someone know those things are on the loose. But we'll have to think of a story. If we say we got chased by giant feral pigs, the police'll think it's a hoax and take no notice."

Rage stared at him. "Pigs? They were wolves."

Logan frowned at her. "Are you nuts? Didn't you see the tusks and their red eyes?" He was already headed for the phone beyond the lockers. Rage followed, bemused.

"Logan, I didn't see pigs, feral or otherwise. I saw wolves!"

Logan turned to her, his face grimly certain. "Look, I know what a boar looks like, all right? One chased me when I was about six. I have a scar from my belly button to my neck to prove it, and I was about three inches from its face when it tried to gut me. I still have nightmares about it sometimes."

Rage was silenced by the vision this summoned up. Was it possible that she had only imagined seeing wolves? Logan was now dialing triple zero, and putting on a much older voice, he described having seen feral pigs in the school grounds near the lower bike shed. He hung up while the policewoman was in the middle of asking for his name and address.

"That was amazing," Rage said. "You really sounded older and totally responsible. Like a doctor or something."

"I can do voices," Logan said gruffly, but she could see that he was pleased by her praise.

Rage remembered something he had said earlier, and after a slight hesitation, she asked, "Logan, what happened to Mrs. Marren?"

Logan gave a short bark of laughter. "You are a cool one, Rebecca Jane."

"Rage," she corrected him automatically, then flushed at what he might say.

But he smiled and made a gesture of surrender with his hands. "Rage, then. I was in the office waiting to get my ear chewed when a phone call came in for you, so I pricked up my ears. It was the Marren woman calling to say she wouldn't be able to pick you up and bring you home because she'd had an accident."

"Oh no!" Rage cried.

"It's okay. It wasn't bad. She drove into a ditch and needed a tractor to get her out. From what I heard, no one was hurt, but I guess she was freaked by what happened. There was a message for Anabel to go to her aunt's, and you're supposed to call that Somersby woman so that she can arrange accommodation for tonight if your uncle can't come and get you. I offered to give you the message. I figured you'd come back to the school when no one turned up to pick you up, so I waited."

"What were you going to do?" Rage asked a little stiffly.

He looked sheepish but also slightly belligerent. "I dunno. I meant to scare you, but you wouldn't scare, so I got mad. . . ." Rage said nothing and he suddenly scowled. "Look, I said I was sorry about the stupid books."

"They're not stupid," Rage said.

"They are if you can't read!" Logan snarled. Then he whitened. "You better not tell anyone I said that. Anyway, it's a lie."

Rage laughed a little. "Logan, tonight we were almost eaten by giant . . . giant *somethings*, and we hid in a bathroom together, so I think that better count as some sort of truce, don't you?"

Logan gave a gusty sigh. "Yeah. Sorry. But look, I was only joking about not being able to read."

"Sure," Rage said. "Look, I better call my uncle again." It was a hint but Logan didn't get it. He stood by while she called and left a message about Mrs. Marren's accident.

"No one home?"

She shook her head, chewing her lip. "I called already on my way back to the school, so he might have got the first message and already be on his way."

"Is that your uncle who went exploring in the jungles?"

Rage nodded, startled at how much he knew about her. "He's taking care of the farm and me while Mam is in hospital. I told him in the message that I'd wait in the library until closing time, so I better go there."

"I'll wait with you," Logan offered. Rage guessed that he wasn't too keen on the idea of going outside alone, and she could hardly blame him.

"What will you do if your uncle doesn't turn up?" Logan asked when they were both sitting by the heater in the library.

"He'll come," Rage said, taking the wet books from her bag and propping them on the floor by the heater fan so that the pages would dry. Logan began to help her, grimacing at the worst damaged.

"Lucky you to have someone to rely on," he muttered with some of his old bitterness.

Rage had opened her mouth to say that she was not a bit certain that her uncle could be relied upon, but then she closed it because she hardly knew Logan. Rage noticed that snowflakes were falling and falling through the blue halo of radiance around a light outside.

"Maybe those things were some sort of experiment

that escaped," Logan murmured. "They'd have to be some sort of mutation to be that big."

"Maybe it will say something about them in the paper tomorrow," Rage said, remembering how big the wolves had looked. Then she realized Logan was still talking.

". . . if you want," Logan was saying diffidently, his cheeks pink.

"Pardon?" Rage asked.

"Forget it," Logan said with an angry shrug.

Rage sighed. "Logan, if we are going to be friends, you have to stop taking everything the wrong way. I didn't hear what you said because almost being eaten has made it hard for me to concentrate."

He expelled a hissing breath and then looked into her eyes. "*Are* we going to be friends? I'm not that easy to be friends with."

"Me neither," Rage said lightly, dabbing at the wetness inside the bag with a balled handkerchief.

Logan hesitated and then said without looking at her, "I was just saying that after the library closes, I can show you this late-night café near the bowling alley that doesn't close until two a.m. Then there's an all-night gas station where they don't mind if you sit, so long as you keep ordering stuff. It doesn't have to be anything expensive, and there's a good doughnut place that opens for breakfast at six. Just in case your uncle doesn't turn up."

Rage stared at him incredulously. "Stay up all night?"

He shrugged. "What else? It doesn't kill you. Unless you want to be sent somewhere by that silly cow, Somersby. Given the way she looked at you the other day, she'll have you sleeping in someone's doghouse."

Rage laughed. "I'd *rather* sleep in a dog kennel than call her. You know her?"

"Unfortunately," Logan said laconically. "Let's just say she makes kids like me her business." He said this in a good imitation of Mrs. Somersby's harsh, malicious tone.

"Hey, you really are good at that," Rage said, laughing in admiration.

Logan said roughly, "Look, what I've been trying to say is that if you like, I'll stay with you the whole time. Show you the ropes, like."

Rage was touched. "Is Logan your real name?"

He nodded. "My mum—my real mum, I mean—she got the name from television. Not the *X-Men* character but a man in this old sci-fi movie. He's a government hunter who chases anyone older than thirty or maybe twenty-five to kill them because they don't want to waste any food or water or anything on old people. All people who get old are supposed to go in this machine thing and die, but some run and he chases them. Then this guy, Logan, ends up being chased, even though he's not old."

"She must have liked the character," Rage said.

"He *was* pretty cool," Logan said with mock modesty. They smiled at one another. Rage thought later that this had been the first moment of true, if unexpected, friendship.

Uncle Samuel came into the library less than an hour later, explaining that he had set off to town as soon as he had played the message. He knew about Mrs. Marren's accident because Mrs. Marren had left a message, too.

Uncle Samuel glanced at Logan, whom Rage had shyly introduced as a friend. "Can we give you a lift home, Logan?"

Logan looked as if he might refuse, but Rage said

quickly that it was a good idea. "You never know what might be out there on a night like this."

Logan blinked twice and accepted. Neither of them had mentioned what had happened outside the school. Rage guessed that Logan was leaving it to her. She decided to leave it until they got home, when she could be sure of being calm about it. The truth was that she felt curiously embarrassed at the thought of trying to explain in front of Logan what had happened.

"It'll be a bit of a squash because I've got a lot of supplies on the backseat. Whereabouts do you live, lad?" Uncle Samuel asked Logan as they walked out of the school. Rage and Logan surreptitiously looked both ways, but there was no sign of the creatures.

"The other side of Lockwood Avenue, Mr. Winnoway," Logan answered politely. "If you can get there, I'll direct you."

Rage climbed into the middle seat, leaving the window seat for Logan, but as he made to enter, Billy growled from the back. Logan froze.

"It's just my dog," Rage said quickly. "Billy. This is Logan. Logan, this is Billy Thunder. Let him sniff your hand," she added.

"Billy *Thunder?*" Logan laughed shakily, offering the back of his hand. Billy hung over the seat and snuffled it thoroughly before giving a soft bark of approval.

When Logan climbed out in front of a nice, ordinary redbrick house twenty minutes later, Rage wondered why she had imagined that he lived in a tougher area. Uncle Samuel honked the horn before pulling away and said, "Your friend seems like a nice guy."

He was a foe before tonight, Rage thought, still amazed at how the whole thing had turned out. She slid over to the window seat and buckled herself in as Billy climbed over to take his usual place in the middle of the front seat. He put his head on her lap with a contented sigh, and Rage slipped into a light doze that did not end until her uncle shook her as they were pulling into the driveway of the farm.

Watching her uncle prepare a late supper of bowls of thick potato-and-leek soup with slices of dark bread, Rage made up her mind to say nothing about being chased. But she must have been tired because suddenly, without planning it, she found herself talking about Mam. Seeing her uncle's face turn to stone, she immediately wished the words unsaid.

"Dr. Kellum called this afternoon," her uncle said in a clipped monotone that was exactly the way Grandfather had sounded. "They will be moving your mother to Leary on Sunday afternoon. They don't want to delay any longer with her condition and the weather worsening. I'll take you to see her Sunday morning."

All the strangeness of the day resolved into angry helplessness. Rage wanted to shout at her uncle that he mustn't let the doctors take Mam away; that he *must* see her because perhaps it was their only chance to make her want to live. But she only watched her uncle rinse out his bowl, too afraid to speak in case he would pack his knapsacks and boxes and return to the jungle.

After he had gone, she gave the remains of her supper to Billy. Whenever would they be able to go all the way to Leary to see Mam? And even if Uncle Samuel should agree to drive them there, the weather made it virtually impossible.

It was not until she was in bed and drifting on the edge of sleep that she thought again about the animals that had chased her and Logan. She was inclined, in the face of Logan's certainty, to believe that fear had made her confuse a boar print for a bear print. The one thing they had both agreed upon, and the footprint had confirmed it, was the animals' extraordinary size. Rather than bringing her more widely awake, this thought drew her into a dream.

It was night and very dark, but a bit of moonlight shone through the ragged edge of a dark cloud, limning what could be seen of the playground equipment and causing it to cast sharp, thin shadows. The moon shadows left by the hillocks of snow were indigo shapes outlined in violet shadows and bluish green pools that gave the whole scene an underwater feel.

The playground swings creaked slowly back and forth. Rage took a step toward them, then heard snow crunching behind her. She whirled to find Billy in his golden dog form flowing over the snow. She felt a muddle of joy and disappointment as she knelt and opened her arms to him, but all at once he was human shaped, and she gave a yell of surprise and fell onto her backside. Billy helped her up, grinning.

Words burst unbidden from Rage's lips. "Oh, Billy, they're taking Mam away to Leary on the weekend! I'm so scared for her."

Billy took her gently in his arms and stroked her hair, making no attempt to soothe her fears with words. It felt so good and right and safe to be enfolded like that.

"You've grown," Billy murmured, sounding surprised, leaning back a little to look down at her. "I didn't notice it when I was a dog."

"You look older, too," Rage said shyly, then she realized that they were acting as if this were a real meeting.

"You want me to go again," Billy said sadly. Rage saw with alarm that he had suddenly grown less substantial. A few more seconds and she could actually see the swing through him, and his arms felt cool rather than warm about her.

She clutched a handful of his jacket tightly and cried, "No! No, I don't want you to go! I want you to stay, and in this shape!" Just like that, he was solid again.

Billy looked around, his nostrils flaring. "Something smells wrong," he murmured.

"What is it?" Rage asked anxiously, looking around, too, and remembering suddenly that he had spoken of the weather as smelling wrong in her dream the previous night.

"I smell the firecat," Billy said with slight distaste.

Rage stared at him. "In my dream last night, you said the weather smelled wrong," she said.

"It did," Billy said. "But the firecat doesn't smell that way. I guess you must have called it the way you called me to your dream."

"Called?" Rage echoed incredulously.

"Or maybe the wizard sent it to your dream," Billy went on, misunderstanding her reaction.

"The wizard would never send it to me," Rage said. "He'd know I would never trust it after what it did to Bear."

"Perhaps he was desperate," Billy said.

Rage shook her head. "He'd know I couldn't do anything to help him."

"You helped him before."

"Only because I had no choice," Rage said stiffly. "But I meant that even if I would want to help him, I couldn't get back to Valley to do it."

"What exactly did it say to you?" Billy asked. Rage told him and he said, "I wonder what the firecat meant by telling you that you would be waking to a nightmare?"

Rage shrugged. "If the firecat was real and not just something I dreamed up, it was probably just a meaningless threat. But Billy, you said I called you into my dream. No one could do that."

"Maybe it has something to do with what Mama meant by what she said when I came through the night gate," Billy murmured.

"Bear talked to you about me?" Rage whispered, remembering with a touch of awe the voice that had spoken to her as she had passed through the world gate that Bear had become upon her death.

"She spoke of many things," Billy said. His eyes were velvety with sadness. "She said that if I willed it, I could be human shaped in this world. But the journey was too quick for me to will anything."

"Oh, Billy!" Rage said, devastated for him. "I'm so sorry."

"It was not your fault that I came after you," he said gently, the gold flecks in his eyes glowing. "I would rather be a dog with you than human shaped without you."

They hugged and Rage wept a scatter of tears that she wiped off on her sleeve before they drew apart so that he would not see them. "Can you . . . tell me exactly what Bear said about me?"

Billy reddened slightly, but he said calmly enough, "She said that you had powers that you didn't know you had."

Rage chewed her lip, thinking about how, when the wizard was trapped in the hourglass, he could not talk to her except when she dreamed. "Maybe the wizard sent that dream of the firecat to me," she murmured. "Maybe something has gone wrong in Valley. The firecat said he needed me. But even if that was true, what could I do? There's no gateway to Valley from here anymore."

Billy's eyes lit up in excitement. "Maybe you could call one of the others to your dreams like you did me. Then you could ask."

"But I don't know how I called you here, if I did."

"Maybe it's as simple as wanting to talk to someone and carrying the wanting into your dreams." Billy gave her a shy look.

Rage gasped. "You must be right! I've just remembered! Last night, just before I fell asleep, I wished for you to be human shaped again so that we could talk, just as I did when we went through the bramble gate!"

Billy opened his mouth to speak, and vanished.

The first thing Rage realized when she opened her eyes was that Billy was growling. It was a low, ferocious dog rumble that would have been terrifying to her if she hadn't known it was him. She sat bolt upright, clutching the warm quilt. Billy was under the window, close enough to the night-light for it to gleam on his coat. He was staring at the curtain, which swayed in a draft.

The hair rose on Rage's arms and neck at the thought that one of the beasts she had seen with Logan might be prowling about the farm. Wild boar or wolf, one smash and the window would shatter. The walls might even collapse if a bunch of the huge creatures threw their weight against the house. Billy would be no match for one of them, yet she knew it would not stop him from attacking. In his human form, he would be smart enough to realize they were too big for him to fight, but in his dog form, he was almost as bad as Elle had been: all fight and courage and not much thought.

Rage reasoned that it was far more likely that Billy was growling at a fox or some small animal in search of food. Sliding her feet into her slippers, she rose, reaching out to catch a handful of the soft fur ruff at the back of Billy's neck. He was still growling, and now she could feel that all his muscles were bunched as if he intended to jump.

To her surprise, instead of straining against her grip as he would normally have done, Billy stopped growling at once and turned to look at her. Her fear evaporated in a thrill of joy at seeing the intelligence of his human self in his eyes.

Billy began to growl again, more urgently than before.

"Okay," Rage whispered. She released Billy and waited anxiously to see what he would do, but he only pawed at her thigh and padded to the door. She followed him because this had been his way of signaling *yes* when they had first returned from Valley. He looked up at her and growled one short, low rumble, as if chiding her to pay attention.

Rage closed her hand around the iron knob in the center of the antique door. It felt icy, reminding her of the burning cold of the bike-shed latch bar. She opened the door. The hall was dark, and cold flowed toward her, making her wish she had put on her bathrobe. She wanted to get to where her uncle slept. It had been added on to the original house and, unlike the rest, was built of double brick. The windows of both the small rooms that made up the extension also had sturdy wrought-iron covers, and a solid oak door separated it from the main body of the house.

Rage crept along the hall past the bathroom door, Billy padding by her side. She passed the door to her mother's empty room and came to the short hall that led to the oak door and the extension. She opened the heavy door as silently as she could, then shut it behind her and pushed the lock. Only then did she relax enough to become aware that her legs were shaking.

The first part of the extension was a little office room where a big desk was heaped with Uncle Samuel's note-books. A night-light lit up a small, uncurtained window behind the desk. Fortunately, a crate on the desk had been pushed in front of the window, so even if something were tracking her movement through the house, it would not be able to see in. She crept through the little office and hesitated a moment at the doorway leading to the tiny sitting room. She could not see where her uncle slept because there was no night-light here and the couch bed was at the end of the room farthest from the door. The only other things in the room were a wardrobe, more crates piled against a wall, and a small case of Uncle Samuel's few personal belongings and clothes.

"What is it, Rage?" His voice came out of the darkness, alert and low pitched.

Rage gasped and then bit her tongue, though her heart was hammering crazily. "I . . . Billy was growling at my window," she said breathlessly. "We . . . I think some kind of animal is prowling around the house." Her heart gave another horrid lurch when her uncle rose to his feet at once, saying that he would go and check.

"We can just stay here until it goes!" she cried too loudly, but he was already brushing past her, bidding

Billy to stay with her and telling her to climb into his bed until he returned. He pulled on a sweater and his shoes in three swift movements, then reached into his suitcase and pulled something out before reaching up to the top of the wardrobe and getting something else. Rage was in shock to see that he was holding a gun, pushing the bullets in with efficient little *snicks*. Only when he had gone through the office to the oak door did she unfreeze to run after him and beg him not to go out.

Uncle Samuel turned toward her. A chink of light from a strip of window not blocked by the crate lit his craggy features, revealing eyes as wild as they were kind, just as they had been when she had first seen him in her dreams. "Sometimes you have to face the things that come after you, Rage," he said.

Then he was gone. Rage pressed her ear to the door, but it was too thick to hear anything. The wind howled, making the house creak. The branches of the big walnut tree scraped against the house like claws. Rage imagined the enormous beasts leaping onto her uncle. If only she had told him about them! If he was killed, it would be just the same as if she had murdered him!

Rage reached for the door handle and Billy gave a slight growl. Looking into his eyes, Rage did not dare to open the door because he was quite capable of nipping her hard to stop her. Before she could decide what to do, there was the *crack* of a gunshot.

Rage's heart seemed to stop for a long minute, as did the howling of the wind and the scraping of the tree branches against the house. It was as if all the world held its breath. Then another shot rang out. Rage told herself these had been measured shots made with a steady hand and not shots fired by her uncle as he was being attacked by one of the huge beasts that had chased her into the bike shed.

"Billy—" she began in a pleading voice, but the door burst open and she staggered back.

It was her uncle.

Rage blinked hard at the sudden brightness of the hall light. She teetered on the edge of an impulse to rush into her uncle's arms and hug him, but shyness and the fear that it would annoy him strangled the notion. He brushed past her, and she watched him unloading the remaining bullets. He tossed them into the top drawer of the desk before going through to the bedroom with the gun. He returned empty-handed.

"What happened?" she asked.

"Prowler, I'd say," he answered. "Might be the same man Mrs. Marren saw that caused her to go off the road. Gunshots scared the hell out of whoever it was, anyway." He sighed and ran a hand through his hair, dislodging a little fall of snow. "Come on, let's go down to the kitchen. We could do with a hot drink."

Rage followed, wondering if whatever had woken Billy had just been a human prowler. It seemed absurd to think anyone would brave such weather to poke around an old farmhouse. "Could it have been a wolf?" she ventured casually. "I heard one howling the other morning when I was waiting for Mrs. Marren."

"There are a lot of weird stories around at the moment about wild animals," her uncle said pensively. "Funny how people always shape their fears as animals. Truth is that humans are the most savage, stupid, and vicious animals in all the worlds."

Rage stared at him. "You said *worlds*."

He gave her a distracted look. "There are a hundred

overlapping worlds in this one world, Rage. Countries that think differently and do things differently, all affecting one another and all trying to pretend the others don't exist. All thinking their way is the right way. Sometimes I think it would be better if we were all caged off from one another like animals in a zoo."

This was surprisingly close to the way the keepers had arranged Valley in the absence of the wizard. Remembering where that had led, Rage couldn't help saying passionately, "You can't cage things that are meant to be free. Even for their own good. And who would do the caging?"

Her uncle looked at her then, really looked at her, for maybe the first time. "You're a bright lass, Rage," he said softly. "But what is the answer, then? How to contain all that viciousness of humanity?"

It sounded as if he really thought that Rage might know the answer. But she could only shake her head and say helplessly, "Not everything is viciousness and hatred and cruelty."

"I know it's not, Rage, but what isn't doesn't have much of a chance against it."

Rage said, "I think you have to try to do the right thing, even if it seems really small." She hesitated. "Uncle Samuel, I know that Mam would begin to get well if she saw you. I think she wants that more than she wants anything in the world."

Simple as that, the words that had been burning to be said for weeks and weeks came out. But Uncle Samuel didn't seem to hear her. He stood up, draining off the rest of his drink, wiping down the bench, and putting the milk carton in the fridge in an unhurried way. As he left the room, he turned to remind Rage not to stay up too long. His eyes looked quite blank, as if he were sleepwalking.

Rage went back to her bedroom, Billy at her heels. The door stood ajar, so the warmth from the little heater had leaked away. Shutting the door behind her, she climbed into the icy sheets, shivering. She called softly to Billy and patted the bed. He looked askance at her, but he came and settled himself on the bed. Then Rage curled her body around his warm, reassuring bulk.

She did not expect to be able to sleep, but almost at once she began to drowse. She had the presence of mind, at the last moment, to picture Billy in his human form. But either she did not dream, or she did not recall it, for it seemed but a moment before her little alarm was trilling its summons into the early morning darkness.

3

Shivering and gritty eyed, Rage pushed Billy aside and clambered out of bed. It took a long, hot shower to bring her properly awake, by which time it was too late to have breakfast. Uncle Samuel was putting on his coat to go out and start the car up even as she let Billy out. Rage hastened to the kitchen to drink a glass of milk. She put a banana and a cereal bar into her pocket before pulling on her outside things and taking up her schoolbag.

It was a luxury to walk only a matter of steps and climb into a waiting car. It was also lovely to have Billy climb in and sit by her knees. He knew he had to sit on the floor when it was wet or snowy, but she felt less comfortable about it, knowing that inside his dog form he was again as he had been in Valley.

Uncle Samuel made no reference to the events of the night on the drive to town. In fact, he said nothing except to utter two mildly blasphemous words about the treacherous road conditions and, as they pulled into the school street, to warn her that he might be a bit late in picking her up. She should wait in the library again until he came for her.

Rage thanked him for driving her in. He gave her an odd look before closing the door and driving away. Rage watched until the car went out of sight because Billy had leapt into the back and was looking back at her. As she turned away, she caught sight of the bike shed. It looked exactly the same as it always did.

"You'd think it never happened," Logan Ryder said from behind her. Rage turned shyly to face him. Logan looked the same as usual as well, except that his green eyes were no longer cold, and though he was not smiling, neither was he sneering. "Feels like I dreamed what happened," he muttered.

"It wasn't a dream," Rage said.

"You didn't tell your uncle, did you?"

Rage shook her head, noticing passing kids giving them curious, sideways looks. "He wouldn't have believed me," she said. She went through the gate and Logan followed.

"Are you sure about that? Your uncle seems a decent sort."

"He *is* decent," Rage said. "I just wish I were sure he'd stay," she added.

Logan's brows lifted into his shaggy hairline. "Didn't you say he was going to stay until your mum got out of hospital?"

"The people in my family are famous for not sticking around when the going gets tough."

"Your uncle didn't strike me like the type who would leave anyone in the lurch."

Rage shrugged. "I think he's just waiting for a reason to leave again."

Logan looked disillusioned. "A couple of the families I lived with looked like they came right out of a Disney movie, but it was more like a horror movie when you got to know them. I guess you never know anyone from the outside." There was a flat edge to his voice.

"How come you lived with so many different families?" Rage asked, glad to be distracted from her problems.

He shrugged. "My mother died having me, and my father didn't want to be left holding the baby, but he didn't want to give me away, either, so he made me a ward of the state. That means no one was allowed to adopt me. I could only be fostered or given holidays. Pretty soon I was old enough that no one would want to adopt me anymore, and that's when he changed his mind. He'd got married by then and his wife didn't want to know about me. The kinds of families who take on older kids are usually sloppy do-gooders, religious maniacs determined to save your soul, or people who want the extra cash the government pays them. Some of the families I was with had a whole lot of kids, all adopted or fostered." He stopped and gave himself a shake and gave her a savage grimace. "I am what you might call a factory recall."

"What about the family you're with now?" Rage asked, thinking about the neat brick house.

He shrugged. "The Stileses are okay. Do-gooders hoping to score on a delinquent. They haven't figured out that I'm a hopeless case yet, but they will." He said this with sour triumph. Rage didn't know what to say. Didn't he want to find a home he liked? But it wasn't the sort of question she could ask. Not yet.

They were inside the front hall now. A voice came over the loudspeaker instructing all staff and students to go to the main assembly hall.

"Maybe they're going to dismiss us," Rage said, wondering what she would do in that case. Then she shook her head. "No, they wouldn't do that because a lot of kids wouldn't be able to contact their parents or get home."

"Maybe it's about what happened last night. There was nothing on the news, but maybe the police don't want to start a panic," Logan said in a low voice. He waited while Rage put her coat and bag into her locker and took out her books and notes. Then he glanced around and whispered, "What if they figured it was a kid making that report and they're going to try to get whoever it is to admit it."

"Maybe someone else saw them or maybe they—" Rage started. Then the bell rang and they had to run to the assembly.

Despite what she had said, Rage would not have been surprised by a dismissal from school, given the dwindling numbers of students and teachers. But the headmistress just assigned teachers to groups of students. From now on, she told everyone, each day would begin with an assembly until the crisis was over. There were a few other general announcements of the sort usually made over the address system, then the students were given a day teacher. Rage's was a short man with reddish hair like a fox's; long, narrow teeth; and a nasty, flowery aftershave. His name was Mr. Pinke.

Logan was put into her group as well. In spite of everything, Rage grinned to think that two days earlier this would have dismayed her.

As soon as they were in the classroom, Mr. Pinke gave them a list of old exam questions, warning that talking would result in additional questions. Usually this sort of approach would have made Logan rebel until he was thrown out, but today he said nothing, though neither did he work. Rage could feel his impatience for the class to end and was oddly warmed by the certainty that he wanted to stay in class with her. She was no less impatient for the end of the period because she wanted to tell him about the midnight visitor to Winnoway. At last the bell rang. Mr. Pinke made them sit until he had collected the sheets, and then he had them walk out single file, like little kids.

"I hate teachers like him," Logan said when they were in the hall.

"I thought you hated *all* teachers," Rage said, but lightly.

"No, I don't." He gave her a surprised look and she bit back a laugh of disbelief. "So what are we going to do?"

"Library?" Rage said.

Logan gave her a sharp look, then shrugged. They walked in silence because half of the school population was in the hallways. Only when they were between the stacks did Logan speak.

"Why do you suppose the head didn't mention those animals during the assembly?" he asked. "It's like she didn't even know about them."

"Maybe the police didn't tell her," Rage answered. "Maybe they don't do anything if a person calls but doesn't say who they are."

"What about the bike-shed roof?"

"It was snowing. By the time the police showed, there were probably no footprints. They'd have thought it was the snow buildup that broke the Perspex."

Logan nodded, frowning. "You know, I've been thinking of those things a lot. Maybe they weren't boars or wolves but some sort of hybrid. They could be mutations caused by experimental chemicals dumped illegally into the high mountains out of helicopters. Maybe those things have been living up there for generations with no one ever knowing until now, and the weather is bringing them down."

"Sort of like teenage mutant ninja beasts?" she asked.

Logan looked angry for a moment, then he laughed. "Yeah, I guess it is pretty wild." He stopped suddenly and she saw that he was staring at the *Librarians' Recommendations* shelf. "I remember that book. It was about these four kids who went through the back of a wardrobe to another world." Rage saw that he was looking at a battered copy of *The Lion, the Witch, and the Wardrobe*, which she had read with Mam a few years back. "I really liked it," Logan went on, almost dreamily, "but I never knew what happened in the end because one of the mothers was reading it, and I went back to the home before she got to the end. I didn't mind about leaving, but I minded about not getting to the end of the book."

"Why didn't you get it out and finish it yourself?" Rage asked. Logan made no response, and she glanced at him curiously, only to find that he was still staring at the book cover. His red face reminded her of what he had shouted the previous night.

"You really *can't* read," she said softly.

He turned on her then, fury, misery, and humiliation in his face and eyes. On any other occasion, she would have shrunk from that look, but now she just held his gaze with her own, much as she might have held him up with her hand if she saw him falling. It felt like that. Like he was leaning his full weight against her. Then all at once he pulled back, turned on his heel, and stalked wordlessly away.

Rage stared after him with pity and exasperation, wondering if the fledgling friendship was over as suddenly as it had begun. She was surprised at how disappointed it made her.

The bell rang again, but Rage decided to stay in the library. Everything was so chaotic, she doubted that anyone would wonder where she was. She took a couple of heavy books from the *Atlas* shelf, carried them to her alcove, and then opened one on her lap. She wanted to think about her dreams and her supposed ability to draw people into them. She had made up her mind that the person to summon would be the witch Mother, Rue. She tried to focus her mind, but the heat in the library was making her sleepy. She struggled against it for a little, then gave in with a sigh, letting her chin drop onto her chest. She was not conscious of slumping sideways, but the book stayed in her lap. A little later a teacher who passed by noted the book and bent head and tiptoed away without coming close enough to see that Rage was sleeping.

Rage was standing on a flat, snowy plain surrounded by a dense, snow-covered forest of dark, spiky trees. She was too close to the trees on one side of the clearing to see anything beyond them, but the other way, she could see mountains beyond the tree line. It was impossible to tell what time it was because there was not the slightest glimmer of moonlight or starlight to offer a clue. The snow gave off a pale glow that bestowed an eerie air to the scene. This was heightened by the lack of animal or bird sounds. The air was utterly silent, unbroken by a sigh or creak from the trees, as if they had been frozen to stony stillness. The air was icy to breathe, and she shivered in her thin school uniform and sweater. "I don't remember ever feeling cold in a dream before," she muttered.

Her voice sounded very loud, and she had the uneasy feeling that she had exposed herself dangerously by speaking. She was so caught up in the brooding atmosphere that it was some moments before she noticed a gray-cloaked figure making its way across the snowy expanse toward her. It was impossible to see a face, but as the person came close, there was something familiar in the long, purposeful strides. Then Rage recognized the witch Mother, Rue. But how old she had grown! Her raven's-wing hair was streaked with pure white. There was a web of lines about her eyes and mouth and stiffness to her movements. The little winged wild thing, Puck, was hurrying in her wake. He, at least, did not look a day older than when she had last seen him.

"It is good to see you, Child Rage," the witch woman said in her stern, lovely voice.

Rage curtsied awkwardly, then said with uncertainty, "I don't mean to be rude, Mother, but are you real?"

Rue laughed. "I am and so are you, Child Rage, and so is Puck here, by the by, for I suppose you must be wondering about him as well. I would have come alone to meet you. Indeed, I intended it but he—"

"I will attend you, Lady," the little man interrupted stubbornly.

Rue sighed. "So it seems, and whether I desire it or not."

Rage hardly heard the exchange, for she was trying to think of a way to ask how the woman had come to age so much. "Has a lot of time passed since I left Valley?" she finally asked.

Rue smiled wryly. "Time has passed, as it is wont to do, even in Valley, but not as much as you may think to look at me. It is three years since you left us by the count of time in your world."

"Three *years*!" Rage cried in disbelief. "It's only been a few months since I left there."

"You mean since you left *here*," Rue said, making a gesture with her long, thin arms that encompassed the forest and the mountains. Rage shivered and Rue looked concerned. "You are half frozen. Puck?"

The little fairy man produced an enormous cloak out of a tiny waist pack, and he flew up to swirl it around Rage's shoulders. It was a lovely thing: silvery gray as a dawn sky after rain, light as a cobweb, silken to the touch, and amazingly warm. All at once Rage was struck by something that the witch woman had said. "What did you mean, 'since I left *here*'?" Rage asked.

"Since you left Valley," Rue said, a line between her brows. "Where we now stand."

"I don't understand. . . ."

"In your world, you are dreaming, but here you are real enough. What you have done is called dream-traveling. Only part of your self is here, and it will remain here until you wake in your own world." Without waiting for a response, Rue went on briskly. "There is much to say before you leave, but we must not stay in the open like this." She glanced about before setting off back the way she had come. Rage followed her to a small clearing in the midst of the trees. A small, pale green silk tent was under the branches of an enormous tree. Rage sat beside a small fire that blazed cheerfully. Tapestry cushions lay atop split logs arranged about the campfire.

Three seats, Rage noted.

"You were expecting me," she murmured.

"Did I not say so?" Rue asked with faint impatience.

Puck fussed with a pot of water that had been suspended over the fire and a teapot. His mistress seated herself opposite Rage. The play of flame-glow highlighted the deep grooves on either side of Rue's nose as she began to speak. "You asked if this was a dream. Better if you had asked if it is a nightmare. You see this dull gray light? This is day in Valley now, and a time may come when this seems bright. You see, the sun cannot shine through the storm clouds that fill the sky. It is so long since we have seen it that I feel that true sunlight was a kind of lovely dream."

"But why?" Rage asked. "What has happened?"

"Almost a year ago in Valley time, the firecat opened a world gate to an unknown land and winter began leaking through it. The firecat claims to have created the gateway, which we call the winter door, but it has not the power for such an undertaking. First winter came to the wizard's castle and Deepwood. Then it flowed to Wildwood. You have just walked upon the frozen heart lake." There was real pain in her face. "Now the River of No Return begins to freeze, and although Fork resists, its powers are limited. It is weakened by the fear and anxieties of its inhabitants. Wildwood and the castle are resisting, too, as best they can, but Fork is the last stronghold. Once it fails, the magical waters in the caverns beneath the land will begin to freeze. When they no longer flow, Valley will cease to be."

"Don't say that!" Rage cried. It was too dreadful to return to Valley, after longing for it, to discover that it was again in danger of destruction. "But where is the wizard? Can't he do something?"

"He is not in Valley," Rue said. "He left some time ago."

Fury rose in Rage's heart. "How convenient for the wizard that he should decide to travel when Valley is in such terrible trouble. What a fearful coward he is not to stay and try to help!" she said.

Rue shook her head. "You are mistaken, Child Rage. The wizard sought to close the gate using all and many magics, and then one day he said he must go through the gate to learn how it had been created, for the more he examined it, the less it seemed like a proper world gate."

"The wizard went through the winter door?"

Rue accepted a cup of steaming tea from Puck. "He did."

"Alone," Puck muttered hotly, bringing a flowered teacup in its pretty saucer to Rage, who was glad to curl her fingers around the scalding heat of it. "He had to do it alone, did he not? All alone and by himself, though he had agreed to be part of an expedition," the little man added fiercely. He turned and stumped away. Rue sighed.

"How long ago did he go?" Rage asked.

Rue's eyes looked into hers. "Nine months ago."

"Are you sure he didn't just go somewhere else?" Rage asked in a voice hard as stone to her ears. "Did anyone *see* him go through it? Maybe he only pretended to go through and then went off somewhere else."

"It is not the place of a child, even one who has done as much as you, to judge as a liar and a coward the one who created Valley," Rue said in reproof. "Since his return, he worked tirelessly to repair the damage that was done here."

Rage wanted to say that she had every right to judge

the wizard, given that he was her great-uncle and responsible for turning his own brother into a monster who had crushed his poor wife and all but destroyed his children. But thinking of her own world brought a new thought, one so awful that it quenched her anger. "Is it possible that this enchanted winter could have begun to leak through into my world?" Rage asked.

The witch woman whitened. "What are you saying?"

"I don't know, but winter in my world is supposed to be over, only it hasn't ended and everyone keeps saying how freakish and unnatural it is. . . ."

"I must consult with Guardian Gilbert," Rue said decisively.

"*Guardian* Gilbert," Rage echoed, wondering if she had misheard.

The older woman nodded briskly. "He who was once known to you by the name Goaty. He remained with the wizard after their return from the shore of the Endless Sea and became his apprentice. His doubts and procrastinations were the cause of his many errors in the beginning, but in time he became the wizard's primary helper. Unfortunately, the loss of the wizard seems to have set him back." She sighed.

"Goaty." Rage shook her head in wonder. "What about the others? Elle and Mr. Walker?"

"Mr. Walker is now Prince Walker of the little folk. He dwells with them chiefly in the caverns beneath Fork. The little folk guard the waters against those who seek to use them as did the Lord High Keeper, curst be his name."

"*Prince* Walker!" Rage tried to imagine Mr. Walker as a prince but could only think of the snappy, high-strung little Chihuahua that he had once been.

"He had to be made a prince so that he could pledge his troth to the king's daughter," Rue continued. "Sadly, Princess Feluffeen died a year past in a plague that came through the winter door."

"Princess Feluffeen?"

"You met her. She preferred to be called Kelpie. She and Mr. Walker were wed."

"Kelpie died?" Rage murmured. A vivid picture came to her of the tiny smiling woman who had led them to the Place of Shining Waters, with her catsuit, high-topped boots, and cloud of pale hair floating like spun sugar about her delicate ears.

"It was tragic, truly," Rue said. "The wizard vanquished the plague, but many died first. The old king was among the last, though I believe he died as much of grief as sickness. Prince Walker became the leader of the little people in his stead and by his dying decree."

Rage was saddened by this list of woes. "He's not the king, though?"

The witch Mother shook her head. "He refuses the title. He says his daughter will be king someday."

"He has a daughter!"

"Her name is Nomadiel. She was a babe when her mother perished."

"Oh, how sad," Rage said, her thoughts flicking painfully to her own mother. "But surely she would be a queen if she is a girl?"

"The fairy folk have only kings, although these may be male or female."

Rage shook her head again. "And Elle?"

The witch woman smiled briefly. "The Lady Elle is an elusive soul whose heart leads her most often to the wildest parts of Valley. If she did not visit Guardian

Gilbert regularly and attend council meetings, I think we should have seen little of her."

"Elle goes to *council meetings?*" It was hard to imagine the impetuous Elle doing anything so tame and rational.

"She attends them in order to take part in the discussions and to vote upon matters concerning all of Valley," Rue said. "She was appointed to the council because, as an outworlder, she sees things differently than those of us born in Valley."

"Then I suppose she is wandering in the wilderness now," Rage said wistfully.

"That was where the Lady Elle preferred to be, but since this fell winter began, she bides in Fork. In truth, I think that she is the reason that Fork is able to resist the winter. But even the sunny courage of the Lady Elle will not hold off the drear winter from Fork forever." The witch woman looked directly at Rage. "But tell me more of this winter in your world. Are you sure that it is not merely an unusually harsh winter?"

"I . . . I don't know," Rage admitted. "I suppose it must be, because how could the winter here go there, since the wizard got rid of the bramble gate?"

"Gates are not the only ways between worlds. There will be many weak places in the matter between Valley and your world. These weak places could act as gateways in the right circumstances."

"You make the winter sound as if it is alive."

"I fancy it so," Rue admitted. "But if you are correct in thinking that it has found a way through to your world, then it is not only our two worlds that are in danger."

"I don't understand what you mean. The wizard made Valley out of a bit of *my* world. He didn't say he had made any other worlds."

"Surely you do not think the wizard the only one capable of such world building? Or that this is the only way parallel worlds come into being? There are many worlds and a multitude of bridges between them. But we must learn if the winter in your world is connected to the winter here. I will go to the castle to see if the wizard left any notes about the possibility that the winter here could flow into other worlds. I will learn what I can before your return—"

"My return?" Rage interrupted her. "But I don't know if I can come back." She thought suddenly of the three seats. "Unless I came here because of something *you* did to make it happen. Is that how you knew I would be here?"

"I used soul magic to ask what I could do to save Valley, and I saw you arriving at the frozen heart lake. So I came here to wait for you."

"Ask what her visions cost her!" Puck commanded in an accusing voice, pointing at Rue's white hair.

"Peace, Puck," said the witch woman with a somber look. Puck hung his head.

"What does he mean?" Rage demanded.

The witch Mother ignored the question. "The visions showed me that the answer to ending this winter can be found in the link between you and the wizard."

"Am I to follow the wizard through this winter door, then?" Rage asked. "I don't see how I could, even if I wanted to, since I am only here while I dream."

"Before you think to refuse what has not yet been asked of you, consider the possibility that you yourself have just raised. If the winter in your world *is* linked to the winter killing Valley, then in time your own world will become the wasteland that Valley has become," Rue said inexorably. "For now, I suggest only that the next time you come to Valley, you dream yourself directly to the wizard's castle."

"I don't think I can control this dream-traveling," Rage protested.

"Of course you can. You would not be here otherwise. You need only think of where you wish to go before you sleep. You willed yourself here by thinking of Valley."

"I *didn't* think of Valley," Rage disagreed. Then she said softly, "I thought about you."

Rue's brows lifted. "An interesting paradox. I am here in this place only because of a vision which showed that you came here, and you are here only because you used me as the focus of your dream magic." She shrugged. "You had better will yourself to Gilbert next time if your dream-travel ability works by focusing on people. He will certainly be at the castle, and I will arrange to be notified as soon as you arrive." She gave Rage a long look. "I wonder how you have this ability, for it is generally only wizards who possess it."

Rage opened her mouth to tell the witch Mother about the firecat, but as she opened her mouth, all strength drained from her and she was pulled away.

Someone was joggling Rage's shoulder.

It was Logan. She blinked groggily at him. "What the heck is the matter with you?" he hissed as Rage sat up. She noticed absently how pale he looked, then she looked around and found that she was in the school library.

"What is it? What's wrong? I must have fallen asleep."

"I've been trying to wake you for about ten minutes! Are you sick?"

"No . . . no," she managed to say. "I . . . I was . . . I had a dream."

His eyes narrowed, but he said more calmly, "You missed the afternoon assembly and I got worried. Luckily, there was no roll call." He sat down beside her. "Are you sure you're okay? You really do look pretty weird."

Rage picked up the book and smoothed the creased pages automatically, saying, "I know. I mean, I *feel* weird, so it makes sense I look weird." She looked at him and remembered how he had stormed away. "Logan, how come you can't read?"

He scowled and grew red again. Then he gave a weary shrug. "I dunno. It was because of being shuffled around, I guess. Everyone thought someone else taught me, and then there was this rotten teacher that made fun of me. Anyway, I started covering it up. I mean, I can read a *bit*, but slowly like some little kindergartner. So I don't bother."

"But what about signs, and what about schoolwork?"

"Signs are okay and I've got a great memory. It helps with school stuff as well. And with homework, I either didn't do it or I got other kids to do it for me. I think some of the teachers might have guessed, but they're just happy if I don't disrupt the class, and they pass me to get me out of their hair."

Rage thought about Mam reading *The Lion, the Witch, and the Wardrobe* to her, and then she was crying. "My uncle says they're moving my mother to Leary Hospital on the weekend. They want to find out why she isn't getting better. . . ."

"Well, that's good, isn't it? I mean, maybe they'll figure it out," Logan said.

Rage shook her head and more tears fell. "She's too

sad to get better. If only my uncle would go and see her, I think that might help her." She stopped because she could no longer speak, for the tears.

"Why doesn't he, then?" Logan asked.

She shook her head, struggling to control the tears. Then she said in a stuffy voice, "The doctors won't let him. They say the shock of seeing him after so long might be too much for Mam. . . ." She blinked back a fresh fall of tears and glared out the window for a long moment. Still turned away, she said, "Don't be nice to me, because it will only make me cry again."

"I could bash you, if you'd rather," Logan offered. Rage turned to give him a startled look and found him smiling sheepishly at her. She laughed, and some of the tight hurt inside her dissolved. "I'm sorry for howling like that. I wasn't even thinking about her and then suddenly I was." He nodded and wisely said nothing. After a bit, Rage rubbed at her cheeks with both hands to ease the stiffness of the dried tears.

At that moment, one of the library monitors came round the stacks and gave them a long look. Rage knew her face must look as if she had been crying because the monitor approached to ask if anything was the matter. His eyes flicked suspiciously at Logan, who immediately stood up, bristling. "What are you looking at *me* for?"

"I wanted to know if everything was all right," the monitor said evenly, though Logan towered over him.

"Everything's fine," Rage said firmly. "Really."

The monitor hesitated, but then he shrugged. "If you say so." The minute he was out of sight, the aggression faded from Logan's features. Rage thought that Logan was as trapped by his bully form as much as Billy was trapped by his dog form.

Logan stopped at the door to the next class, but Rage persuaded him to go in. Everyone, including Mrs. Gosford, gaped when they walked in and sat together. Rage had to look down to stop from laughing aloud.

Mrs. Gosford began to speak, and Rage forced herself to pay attention. The teacher announced that everyone in class was to read the same piece aloud, one at a time, so that they could get the feel of the language. There were groans, a few from kids who had joined their class because of the shortage of teachers and who were supposed to be silent-reading.

They started. Some of the kids read badly, stumbling over the words, hesitating, and making mistakes, so if one hadn't already heard it seven times, it would have been incomprehensible. Bit by bit, Rage saw the point of the exercise and so could most of the class. The repetition forced everyone to think about the meaning of the lines, even the dullest students. When the first student in the back row began to read, Logan shifted restively in his seat. Rage knew that he was about to make a fuss that would get him kicked out of the class.

She elbowed Logan, and when he leaned closer, she whispered, "You can do this just like everyone else."

He glared at her. "Are you crazy? You know why I can't," he hissed.

"Yes you can!" she insisted. "You said you have a really good memory, and even *I* can remember the lines because we've heard them so many times. Now just *pretend* to read them."

"Rage Winnoway, perhaps you would like to share your news with all of us?" Mrs. Gosford said. She hated students to be inattentive to a student who was reading.

"I'm sorry, Mrs. Gosford," Rage said penitently. The

teacher's eyes shifted to Logan, and fearing that she might suggest Rage's behavior was degenerating because of the company she kept, Rage said quickly, "Logan forgot his book and I was just offering to let him use mine."

Mrs. Gosford's mouth all but fell open, but she collected herself and said mildly that perhaps Rage ought to read before passing the book on. Rage read badly because she was worried about what Logan would do. When she finished, she sat down and handed the book over without daring to look at him.

There was a long pause, and mentally Rage crossed her fingers.

Then Logan laid his fingers on the book and began to speak the lines without standing up. He was reading the part of a character called Bottom, who was playing the part of a donkey that had wandered into the forest and had got caught up in a magical competition between the king and queen of the fairies. It was meant to be funny, but it hadn't been until Logan said the words. When kids in the class started laughing, he stopped and glared furiously about, but Rage hissed, "They're laughing because you're *good!*"

Logan's tension faded and he looked about with dawning wonder, seeing that she was right. There was enough laughter that her comments and his hesitation went unnoticed, except by the teacher, who only nodded for him to go on. Logan read to the end of the speech, saying the lines perfectly except in one place, where Rage was able to prompt him softly. He finished to a storm of applause. Logan looked around, almost purple in the face with pride and scowling embarrassment. Rage had to laugh at his expression, and then at last he laughed, too, shaking his head.

"That was brilliant," Mrs. Gosford said enthusiastically, waving her hands to quiet everyone down. "Logan, I had no idea you were hiding thespian talents."

The class ended with students who normally steered clear of Logan slapping him fearlessly on the back and telling him how great he was. Mrs. Gosford kept Rage and Logan back, and when the others had gone, she wagged her finger at them.

"Don't think I can't guess what this is all about."

Rage didn't need to look at Logan to feel him tense up, but before he could react, Mrs. Gosford said, "You have been *rehearsing* the play together, haven't you? I can't tell you how impressed I am with both of you, and I shall say so in the end-of-term reports later in the month. I insist on seeing both of you next week at the play auditions."

Rage muttered something noncommittal and hustled Logan out of the classroom. In the hall, students were milling around opening lockers, getting ready to go home. Several of them stopped Logan to tell him how they had liked his performance.

"I can't go to that audition," Logan said when they got to a passage that was relatively empty.

"Why not!" Rage protested. "Why shouldn't you try out?"

"What are you talking about?" Logan demanded. There was an accusing note in his voice.

"You can learn the audition piece by heart," she insisted warmly. "You've just shown what a great memory you have, and actors on stage don't *read* lines. They learn them and then they say them from memory, just as you did in class."

"I can't remember a *whole play!*" Logan argued again.

"I bet you could if you tried, but you don't have to. Try for the part of Bottom. It's not that long. I can read the lines to you over and over, and you can learn them that way. We can start out by learning another of his speeches for our audition piece. There are even tapes of plays in the library, and I bet they have *A Midsummer Night's Dream*. You can listen over and over. And there's a film of it, too."

Logan was staring at her, partly in hope and partly in apprehension. Rage decided not to press him to an actual agreement. *Let him think it through and see how easy it would be.* In a funny way, because of not being able to read, Logan had actually trained himself to learn just as real actors did.

Rage changed the subject, saying they ought to get to the library. Once there, she went to the shelves and got out *The Lion, the Witch, and the Wardrobe*, then she went into one of the little study rooms along the library wall. Logan followed her, closing the door, as she asked, with a puzzled frown. Rage sat down, opened the book, and began to read aloud. From the corner of her eye, she saw him pale then flush, then he looked around self-consciously. Finally, he sat stiffly, his arms crossed over his chest. Rage became engrossed in the story herself then and did not look up again until her voice was beginning to crack. Disappointment flitted across Logan's face, but she pretended not to notice as she matter-of-factly closed the book, saying her uncle would arrive at any moment. Then she suggested checking out the audiotapes of both *The Lion, the Witch, and the Wardrobe* and *A Midsummer Night's Dream*. Logan's eyes lit up before he shrugged and said casually, "Yeah, okay."

A little while later they were outside in the icy air. Rage shivered, wondering again if the deadly winter in Valley was stealing into their world.

"Want my coat?" Logan offered.

Rage nodded, sensing that he was thanking her. But even the heavy jacket did not ease the cold. Fortunately, Uncle Samuel arrived and offered Logan a lift home. This time it was accepted at once. Billy sniffed Logan as he got in and wagged his tail in recognition.

"He remembers me," Logan murmured, rubbing Billy between the eyes.

"Billy smells that Rage likes you," Uncle Samuel said, surprisingly.

When Logan got out, he thanked them and ran lightly across the road, despite the fact that *The Lion, the Witch, and the Wardrobe* audiotape and another of *A Midsummer Night's Dream* were stuffed into his pockets, making the sides of his coat bulge. Rage wondered, smiling, what his foster family would make of him suddenly listening to Shakespeare.

Rage thought happily about what had happened in English that afternoon. But the good feelings faded as the car began to climb the hills above the town, for here the bleakness of the winter was evident on all sides. Rage thought of the creatures that had chased her and Logan.

Then a truly awful thought assailed her.

What if the beasts had come through the winter door? What if *they* were what the wizard had sent the firecat to warn her about? Rage tried to remember exactly what the firecat had said. It had said something about needing the wizard. Then it had offered to take her to him. It could only have made that offer if it had possessed the power to take her to the wizard.

A picture came into Rage's mind of the tiny hour-glass. What if it had contained dream-traveling magic? Perhaps the spell had been designed to activate as soon as it was near her. Then she might have been meant to dream-travel to the wizard, who would have told her how to block the gap between her world and Valley to keep out the winter. Or maybe she would have been told how to close the winter door, thereby saving both worlds.

Rage began to smooth Billy's fur with her fingers. It soothed her as much as it did him. She focused on the world outside the car again. The snowy world of hillocks and trees flew past, shadowy and as full of jumps as the old Charlie Chaplin movies that Mam loved so much. It was only when they were coming up the hill road to the farm that Rage glanced at her uncle and noticed a little nerve jumping crazily in the side of his neck.

Rage told herself that her uncle was no different than usual. His coolness might only be because he was irri-tated at having to ferry her to and from school. Worry-ing about her uncle on top of worrying about Valley made her feel strangely hollow, as if fear had claws and were burrowing into her.

Dinner was a frozen pizza to which they added fresh toppings. Rage had extra cheese and slices of tomato. Uncle Samuel put butter beans and feta cheese on his, then he drizzled on olive oil, saying it was better that way. While the pizzas heated, he unwrapped some bones he had gotten for Billy and put out a bowl of water. The news came on and Rage listened to it, half hoping that some expert would come on and talk about mutated boars.

The first half hour was world news. Unusually, Leary got a mention because of its weather. The attention of the world was beginning to focus on the phenomenal weather pattern around their part of the globe. The announcer said that the freakish weather was spreading and continued to baffle experts. Rather than being the result of high- or low-pressure fronts, or hurricanes out at sea, or even of volcanic activity, this weather seemed to be spontaneously roiling out of the skies above Leary.

Rage stiffened. If the weather was flowing from an opening in Valley, it would probably be near Leary.

The announcer went on to say that experts from all over the world were coming to Leary for an emergency weather summit. Then a local news announcer came on and repeated pretty much all that had been said, only adding that the weather had immobilized all transport outside Leary. Snowplows were facing a struggle to keep open the main roads to smaller towns such as Hopeton and Cally to the north and south.

Rage knew this would affect the possibility of visiting Mam in Leary. It was even possible that the hospital authorities would decide the journey was too dangerous for Mam and change their minds. But Rage could not really hope for that because maybe Mam did need more specialized care. The broadcast dissolved into loud crackling, and Rage didn't know whether to be glad or sorry.

She glanced over at her uncle and was alarmed to notice that he was staring curiously at Billy, who looked exactly as if he was trying to hear the faint words under the static. Rage coughed loudly and Billy dropped his muzzle to his bowl.

Dessert was a tin of peaches, then Uncle Samuel made himself a coffee and said he would do some work in his room. Rage was surprised because he had not touched the piles of notebooks and boxes of specimens in his room, let alone the battered typewriter he'd spent such care in cleaning and oiling. Then she realized that it was probably just an excuse not to stay in the kitchen with her. As he went out, her uncle looked back and reminded her to finish her homework and not to stay up too late.

Later Rage snuggled into her blankets and yawned widely, forcing her tired mind to imagine Goaty. *Not Goaty*, she reminded herself dreamily. *Gilbert.* She mustn't forget to use the name Elle had given him.

columns supporting a balcony and gasped to see a fall of lush marble blossoms with petals so thin as to be translucent. Reaching out to touch one of the flowers, Rage was disconcerted to discover that the marble was faintly warm.

She continued along the path. The warmth in the carved flowers extended to the flagstones under her bare feet, but Rage was distracted from wondering about it because the stream suddenly curved out of sight. Then, around the bend, the pale stone altered slightly in hue. It had a delicate greenish tinge, and here and there were streaks of dull purple that looked oddly bruiselike. Touching one of these streaks, Rage discovered that unlike the surrounding stone, it was quite cold. On impulse, she went to the bank and knelt down to dip her fingers in the water. She half expected it to be hot, for a slight mist lay over it, but it was so cold that her fingers hurt. She frowned at the water, trying to think what the milky aqua color reminded her of. Both the water and the misty air had a luminous quality that suggested that the sun was somewhere above, shining brightly.

It was growing colder, or perhaps the chilly mist was beginning to make Rage cold, so she started walking again, wishing that she were wearing something warmer. She couldn't remember feeling so cold in her dreams before. But she had been cold in the playground dream, too.

Only that had not exactly been a dream.

She drew in a slow breath, for this was not *just* a dream. She had obviously dream-traveled again. She turned slowly, trying again to figure out what it was that bothered her about this place. She noticed the way the mist coiled and swirled in her wake, while elsewhere it hung motionless. It was as if she were the only thing in the whole city that moved. Wishing she had willed Billy along in his human form, she went on uneasily. The canal path curved again, and when it straightened out this time, Rage saw a small wooden bridge spanning the stream a little way ahead. She stopped abruptly, realizing where she was.

"This is *Fork*!" she whispered.

"Are you sure?" Billy asked doubtfully.

Rage whirled to find him standing behind her in his human form!

"The smell of places doesn't change and this doesn't smell like Fork," he said.

Rage's delight faded as she turned to look around. "But it *is* Fork, Billy. Look at the canal streams and the paved banks and the way the houses don't have any spaces between them."

"Fork was black."

"It was, but remember, that was only because of the High Keeper and the conservatorium." A shadow crossed Billy's face. "Remember the wizard said he was going to go back to Valley and fix Fork up so that it would be the way it was before the High Keeper took over?"

"Where are the people and animals?" Billy asked.

"People didn't live in this part of the city before," Rage reminded him. "Maybe they still don't."

Billy sniffed again. Then he looked at Rage. "Why did you bring us here? I thought you wanted to see if the firecat would contact you."

"I didn't bring us here. At least, I didn't mean to if I did. Maybe this dream-traveling doesn't work the way the witch Mother said it does."

"Should we try to go to the castle?" Billy asked.

"I don't see how we could get all the way there before we wake up," Rage said. "We had better try to see if we can find someone to take a message for us. And maybe we can get some idea of how much time has passed since I was at the heart lake." She glanced down at her pajamas ruefully. "If only I had dreamed myself here in something more sensible!"

Billy had moved away from her a little and was examining the carvings on the building facades with an expression of puzzled wonder. "These leaves look real. I wonder what made Fork create them."

Rage gave a little gasp. "Oh, Billy, I've just remembered! Rue told me that Elle is here in Fork trying to help the city to resist the winter. Maybe *she's* the reason it's not frozen here like the heart lake was."

"You think we're here because of Elle being here?" Billy asked.

"I don't . . . oh, of course! It must be that!" Rage clutched at Billy's hand. "Just as I was falling asleep, I was thinking about the way Elle named Goaty—I mean Gilbert—so maybe I dreamed myself to her instead of to him."

"Let's go and find her," Billy cried eagerly.

"But *how?*" Rage muttered. "Fork could help if we knew where she would be, but I can't imagine she'd be at the Willow Seat Tower or the conservatorium or any of those places we know. The best thing would be to find someone to ask where the Valley council sits. Elle might even be there now, since she is a councillor."

Billy nodded absently. "If this dream-traveling works the same as when you went to the heart lake, shouldn't Elle be somewhere near?"

"Maybe she just went somewhere else."

Billy shook his head. "I would have smelled it if she had been here."

"Maybe we can get the city to help us find her. After all, she's helping Fork, so it must know where she is. Let's try to do it together now."

"Do what?" Billy asked.

"Imagine Elle," Rage said impatiently.

"I can think about the smell of her," Billy offered hesitantly, and Rage remembered that it was unnatural for animals to imagine things. Billy might be a wonderful thinker, but he was still too much of a dog to be able to imagine things.

It was up to her, then.

A cold breeze began to blow. The mist shifted and coiled about them as Rage closed her eyes to concentrate. She thought of Elle as she had been before they had parted on the shore of the Endless Sea: a lithe, gold-haired, tan-suited woman with almond-shaped eyes, pointed ears, and white teeth that flashed when she smiled. With the picture fixed firmly in her mind, Rage started to walk, hoping that the city would see fit to guide her steps.

Billy came along behind her.

Rage had no idea how long they walked, but when she stopped to rest, it had grown darker and her head was pounding from the effort of trying to keep thinking the same thing over and over. It was colder, too. Her feet were the only part of her that was not freezing, because of the warm stone underfoot, but they felt sore and grazed. She would not be able to walk too much longer without finding shoes or at least something to bind her feet.

Through the mist she saw some sort of crossroad

ahead. At the center was a large monument, but it was impossible to make out what it was. Rage walked faster, certain there would be some sign or clue to indicate which direction they ought to take next, since thinking about Elle wasn't getting them anywhere.

Rage was more troubled than she wanted to admit that they had not seen a single sign of life so far. Maybe everyone in Valley had died and Fork was all that lived. If that were so, maybe the city held enough of a memory of Elle to have called them here.

She stumbled over a tuft of the whiskery stuff between the flagstones and, on impulse, bent to feel the wiry threads. It was a dead, mossy sort of grass and had obviously been alive once. Probably the cold had killed it off, but she could imagine how this street must have looked when the mossy grass growing between the pale flagstones had been bright green in the sunlight. There would have been other colors as well, for the many niches built into the facades of the buildings held wispy sticks that might once have been blossom-laden creepers or flowers.

Rage wondered if Fork had created the carvings to compensate for the loss of living plant life, once the winter sapped the green life threaded through it. If there *had* been plants, there would have been insects, birds, and maybe even animals, which would explain the ornate little drinking troughs along the front of buildings every few meters. Oh, how she would have loved to see a city with green streets where humans and little folk and animals lived in harmony!

Billy and Rage came to the meeting of roads at last, and despite the cold and her sore feet, Rage was dazzled to see that the monument was a fountain shaped like a huge, gnarled tree. Water trickled from under its leaves and down its trunk into puddles around its stone roots. Billy snuffled at the water, then lapped thirstily at it. Taking her lead from him, Rage scooped up a handful and drank, too, gasping at the coldness of the water. Only then did she notice that there was a thin crust of ice about the outer rim of the fountain. It occurred to her that the sluggish movement of the canals might mean the water there was beginning to freeze as well.

As she straightened up, a gust of wind whistled along the street and huffed coldly into her face. Rage thought she could feel tiny specks of ice in it. Shuddering, she wrapped her arms about herself and wondered if it was possible to catch pneumonia when you were dream-traveling. She was beginning to feel sick with cold. Billy leaned closer and sniffed at her anxiously. Then he shed his bomber jacket. Rage was too cold to resist as he put it on her.

"I should have given it to you sooner," Billy said contritely. "I just forgot that I was not wearing fur."

Rage frowned at him because the skin of his arms was already rising into gooseflesh. "We need to find somewhere to warm up," she said. The trouble was that the streets leading away from the monument all looked the same: lovely, pale, and empty. Rage tried to imagine the kind of place she wanted to be. Her mind produced a memory of a tavern that she and Mam had visited before they went to Winnoway Farm to live with Grandfather Adam. It had been a rather dark place smelling of ale, stew, and fresh-baked bread, with a noisy, friendly press of people. The vision was very strong, and as it began to slip away, Rage felt that *something* had noted it. Then *something* nudged at her mind. Obeying the gentle push, Rage walked down one of the streets.

Billy followed, sniffing at her in puzzlement. "Where are we going?"

"I don't know," Rage admitted, but dreamily, because the compulsion was making her feel beautifully safe, like when she was a little girl and Mam held her hand to cross the street.

They came to a smaller side street, and Rage followed the prompt to turn into it. "I think Fork is taking us somewhere," she murmured.

"Fork!" Billy said. He sniffed at Rage again, but she was walking faster now, despite the fact that her bare feet were beginning to feel tender. In a very little time, they turned another corner into a lane. They had not gone more than a few steps down it before Billy stopped with an exclamation that was more bark than shout. Rage stopped, too, slightly dazed to feel whatever had been shepherding her withdraw.

"What . . . ?"

"I smell people and smoke and food!" Billy said, mistaking her word for a question. He caught hold of Rage's arm and dragged her to the door of a building. Steps led darkly down, but there were lanterns hung on hooks. Now even Rage could smell food and smoke. They descended and found themselves in a short hall that led to a set of carved wooden doors. Rage hesitated, but Billy pushed at the doors, and in a moment, they were standing in what was clearly some sort of public tavern. It bore an astonishing resemblance to the tavern of Rage's memory. Two girls were serving ale that frothed golden at the top, and another woman pushed out through a set of doors carrying a tray of fresh-baked bread.

Rage's stomach rumbled, and she remembered that they had no money. Indeed, she hadn't any idea what passed for money in Valley. Billy sniffed hungrily beside her, and she elbowed him to make him stop. The woman with the bread glanced over at them and stopped dead.

"Mercy me! What have we here?"

Everyone in the room turned to stare at them. Rage felt blood rise in her face, knowing that they would be seeing a barefoot girl in nothing but a thin nightdress and a bomber jacket, and a boy with no jacket and no shoes.

"Hello," Billy said easily. "I am Billy Thunder and this is Rage. We are trying to find Elle."

Concern passed over the woman's red face, and strangely, she lifted her finger to her lips and shook her head. Then she turned and scowled at the gaping patrons. "Get on with your own business," she snapped, sharply enough that most turned away. Those that continued to stare did so discreetly once she had turned her back. "Come and sit over in this wee corner. Truth to tell, you look froze, and isn't the weather an awful thing? Our poor city does its best, but it's a cruel winter and no mistaking it. Sit now and have a warm bit of bread. I'll get some butter and soup, and that will put some color into you."

The woman ushered them to a table in a niche, and when they were seated, she set down the tray of bread and hurried away.

"She smelled nice," Billy said, helping himself to a chunk of fragrant bread. Rage took a piece, too, and made herself eat. Her face and hands ached as the warmth restored her circulation, and her feet felt bruised and sore. If she had been Billy, she thought wryly, she would simply have asked the waitress if she had any shoes, but being human, she could not bring herself to ask.

It occurred to her that they had done exactly what Mr. Walker had advised the last time they had come to Valley, based on his devotion to the fairy tales. They had found a tavern in order to ask directions. Rage smiled and some of her tension dissolved. After all, there was no need for them to hide their errand or their identities this time.

The waitress returned with two bowls and spoons, a steaming jug of thick soup, and a little pot of golden butter. Billy reached out at once, but Rage caught his hand. "You are very kind, madam, but we don't have any way to pay for this."

The woman laughed. "Why, wild things and witch folk don't need tokens in such a time as this, child. Did no one tell you that on the ferry? Fork loves to have you visit us, and anything that makes our dear city happy is fine by us. Especially now." A cloud passed over her features again, and she busied herself pouring the soup out. Billy thanked her and began to eat hungrily.

Rage opened her mouth to say that they were neither witch folk nor wild things, then thought better of it. There was something odd about the woman's manner for all her kindness. It was this thought that prompted Rage to repeat their earlier question. "Do you know where the Lady Elle can be found?"

The woman all but cringed despite the softness of Rage's question. "*Hsst.* You must not speak that name," she hissed with genuine anxiety in her face. "Do not remind poor Fork of its despair, lest it further lose its will to fight this deadly winter."

She glanced about and then in a loud, jovial voice bid

them sup well. Rage caught at her apron and the woman gave her a look of impatience mingled with despair. "Can you tell us where the Valley council meets?"

The woman's face cleared miraculously. "I am surprised that even outlanders don't know that the council meets at the council house. Did you not ask the river folk? It's close by the ferry port, and you all but passed by its door to come here."

"It's the mist," Rage said vaguely.

The woman nodded sagely. "It is true that the mists grow thicker each day that passes, and I do suppose that one not accustomed to the city might lose themself. All you need to do is think of the ferry port and Fork will take you there, then one of the ferry folk can direct you to the council house."

"Thank you," Rage said.

The woman frowned a little. "I do hope it is good news you bring them from the witch Mother, for anything that lifts the heart of the city will serve us better than bad news."

"I hope that what I have to tell the council will help," she said.

"I hope so, too," the woman said, and went away.

Rage ate a few spoonfuls of her soup, but she had no real appetite. She supposed this was because she was not truly in her body, but Billy finished his bowl off and looked so longingly at hers that she slid it over to him. She wanted them to hurry, but she was dreading walking again. It was not that the flagstones were so hard, but she was simply not accustomed to going without shoes.

"Let's go," Billy said.

Rage rose, wincing slightly. Billy frowned and sniffed at her.

"Stop that," Rage whispered, seeing a man look over at them curiously.

"You need shoes," Billy said decisively. Before she could stop him, he had turned and gone over to the bar. Rage stood there, feeling her face flush brighter and brighter, but Billy returned with a well-worn pair of slippers.

"It's all she has, and she says that I must beg your pardon for her not offering them sooner, but she didn't know folk like us needed such things." He so exactly mimicked the waitress's singsong way of talking that Rage's embarrassment faded. After all, wasn't it better that he had asked than that she had walked herself to a limp? She pulled the slippers on and sighed to feel their softness. She would have liked to thank the waitress, but she had vanished.

Outside, Rage pulled the bomber jacket more closely about her. The mist had grown thicker but so had the darkness. It was definitely night now. She closed her eyes, but before she could begin to summon up a memory of the ferry crossing, Billy elbowed her. She opened her eyes. "What is it?"

Instead of answering, he nodded, and Rage turned. Her breath caught because there was a black crow sitting on a jutting piece of stonework a little above their eye level. It watched them with its head cocked.

"It's a crow," Billy said.

"I know," Rage whispered.

The crow launched itself from its perch and flapped to a lantern post alongside them. The lantern flared to life, throwing out a soft buttery light over the pale stone. The crow regarded them again for a long moment, then rose into the air with a grating *caw* and flapped away.

Watching it blur and dissolve into the misty darkness, Rage wondered if it was one of the animals in Valley that could talk. Then she dismissed the thought and turned back to the task at hand, closing her eyes and envisaging the ferry. She held the image until the cold began to bite into her bare legs. Then she opened her eyes to find Billy peering worriedly into her face. Staggering back in surprise, she almost fell because the slippers were too big, but Billy's hand shot out and he caught her. She was about to scold him when she felt *something* touch her mind again. She summoned up the image of the ferry port. At once she felt a nudge.

"Come on," she told Billy, and began to walk.

They had not gone far when Billy gave a start. The ferry image slipped from Rage's mind and she felt Fork withdraw. Billy was staring at a crow that was now sitting on a lamp just ahead, watching them. It looked like the same one from before.

"Good dusk, Master Crow," Rage said politely. She was less frightened than curious. After all, what harm could a crow do them? It might dive and peck their heads, but both she and Billy had been swooped any number of times by magpies on Winnoway. "Can you talk?" she asked, for it looked both dignified and intelligent.

The crow only stared harder than ever.

"I guess you don't, then," Rage said, slightly disappointed.

"His name is Rally and he talks only when he has something to say. Not like humans, always talking about nothing." Rage and Billy turned toward the voice. It came from a young girl so small that she could only have been one of the little folk. Slight of build and wearing a long cloak with the hood up, nothing could be seen of the girl but her small serious face, the toes of her pale boots, and a lick of golden hair falling across her forehead.

"I am Nomadiel," she introduced herself imperiously. It was the name of Mr. Walker's daughter. But this could not be her, for she had been born only a year ago.

Billy gave a cry of joy. "You smell of Mr. Walker!"

The severe little features softened. "Prince Walker is my father." That meant she had aged in dog years, seven years to a human year!

"How did you know we were here?" Billy asked.

"Rally came and told me that there were two people asking about *a certain person*," Nomadiel said, gesturing at the crow.

Rage frowned. "He heard me ask about Elle?"

"You shouldn't speak of the Lady." Nomadiel glanced about with real anxiety. Then she crooked a finger at them and strode off.

Billy and Rage exchanged a startled glance before following her. Rage hurried as best she could, but the slippers made her clumsy. Finally, she caught at Nomadiel's cloak, forcing her to slow down. "You had better tell us where you are taking us."

Nomadiel gave her a cross look. "You are Rage Winnoway, are you not? And he is Billy Thunder? You don't look heroic, but things are not always what they appear to be."

Rage gaped. "I am. I mean, we are. But how did you know?"

"From Rally's description, and because of how you asked openly about . . . *a certain person*. No one from here would do such a thing."

"Why do you keep calling Elle 'a certain person'?"

Rage asked impatiently, annoyed by the child's dis-approving manner.

"Please, do not name her again," the child said in a pained voice. "I will explain why when we are—"

"You had better explain now," Rage interrupted. She stopped.

"I *can't* explain here without increasing the harm you have already done! We must go somewhere I can speak freely." Nomadiel stamped her foot, looking so much like her father that Rage's irritation was quenched.

"All right. But at least tell me, where are you taking us?" said Rage.

"We must go to the other side of the river, where Fork cannot hear us."

"Fork? But why shouldn't Fork hear us talk about—" Rage stopped at the anguished look on Nomadiel's face. "All right, why shouldn't we speak about *a certain person?*"

"I can't explain here," Nomadiel repeated.

"Look, we don't have the time for this," Rage said crossly. "If you could just take us to where the council meets . . ."

"If you go to the council, you will never get to the castle, and I think that is where you wish to go."

"Are you saying the council would stop us?" Rage asked in disbelief.

"No one would mean any harm, but they would delay you," Nomadiel said. "You see, Hermani is in charge, and being so old, he is cautious. He would want to send a messenger to the castle, and it would take days before he and the other councillors would be able to agree on the right messenger. There would be endless meetings and discussions, and you would have to tell your tale ten times. It would be better if Fork were itself, but it is grieving and that makes everyone nervous. Do you see?"

Rage saw, but there was still one question she wanted answered. "Is *the certain person* here in Fork?"

"No, of course she is not," Nomadiel said. "That is what hurts Fork so. She left to go to the wizard's castle days ago to meet you! The city is suffering horribly because of her absence, and that weakens its strength so much that the winter gains a foothold here at last."

Rage was confused. If Elle was not in the city, then why had they come here? She might have asked but for the soft probing at the edge of her mind, which she now identified as the mind of the sentient city.

"You must not!" Nomadiel cried, and pinched Rage hard enough to bring tears.

Rage glared at her. "What did you do that for?"

"You were thinking about her, weren't you? I can feel the city wondering about you and soon it will know more. If you do not care about the city, then have a care for yourself. If Fork wishes, it will simply make it impossible for you to leave, as it did *a certain person.*"

"Fork would stop me from leaving?" Rage murmured. She remembered all too well how the city had shepherded her toward the dreadful dark conservatorium.

"It would if it thought that keeping you might bring . . . *a certain person* back." She glared at Rage. "Now let us go before your carelessness prevents us leaving."

Rage made her mind a careful blank as she followed Nomadiel. In a surprisingly short time, the River of No Return lay ahead of them. Like the last time, a thick mist lay over it, and Rage had a moment of déjà vu. It was not until they were at the ferry port that Rage could see that there was no longer a gateway to the landing. She was relieved to note that the ferry tied on their side of the river was unchanged in the lantern light. There was still a simple cabin in the middle of its square, flat deck, an enormous wheel on either side, and an enormous cable that pulled the ferry to the other bank.

"It will leave soon," Nomadiel said. "We should board at once, but it is better to wait until we are well away from the bank before we speak freely."

Rage nodded and let Nomadiel speak to the riverman at the gangway.

"Two humans," Nomadiel said firmly. She took two greenish metal lozenges from a pouch at her waist and laid them in the man's palm. He pocketed them, barely looking at her or her two companions, and they went aboard without further ado.

Rage made her way to the front part of the ferry, noting that it was distinctly colder on deck. She was cold even through Billy's bomber jacket. Most of the other passengers wore thick coats, except for a few sprites in glittering draperies that barely covered their long, pale limbs. No wonder the people in the tavern had thought she and Billy were wild things, given their scanty attire. It was well known that wild things did not feel the cold.

Nomadiel stood beside Billy, her little face preoccupied. Now that Rage knew who she was, she could see Mr. Walker in her, even though she had Kelpie's silky golden hair and pretty features. Nomadiel seemed to have her father's snappish, irritable temperament, too, although that was probably the result of her being brought up by her father. Rage felt a thrill of excitement at the thought of seeing him again, and Goaty, too. Though she must remember to call him Gilbert now. And Elle! How wonderful to see the lovely dog-woman that Elle had become in Valley. She wondered if they would have changed much. Three years was a long time, and they had been part human for all of that time.

The deck lurched as the tether ropes were cast off. They were now moving smoothly away from the city. Rage went to the edge and watched it grow less and less distinct as the mist coiled between the ferry and the bank. The last time Rage had seen it from the ferry, Fork had been dark with malice. Now it was as pale and melancholy as a ghost city. At length, it dissolved into whiteness, and Rage turned to find Nomadiel watching her with a curious expression.

"Rally and I will lead you to the castle," she said firmly.

"You said Elle went there?" Rage asked.

The child nodded.

Rage looked at Billy. "I just don't understand how we could have come to Fork if Elle isn't there. I was thinking about her, so we should have been drawn to her."

"Perhaps you were drawn to Fork's dreams of the Lady Elle," Rally offered in a startling deep voice.

"Fork dreams a dream of the Lady Elle which is more bright and pure than the reality of her," Nomadiel agreed. "And it is not just the city that dreams of her. All who dwell here share its dreams, just as Fork shares and absorbs their dreams. Indeed, Ania says that those who live here reflect the city as much as Fork reflects them."

"Ania," Rage murmured, remembering the young witch spy who had risked so much to help her when the ruthless High Keeper ruled Fork.

Nomadiel took this as a question. "*She* might have persuaded Hermani to let you go quickly, and even to give you aid, but she is not in Fork, either."

"She is not a councillor?"

Nomadiel shook her head. "She is the trusted personal journeywoman for the witch Mother and carries much of her authority."

"The witch Mother?" Rage asked.

"She will be at the castle. Unless she has returned to Wildwood. They have need of her there, and it was thought that you would come two seven-days past."

Rage was aghast. They had been expecting her for two weeks! That meant more than a fortnight must have gone by since she had been in Fork, though less than a day of her own time had passed.

"At least it won't take long to reach the castle," Billy was saying. "It took us two days to get from the hill where we came out of the bramble gate to the ferry last time we were here, and it didn't look that far to the castle."

"It is said that travel was once much swifter in Valley," Nomadiel said. "These days it takes a seven-day to reach the castle on foot, *if* there are no storms and *if* all goes smoothly in Deepwood."

Rage realized that Nomadiel had little or no memory of Valley before the winter door had opened. Maybe *that* was why she was such a sullen little thing. Anyone might be the same if they had only ever known winter and grayness.

Billy expressed dismay at the length of time it would take, but Nomadiel laid a tiny hand on his arm to silence him. "I said it would take that long if we made the journey afoot. However, once we leave the ferry, I will send

Rally to some friends of mine who dwell nearby. They will carry us as far as the entrance to Deepwood, once they know who you are."

"Only to the entrance?" Billy asked before Rage could voice the question.

"We must make our own way afoot through Deepwood to the castle, else it will not allow us to pass."

"What won't let us pass?" Rage wondered.

"Deepwood, of course," Nomadiel said. "It will test us, and only if we prove worthy will we be permitted to pass through it to the castle."

"Test us! We don't have time for tests, and what on earth would it test us for anyway?" Rage demanded. Cold was biting into her bare legs and making her feel out of sorts.

"Its nature is to test, just as Fork's nature is to respond to its inhabitants," Nomadiel said coolly.

Rage stared at her. "You mean that Deepwood is like Fork?"

"It is sentient," Nomadiel answered. "But it is no more like Fork than I am like you or him. It has its own nature. The wizard did not desire to have people and creatures coming to him every time they had some small problem, so he gave the forest about the castle sentience and required it to keep away all but the most determined and worthy supplicants."

"Worthy of what?"

Nomadiel shrugged. "That is something Deepwood decides."

"What sort of tests?" Billy asked, sounding intrigued, and Rage remembered how much he had loved puzzles and questions when he had been human shaped before.

"The tests are different every time, but I have traveled

to the castle many times and I will help you."

"Is that allowed?" Rage asked rather bitterly.

"Of course," Nomadiel said, looking surprised. "Is not the choice of companions a sort of test in itself? One must have wisdom to choose clever companions."

The crow gave a dry croak that recalled them to the present, and they realized that the ferry was about to touch the other bank. Once the gangplank was laid down across the gap, they went ashore with the other passengers. It was true winter here, and Rage began to shiver uncontrollably.

Nomadiel frowned at her in concern. "I will ask Rally to tell my friends that you need proper clothing. I hope they will have some human clothes. I should have thought of it when we were in the city, but I was worried that you would talk about Elle again. I think we had better wait in the hut until they come."

Nomadiel conferred briefly with the crow, who rubbed its beak gently on her cheek before launching into the icy air and flapping away. There was less mist on this bank but no streetlights, and Rally soon vanished in the darkness. Nomadiel ushered Rage and Billy into a hut. There was no heat, but at least they were out of the chill air. The floor was dry earth rather than snow, and two lanterns offered a golden glow that let them see one another clearly. Now Billy was shivering, too, and Rage stripped off his jacket. They pulled it around their shoulders and sat close together.

"I do think you might have worn better clothing," Nomadiel said with faint but definite disapproval.

If Rage had not been so very cold, she would have had plenty to say to the haughty little creature, but instead she asked a question nagging at her. "Nomadiel, back there, you said something about Fork not letting Elle leave?"

"Fork did not want to let her go. At first it pleaded and remonstrated, then it simply made it impossible for her to leave. It would not let her come to the ferry port."

"How did she get away?" Billy asked.

"She jumped into the River of No Return. She must have done it without thinking about it in advance, for Fork would have seen it in her mind and prevented her coming to the shore otherwise. I think few would do such a rash thing, for the river current might have slowed in these days, but it is colder than an ice bath. But she managed to swim to the ferry as it was crossing, and the river folk pulled her aboard."

"She was all right, though, wasn't she?" Rage asked worriedly.

"If she had not been, she would not have gone on," Nomadiel said.

Billy said, "I suppose the city didn't want Elle to go because it was frightened to face the winter alone."

Nomadiel gave him a scathing look. "Fork is not cowardly. It was not fear of the winter that made it try to stop the Lady Elle leaving. It cares for her. Everyone knew it because the city sang of it. That is why everyone in Fork dreams of the Lady."

Rage thought she must have misunderstood, and so she said it again. "The city cared for Elle?"

"Did I not say so?" Nomadiel asked, sounding annoyed. "Elle was its friend. For a time, it was wonderful here, even in spite of the winter door, for the city was happier than it had ever been, but then the Lady Elle said she must go and . . . well, I have told you." After a moment, Nomadiel added morosely, "She didn't mean to hurt it, but since she left, the city has lost heart and we begin to lose it to winter. She should not have left, once she had made the city care for her!"

"Elle is not the sort that can be held down when she wants to go," Billy said gently.

Rage said nothing, for Nomadiel's words rang true for her. Hadn't she herself felt exactly this same sense of betrayal when Mam had fallen into a coma? Or whenever she thought about her uncle leaving? Then another thought occurred to her. She cared very much for Billy, but she had been prepared to leave him when she chose to return to her own world for Mam's sake. She had wanted to leave him in Valley, but he had wanted to stay with her more.

"You said the city pleaded with Elle," Billy said, breaking the silence that had fallen. "Do you mean it spoke to her?"

"The city communicates more deeply with some than others. Ania told me that she sometimes hears it, though it has never spoken to her. I have heard it sing," she added with grave pride. Rage wondered if she ever smiled.

On impulse, Rage decided to put some of the questions she wanted to ask Rue to the child. "Where did the winter door come from in the first place?" she asked.

"No one knows," Nomadiel said.

"What does the witch Mother think?" Billy asked.

Nomadiel shrugged. "She does not confide her thoughts to me, but my father believes that it was the firecat that made it, even though the wizard said it is impossible. My father says the firecat is a desperate, wicked thing whose hunger for power is great enough for it to have found a way."

The sound of hoofs came drumming out of the darkness. Moments later, two centaurs galloped up and came to a halt at the door of the hut, plumes of steam rising from their nostrils. Rage, Billy, and Nomadiel went out to meet them. The human part of the older centaur was a matronly woman, while the other was a young, bearded man. Rally sat upon his shoulder.

"Good dark, Rage Winnoway," said the male centaur in a thrumming voice. Rage recognized him as one of the witch Mother's attendants.

"Greetings, Centaur," Rage said.

"You have reached the changing time," the centaur observed. "You are no longer a child, though you are not yet a woman. It is a time of great power and confusion among my kind and maybe your kind, too. This is my mother, and the leader of our tribe, Suria Lightfoot," he added proudly, gesturing at the other centaur.

"Greetings, Rage Winnoway and Billy Thunder," the female centaur said regally. "I hope that you will be able to find a way to end this deadly winter."

"You honor us, Lady Centaur," Billy said courteously. "I hope we can help."

"Greetings, Princess Nomadiel of the little folk. How fare you?" Suria Lightfoot addressed the child with grave courtesy.

"I fare as well as we all do in this dark time," Nomadiel said surprisingly softly.

"We have human garments that, though not beautiful, will serve to keep your friends warm," Suria said, taking a pack from her back and dropping it into the snow. She nodded to the male centaur, who removed his own pack and dropped it beside the first. "There is food and other supplies such as you may need in the other pack."

"Will you carry us to the castle trail?" Nomadiel asked.

"I will bear you there," the male centaur said. "I did not know that you would travel, Princess, but I can carry all three of you, if you desire it. I am Galantir Longleg."

"Thank you, Galantir Longleg," Nomadiel said with dignity. She turned to Billy and nodded at the packs. "You had better dress so that we can go."

Rage and Billy picked up the packs and carried them into the hut. Rage was relieved to find warm leggings, undershirts, and soft hide boots. There were also thick overtunics and warm, hooded coats. All the clothes were mud colored, roughly made, and scratchy, but they were warm, and that was the main thing. As they dressed, Rage asked Billy what he made of Nomadiel's manner.

"She smells wounded," he said, but before he could elaborate, Nomadiel came to the door and asked if they were not ready yet. "We must ride at once, for Suria Lightfoot says another storm cycle will soon begin."

They quickly gathered their things, then clambered onto Galantir's broad back, apologizing for their clumsiness. There were no stirrups or saddle to help them. Once they were mounted, Billy in front of Rage and Nomadiel behind her, Billy was commanded to tangle his fists in Galantir's flowing mane. Then the centaur gave a wild neighing cry and broke into a canter that soon became a gallop.

The wind in Rage's face was so cold that her eyes watered. She was glad not to be in front; Billy was shielding her from the worst of the icy wind. After a little, she found a way to peer over his shoulder. She was disappointed to see only a snowy road winding between two high, snowy banks. Before long, she felt drowsy from the rough monotony of the movement and the sameness of the view. She dreamed that she was walking in a dark, desolate place.

"See what will coming now, stupid ragewinnoway," snarled the firecat.

Rage stiffened and whirled, but she could see no sign of the brightness within which the wretched creature hid its true form. "Where are you?" Her voice was sharp with anger and frustration, and she quickly modified it. "Will you come and speak with me? I'm sorry I didn't listen before but—"

"Too late," the firecat hissed.

This time when it spoke, there was a flare of light. It seemed to be coming from a puddle of oily liquid caught in a depression. Rage crossed to it and looked in. Sure enough, a reflection of the firecat glared out at her, its red eyes glittering.

"I said that I was sorry," Rage said, trying to keep her voice even. "Now, if you want me to help the wizard, you must tell me what he sent you to tell me. Was it something about closing the winter door? Something about the gap between Valley and my world?"

The firecat gave no response.

"Please," Rage said. "If you don't tell me, I can't help the wizard."

"Ragewinnoway hates wizard," the firecat said triumphantly.

Rage could not bring herself to lie. "I don't much like him, it's true. But that won't stop me helping him."

A cunning look shifted in the molten eyes. "Maybe firecat bringing you to wizard. You wanting that?"

Some instinct held her from agreeing. "Where is the

wizard?" she asked. "Why didn't he come himself, rather than sending you?"

The firecat glowed. "Ragewinnoway trying to trick firecat!"

Confused, Rage shook her head. "Trick you how?"

But there was no answer because something was dragging Rage away.

Rage opened her eyes to find that she was lying in the snow looking up at Nomadiel. She was carrying a small lantern, and all about them was impenetrable darkness.

"Are you all right? You fell off," Billy said apologetically. "Luckily, you fell into a snowdrift."

"Luckily," Rage echoed wryly, struggling to her feet with Billy's help. The road was bordered on either side by trees half buried under mounds of snow. Beyond the light given off by Nomadiel's lantern, the darkness was as thick as molasses. There was no sign of the centaur.

"What happened?" Nomadiel demanded worriedly.

"I fell asleep," Rage said, feeling stupid.

"Asleep!" Nomadiel snapped. "Our world is in deepest danger and you sleep!"

Rage opened her mouth to snap back but bit back her retort, remembering what Billy had said about Nomadiel smelling wounded. "I'm sorry. What happened to Galantir Longleg?"

"I told him to go back to his village. If he had stayed with us any longer, he would have been caught on the road in the storms. In fact, as it is, *we* may be caught if we do not hurry. We are not too far from the entrance to Deepwood. We can still get there if you can manage to stay awake long enough."

Rage did not react to the small girl's tone because she

was impressed that Nomadiel had cared more about the centaur than about their own welfare.

"Maybe we can find some shelter and wait out the storm," Rage said. "There used to be a village near here."

"There is no waiting out the storms that come through the winter door," Nomadiel said. "They are not natural storms but sick black conflagrations bent on destruction, and if we are not within Deepwood when this one strikes, we will die." She turned and began to trot up the road.

Rage and Billy followed. "We can't get to the wizard's castle before the storm arrives," Rage puffed.

"We don't have to," Billy assured her. "Nomadiel told me that we just have to get to the entrance to Deepwood. There is a hut close by where we can take refuge."

"How can a hut be any use if those stone houses that were in the village can't protect us?"

"The hut is part of Deepwood," Billy said, "and Deepwood opposes the winter because it is not natural."

"I hope it doesn't decide that *we* are not natural," Rage said.

"If it let Gilbert through, it will let us through," Billy said reassuringly. Then he began to sniff the air.

"What is it?" Rage puffed.

"I can smell the storm. It smells . . . wrong."

That word again. "Wrong how?"

Billy shrugged, annoyance tugging at his features as it always did when he couldn't find words to explain a dog thought or experience.

"Use your energy for walking, not talking," Nomadiel snapped over her shoulder.

All at once the darkness about them thickened, and the wind began buffeting them from all directions, sending powder snow into dervish spirals. Rage tried to ask Nomadiel how much farther it was to Deepwood, but there was a peculiar vibration in the air that tore her words away. One vicious gust extinguished Nomadiel's lantern, and they were plunged into darkness so complete that Rage could see nothing at all, not even Billy or Nomadiel. She opened her mouth to call out, but the wind actually sucked the air out. She gasped with relief as Billy suddenly caught her hand in his. Her eyes adjusted to the slight glow given off by the snow, and she saw that he had also taken Nomadiel's hand. The three of them struggled forward, but it was as if the wind deliberately opposed them, for it battered them spitefully as if trying to pluck them apart.

Rage thought of her mother and began to cry.

"Oh, Mam," she whispered. The wind snatched the words from her lips and turned them into a mockery of wailing filled with self-pity. Rage felt a surge of disgust at herself. At her stupidity and selfishness. No wonder Logan and Anabel and Mrs. Somersby disliked her. No wonder the people she loved left her. She was stupid and dull and ugly.

Billy didn't leave, even though you would have left him, she reminded herself. *And Logan is your friend now. . . .*

Rage clung to the reminder, and to the truth she sensed in it, because Billy hadn't left her, and she knew he would never willingly do so. And Logan might be a new friend, but there was something in him, too, that she felt to be as steadfast as Billy. *If I am worthy of their friendship and love, I am worthy of Mam's,* Rage thought, and it seemed that the storm winds hushed for a moment. Only then did she become aware that they were no longer running against the wind but barely shuffling forward.

The others were hardly visible in the dimness, but Rage saw their dull, sorrowful expressions and understood that they must have been hearing their own voices of doubt. "It's the storm!" she shouted at them. "Don't listen to it!" Rage saw the other two stir and shudder as if she had awakened them. Billy gave her a strange, desperate smile, and on impulse she threw her free arm about him and kissed his cheek. "I love you, Billy," she shouted.

Billy must have heard her, because his arm tightened, squashing the breath out of her. Then he turned and hugged a startled Nomadiel, too.

"How much farther to Deepwood?" Rage shouted.

Nomadiel looked about, she sniffed, and her face changed. Eyes alight, she pointed, then nodded so dramatically that Rage knew they must be very close.

5

The moment they stepped onto the path leading into Deepwood, the pounding force of the storm was muted. Rage wondered if this was magic or merely the closeness of the trees. Then she saw that there was no snow on the trees except for those bordering the road at the edge of Deepwood. Nomadiel led them off the main Deepwood trail to a round, windowless bark hut with a solid door and roof.

Once the rickety door had been pushed closed behind them, the deafening growl of the storm was cut even more. It was pitch black, but Nomadiel lit a rush torch and set it in a groove in the packed-earth floor. There was a small fire pit at the center of the floor, and once a fire had been lit, Nomadiel filled a pot with water from an earthenware jug set by the door and set it to boil on crossed sticks. She added potatoes and onion from the knapsacks given them by the centaurs, then cut bread from a brown loaf. Handing a fork brusquely to Rage, she told her to toast the bread.

Rage did not mind being ordered about. The savagery

of the storm had beaten all the will out of her. It was not until they had eaten the soup that she felt restored enough to ask questions.

"What happened to your crow?"

"He is not my crow," Nomadiel said in the disapproving voice she seemed to save especially for Rage. "Rally flew ahead to the castle when we mounted Galantir Longleg," Nomadiel went on. "He will have let my father and Elle and the others know we are coming."

Rage went out to relieve herself. It was raining quite heavily, and the wind seemed louder than ever as she made her way to the nearest tree. On her way back to the hut, a hand descended on her shoulder.

Rage screamed and leapt around, only to find Gilbert and Mr. Walker staring at her. She was slightly taken aback to see that Gilbert's long ringlets were glowing as well as saturated. But otherwise he looked his dear, familiar, gloomy self, and she flung her arms around her friends and hugged them hard. Then Billy threw open the door, his face wreathed in smiles as he announced that he had smelled them. He pulled them all inside, banging the door closed behind them.

"It is so good to see you both!" he cried, hugging Goaty and Mr. Walker exuberantly.

Gilbert! Rage reminded herself firmly, knowing how much it had meant to the faun to have his own name at last.

"You're wet!" Billy said.

"Just a minute." Gilbert lifted his fingers and made a peculiar twisting motion. Just like that, he was dry.

"You can do magic!" Billy cried.

"I am the wizard's assistant now," Gilbert said shyly.

"What about me?" Mr. Walker demanded.

"Oh, sorry." Gilbert made the same twisting gesture toward Mr. Walker, but this only made the tiny man wetter. Water puddled on the floor under his feet. "Sorry! Sorry!" Gilbert muttered. "I'll just try that again—"

"No!" Mr. Walker said, looking exasperated. "With my luck, I'm likely to explode."

Rage gazed at the little man, seeing in his pointed ears and nose and his bright eyes the tiny Chihuahua that he had once been. Then because she could not help herself, she gathered him into her arms. He had grown, she realized, almost doubling the size he had been when he had first come to Valley, while Nomadiel was the size he had once been.

"It is good to see you," he said softly. "And you," he added, looking up at Billy. "We hoped that you had gone with Rage, when you jumped after her so suddenly, but we never knew because the wizard straightaway dismantled the bramble gate. I thought that I would never see you again, and yet it seemed impossible that I should not. Like a story with the last page left out." Mr. Walker suddenly spotted Nomadiel, and his weary smile faded to a grimness that Rage had never seen before.

"What are you doing here?" His voice was so cold as to be almost unrecognizable.

"I had to show them the way, Father," Nomadiel said calmly, but her face was pale. "If they had gone to the council house as they intended, Councillor Hermani would still be discussing whether or not to send them."

"I told you not to leave the city," Mr. Walker said. "It is dangerous on the road. This storm cycle might have caught you in the open—"

"It *would* have caught them in the open if I had not been with them," Nomadiel pointed out tightly.

"You disobeyed me," Mr. Walker said.

Nomadiel flinched. "You speak as if I am not your daughter who will someday be king of the little people. It is you who told me that a ruler must know his own mind."

"A ruler who cannot also obey at need is one who will rule by whim and self-indulgent fancy. I will not allow you to become such a one."

"Sometimes rules must be broken," she said. Her voice had taken on a formality that suggested she was quoting someone else, and from her mutinous expression Rage gathered that her father must have said these words. "If I had not disobeyed, your precious Rage Winnoway would have perished in the storm. Then where would Valley be if it is true that she is its last hope?"

"You are arrogant, daughter. You make too many judgments based on your certainty about a future that can only ever be uncertain. You must act based only on what is right in the moment that you act, and upon things that are known to you."

"She is right, though, Mr. Walker," Billy put in apologetically. "If she hadn't helped us, we would have been in trouble when the storm came. As it is, we are only here so swiftly because she sent her bird to get help from some centaurs. . . ."

"*Her* bird," Mr. Walker echoed, still staring at his daughter.

"I do not call Rally mine," she said tightly.

"No, but why do others name it so if you do not claim him with your manner?"

"If I claim him, then it is no more than he claims me, and I do not object to it," Nomadiel said.

"Perhaps this is not the time . . ." Gilbert interrupted gently.

To Rage's surprise, Mr. Walker turned from his daughter to bow slightly to Gilbert. Rage caught the look of hurt, quickly masked on Nomadiel's face.

"Rage," Mr. Walker said, turning back to her, "we came because Rally told us that you had arrived in Fork and were journeying toward Deepwood. Rue told us that you would come directly to the castle."

"I meant to," Rage admitted. "But something went wrong. I guess I haven't quite got proper control of this dream-traveling stuff yet. I thought that we ended up in Fork because I was thinking about Elle right before I went to sleep. But Nomadiel said she left Fork days before we got there, so I don't know why we went there." Rage stopped, struck all at once by how unlikely it would be for Elle to have stayed at the castle while Gilbert and Mr. Walker braved the foul weather to reach them in the hut.

Billy might have read her mind because he asked why Elle had not come. Gilbert and Mr. Walker exchanged a glance, then Mr. Walker said, "I think we ought to go up to the castle before we speak of Elle. The center of the storm will pass over Deepwood soon, and we must be ready to move when it does."

"Wouldn't it be better to wait until the storm is over before we leave this hut, if it is so dangerous?" Rage asked.

Gilbert gave her a morose look. "One storm is followed by another, in a cycle that lasts for weeks at a time. The gaps between the cycles grow shorter and shorter. One day soon there will be nothing but endless storms."

"What is the center of a storm?" Billy asked curiously.

"Each storm has a center of stillness," Gilbert said.

"We cannot predict how long the gaps between cycles are, but the center lasts for about one hour. In that time, we can reach the castle."

"You came here without waiting for a center," Rage objected.

"I used magic to shield us," Gilbert said.

"His magic makes you feel as if someone is chewing your brain out," Mr. Walker said flatly. "It is a very unpleasant experience."

Gilbert looked upset. "It ought not to be, but since my master left, I have been so worried that I can't seem to concentrate properly, and it is terribly important to concentrate with magic."

The wind abruptly stopped its shrieking, and they all instinctively looked up.

"It is the center!" Gilbert cried, wringing his bony fingers. "We must leave *now*."

Outside, it was utterly silent, but it was not as dark as it had been. Now Rage could see the clouds overhead, a great boiling mass streaked with livid yellow. Such a sky arching above such stillness made her feel uneasy, as if the storm were watching them with some great malevolent eye. Perhaps Deepwood felt the same, because the trees seemed to rustle of their own accord.

"I wish that you would tell us what has happened to Elle," Billy said as they hurried along the path, following Gilbert's glowing shape. "It's obvious she is not at the castle."

"She went through the winter door," Mr. Walker said flatly.

"No!" Nomadiel cried, looking at her father in dismay.

Gilbert made an agitated movement with his horns,

which caught in the branches of the tree overhead. They stopped while he untangled himself.

"Now see what you have done!" Mr. Walker snapped at his daughter.

They went silently after that, in weariness. Deepwood was very similar to Wildwood, except that the trees here grew so entwined that you could not see where one ended and another began. There was also a brooding sense of purpose about the trees, but Deepwood made no effort to test them or to put any barrier in their way. It was a long, tiring climb, but they came at last to an open field. Across the field, they could just make out the castle, no more than a great blot of darkness with a few lit windows set high above an encircling wall. They were nearly across the field, approaching the wall, when Rage felt a queer vibration in the air.

"Run!" Mr. Walker shouted. "The center is passing!"

Billy scooped up Nomadiel as they all ran. The first raindrops fell, stinging viciously, but it was only a few steps to the arched doorway in the wall. Passing through, they found the wall was so thick that they were in a short tunnel. Rage went to the other end and peered out. The castle was still largely invisible because of the driving rain. Rage turned back to see Billy setting Nomadiel gently on her feet. Gilbert and Mr. Walker opened a door in the side of the tunnel, and as soon as the glowing faun went through it, the tunnel fell into darkness. The rest of them followed his glow through the door. It led to an enormous chamber constructed within the wall. Mr. Walker and Gilbert began to light rush torches.

"What are you doing?" Rage asked.

"It is too late to reach the castle now," Mr. Walker said. "We will have to wait here until it is safe to leave."

He knelt to poke at the ashes of an old fire in a shallow hearth.

"But we're almost there!" Rage said.

"If you went out in it now, you would discover that the rain will burn your skin. And then after the rain will come hail the likes of which you have never seen in your world, or in Valley before the winter door was opened by that hell-born firecat," Mr. Walker said.

"Does such rain fall in Wildwood?" Rage asked.

"No, because the witch folk stop it, but they can only do that while magic flows," Gilbert said. He sniffed despondently. "If only I were a better apprentice wizard. My master—"

"Be quiet," Mr. Walker snapped. "We do not need your gloomy talk now."

"We can't stay here forever," Billy murmured, having come to stand between them.

"Not forever," Gilbert said. "You see, the rain is part of the cycle of each storm, and they always follow the same pattern. Last of all will come a sleety snow. That is when we can cross the yard to the castle."

"It doesn't make sense," Billy said. "If the storm is a circle, then the same things ought to be on both sides of the center."

"I don't know what makes sense, but that is what happens," Gilbert said tiredly. "The wizard said the storms are sentient. Well, you must read his notes if you want to know more about it. I am far too stupid to be able to understand them." He gave a half sob. "I do not deserve the name given to me."

Rage took a deep breath. "You'd better tell us why Elle went through the winter door."

Mr. Walker bent to poke at the fire. It was alight now,

but the wood must have been wet because all it produced was black smoke and a feeble flame. Still staring into it, Mr. Walker said, "We waited for you as the witch Mother advised, though the storms grew worse and fell beasts roamed about: dark shape-shifters that rend the soul before they rend flesh. And illness. More plague and a strange disease that affects natural animals, humans, and little folk, making them waste away. Horrible. Elle woke this morning and said she could wait no longer."

"How could she leave?" Nomadiel cried. "What of Fork? How will it bear her loss?"

"Fork must endure, as do others who have lost those they care for," Mr. Walker said.

"Why would she decide to go so suddenly?" Billy asked.

"The wizard went suddenly, too," Rage murmured, but no one heard her.

"Elle spoke of a dream this morning," Gilbert said. "Then she said someone must go at once, and that it had better be her. She said the rest us should follow as soon as Rage arrived."

Billy stiffened. "She went through the winter door *this morning?*"

Gilbert nodded. "Then that's it!" Billy said. "That's why we were drawn to Fork! Elle must have gone through at the same time as we were coming here, and once we were here and Elle wasn't, the magic just took us to the closest thing to Elle. Fork's dream of her."

"What did the witch Mother say about Elle going?" Rage asked.

"She doesn't know yet," Mr. Walker said. "She was called away to Wildwood, for they had need of her magic. Ania arrived yesterday to take her place."

"Perhaps it was the wrong thing to do, letting Elle go," Gilbert said mournfully. "My master would have been able to stop her."

It gave Rage a strange feeling to hear Goaty calling the wizard *master*, for wasn't that what animals called their owners?

"So both Elle and the wizard had dreams that made them go through the winter door," Billy mused. "I wonder if they had the same dream."

"I do not know what the wizard dreamed, but I heard him tossing and turning, and several times he shouted out something about the winter door," Gilbert said, wringing his hands. "I thought nothing of it until I found that he had gone. Then I went straight to the door."

"Is it somewhere near?" Rage asked.

"Near, yes, but still it is a dangerous journey unless you pay strict attention to the storm cycle."

"Did the wizard make the winter door?" she asked, wondering if that was why he had been so sure the firecat had *not* made it.

"The firecat made it," Mr. Walker said in a harsh voice. "It let in the plague that killed Feluffeen. It deserves to have its head bitten off."

Gilbert shook his head sadly. "My master believed the firecat *thought* it had created the door, when it merely activated it. He wrote about the door in his notes. Maybe you will find something I missed. I often muddle things. It is my fault—"

"For Bear's sake, Gilbert, stop blaming yourself for everything!" Mr. Walker snarled. "I thought you had gotten over that!"

Gilbert looked hurt. "I am sorry, Prince Walker. I know that I am . . ."

"I am sure you are a very good assistant, Gilbert," Billy said in a soothing voice. "Did the wizard say anything at all to you that might help us understand why he went through the winter door when he did?"

Gilbert shook his head, his eyes suspiciously bright. "There are only his papers, as I told you."

"Did Rue look at them before she left?" Rage asked.

Gilbert nodded. "She began, but then she received the message from Wildwood and had to leave."

Rage thought of something. "If you didn't see the wizard go through the winter door, why are you so sure that he did?"

"What do you mean?" Gilbert asked in bewilderment. "Where else would he have gone?"

Rage found that she could not say outright that the wizard might have used his magic to escape from troublesome obligations. But if the wizard had sent the firecat to her, that must mean he had not shirked his responsibility this time. Thinking of the firecat reminded Rage that she still had to tell Gilbert and Mr. Walker about its visit, but as she opened her mouth to speak, she felt the unmistakable pain of a pinch. Then she felt the familiar tugging that preceded the dizzy free fall back to her own world.

When Rage opened her eyes, she rubbed at her arm where she still felt the pinch, but no one was in her room other than Billy in his dog form, lying deeply asleep beside her. Her first impulse was to shake him, but she held herself back, reasoning that his dream self was still in Valley. With luck, *he* might think to tell the others about her dream of the firecat.

Glancing at the clock, she saw that she had better get

up if she was to be ready to go to school. Slipping out of bed, she scooped up her clothes and went to the bathroom to dress, thinking how odd it was to go from magic and missing wizards to getting ready for school. The bathroom was cold after the warmth of the bedroom and the water was only lukewarm, so her teeth were chattering by the time she was ready. In the kitchen, she peered into the fire hopefully, but the embers were all dead. She had forgotten to close the flue the night before! There was not enough time to light another fire, so she lit the gas stove and hunched over it, waiting for the kettle to boil. Then she ate toast and sipped at some hot cocoa, trying to shake off the strangeness of being so suddenly transported back to her normal life.

By the time her uncle appeared, his coffee was made. He drank it down quickly and announced that they had better get moving. Rage asked her uncle if they could leave Billy to sleep, as he had seemed not quite well to her the night before.

"Maybe we should take him into the vet," her uncle said.

Rage shook her head. "Mam always says dogs ought to be allowed to have sick days like anyone else," she said truthfully.

A smile glimmered in her uncle's amber eyes. It was as dark as night outside, reminding Rage that Valley and her world were certainly linked by the danger of the winter door. The inside of the car soon warmed up. Rage found herself thinking about Fork, transformed from the black, twisted labyrinth it had been when the keepers dwelt there into a pale, near-frozen beauty haunted by Elle. How had the dog-woman reacted to being adored by a city? she wondered. Had Elle been angry at it for trying to stop her leaving? Had she pitied it as Nomadiel did, or had she shrugged off the city and its feelings for her the moment she left it, her mind on the journey to the wizard's castle?

"You are very silent this morning," her uncle said.

"I . . . I was thinking about Elle," she said. Then she bit her lip hard.

"Elle is one of the dogs that disappeared?" Uncle Samuel asked. Rage nodded and said nothing in the hope that the subject would be dropped. "Did Mr. or Mrs. Johnson ever ring the pound?"

"I think so," Rage said. "Uh, will I wait for you in the library again tonight?"

"No, I'll be waiting out front when school ends." The car went slowly round the corner, passing between two piles of black-streaked snow, and pulled up outside the front gate to the school. "There's your friend," Uncle Samuel said. "We can give him a lift home this afternoon if you want."

Rage turned to see Logan standing by the gate. He lifted a hand in response to her uncle's wave. The sight of his smile gave her a shock because it was so nice to find a friend waiting for her. It seemed ages since she had seen him. She bid her uncle goodbye and scrambled out, dragging her schoolbag after her and slamming the door.

"Hi," Logan said. Up close, she saw that the smile did not reach his eyes.

"What's wrong?"

He shrugged and said tersely, "The do-gooders are thinking of moving to Leary."

"Why?" Rage asked, devastated at the thought that her first real friend was to be snatched away.

Oddly, Logan flushed darkly. "I . . . uh, it's because of

me, can you believe it? They think I'm not doing well at school here and so they want to try me at some school there. A school for gifted kids."

This was offered as a sneer, but Rage saw Logan's wonder underneath it and swallowed her own disappointment. "They . . . I guess they think a lot of you."

He laughed. "Well, it was last night. I was practicing the play. Bottom's part, like you suggested, and I'm standing there raving on, and when I finish the speech, the do-gooders are there in the doorway applauding like crazy. She was actually crying. They knocked, but I guess I didn't hear them. Anyway, they said they hadn't realized how talented I was, and they apologized for . . . well, for treating me like I was . . . well, they told me they knew I couldn't read properly." He grimaced. "Here I was thinking I had kept it such a secret and the caseworker wrote it in my report so they knew all along. Anyway, they said not being able to read properly didn't mean I was dumb and that maybe I needed to approach learning differently than other kids. The next thing I know it's morning and they are talking about this alternative school."

Rage forced a smile. "I guess . . . it might be a good school."

"It sounds . . . well, there are no uniforms, no classes, no rules and regulations. You have these tasks that you help come up with, and there are people to help you complete them, and you don't have exams or tests. You don't even have to go every day and *you* decide when to go home. They said it's a school for kids who are self-directed." He laughed. "I guess that's me. The school even has a theater program. . . ." His enthusiasm faded and he hesitated. "The truth is that I'd have been rapt a few weeks back, but now . . ." He stopped again, and flushed.

"When will you go?" Rage asked. Her voice sounded stiff and strange.

Logan frowned. "I don't know. I don't think they could move that fast. Probably next year."

"I wish—" Rage began, then the bell rang. "Look, I'll see you in the hall," she said abruptly, horrified to realize that she was close to crying. She brushed at her eyes furtively as she closed her locker.

Joining the drift of students to the main hall, Rage noticed that all the lights were on. They hadn't been on the previous day, and since they went on automatically once the light fell to a certain level, she reasoned that it really was darker today. She thought of the radio announcer the night before saying that the weird weather was coming from somewhere around Leary, and wondered again if there was not some sort of opening to Valley there. It was hard to imagine how that could be, since Valley had begun as an alternate version of the valley flooded by the dam. But it had grown since its beginning, and it was ruled by laws of magic that did not align with the rules of science, or at least with science as humans understood it.

Entering the hall, Rage saw that Logan was sitting in the same place they had occupied the day before. She went over to him, ignoring a leer from Anabel Marren, who was also sitting in the back row.

"Are you okay?" Logan asked, giving her a searching look.

"I'm fine," Rage said softly. "Look, about your going. The truth is that I took off before because I was upset to think about losing the first friend I ever had." *First* human *friend*, she amended inwardly. "But I think the school sounds fantastic, and I think your foster parents sound pretty nice as well."

Logan managed to look both pleased and embarrassed. "I felt the same when they told me, but then I got to thinking about your mum being transferred to Leary Hospital and you going to visit her every week. I thought that maybe we could meet when you come and maybe . . . maybe you could even stay over sometimes. If it's okay with your uncle. If you wanted to . . ."

"Of course I would want to," Rage said, thinking distractedly of Leary and the possibility that there might be a way open from the city to Valley. She wondered if she couldn't find a way to close the winter door in Valley if she went to Leary sometime soon.

"You have a strange look on your face. What are you thinking about?" Logan asked curiously.

Rage looked at him, and it came to her that she should tell Logan about Valley and the winter door because after seeing those beasts, he might be able to believe there was more to the world than the science books and newspapers said.

"I'll tell you later," she said. "I promise."

Somehow, though, the right moment never came.

Rage spent the day planning to tell Logan everything that had happened to her, but they didn't have any classes together. At lunchtime, although there were even fewer students than the day before, it was harder to be alone because groups were beginning to form. Somehow, Rage and Logan were the center of one of the groups, which included most of the students from the English class the day before, as well as drama students from other classes. They all wound up talking about the parts they would like in *A Midsummer Night's Dream*. Logan said nothing about the proposed move. At the end of lunchtime, a tall, thin boy with glasses commented to Rage that they ought to form a drama club.

Rage was surprised how much she enjoyed being part of a group for a change. It never would have happened if school had been operating as usual. There was every chance that she and Logan would go back to being outsiders the second everything was as it had been, but even so, it was nice to belong for a change. Her getting to know Logan and his finding out that he could act were more things that would never have happened if not for the storms.

On the way to her locker after the last class, Rage thought how weird it was to try to figure out how something came to happen. She and Logan might never have become friends if not for the pig beasts. And if the beasts had come through the winter door to Valley, and then to their world, you could say that they had become friends because of the wizard. But *then* you had to go back and point out that the wizard had only made Valley because the government had decided to make a dam, so the government had caused her and Logan to be friends. But you could go back further again and ask why the government had decided to make a dam. . . .

"Why are you laughing?" Logan asked, coming up to stand beside the locker as she dug her key out.

"I wasn't exactly laughing," Rage said as she excavated the mess to find what she needed. "I was trying to figure out the exact cause of us becoming friends."

"It was you shouting at me to run when those things came after us," Logan said. "I mean, you didn't just take care of yourself."

Rage was surprised at his view, but she nodded. "Well, you could say those creatures are the reason we became friends, but you could also say that why ever those things were there is the reason. You know what I mean?" Logan gave her an odd look, and she realized that she had better steer away from the subject of the beasts until she could talk freely to him.

"It's funny you should mention the creatures because I've been thinking a lot about them. I mean, they were here at the school, and at least one of them was at your place sniffing around. Now, if the one at your place was one of the three that came after us, then it had to have followed you, in which case, why? And if the one at the farm was only one of a whole pack of those creatures roaming all around this area, then how come no one else has seen them?"

"There were reports on the radio of slaughtered animals."

"It might have been them, but the point is that no one saw them. Only us."

"Maybe someone else saw but didn't want to report it."

A group of girls came by laughing, and Logan hissed, "Let's go to the library."

"I can't," Rage said regretfully. "My uncle will be here early today. He's probably out there now. But we can give you a lift home if you want."

It was Logan's turn to shake his head. "The do-gooders are picking me up in an hour. I told them to come later because I thought you would be around for a bit."

"Sorry," Rage said.

"Me too, but we can talk tomorrow."

Rage swallowed all the things she wanted to say and smiled. "Tomorrow's Saturday."

Logan blinked and then slapped his head. "Damn. I forgot. Hey, that's a first. I'm actually sorry the weekend is coming. Maybe I'll give you a call."

"That would be great," Rage said, meaning it, though she didn't think she could tell him about Valley over the phone.

Outside, Anabel Marren was standing by the gate. "My aunt is picking me up," she said, sidestepping in front of Rage so that she was forced to stop.

"My uncle is taking me home," Rage said. "He could take you, too, if you wanted." She hoped she didn't sound as reluctant as she felt.

"Yeah, sure! Like I'd ride with the Wild Man of Borneo. You know he ate people when he was out there in the jungle all those years? That's what they do."

A familiar horn blared, and Rage turned with relief to see her uncle waving from where he had parked on the other side of the street. "Bye," Rage said blithely to Anabel, figuring that acting as if she wasn't bothered by what the other girl had said would annoy her worse than anything.

Her uncle held open the door as she slipped inside the car. Billy hung his head over the back of the seat and gave her a slobbery lick right on the mouth. "Yerk! I hate it when you do that!" Rage laughed. He gave her a quizzical look, then did it again. "Ack!" she cried, pushing him away as her uncle climbed into the driver's seat. "You went back home and got him?"

"I wanted to check on him because it was so odd him sleeping late like that this morning. He was still asleep when I got there and that really bothered me, so I brought him in to the vet. He was in the middle of being examined when he sat up and suddenly started barking." He laughed. "The vet nearly fainted. It seems Mary was right about him needing a bit of a layin because, as you see, he's in fine spirits now." It was the first time Rage had heard him mention Mam by her name, and without any ominous overtones. It must have surprised him as much as it did her because, for a moment, his face went all peculiar and rubbery. But a second later the mask was back in place as her uncle reminded her to fasten her seat belt.

Rage buckled up. Billy took the chance to climb into the front seat, where he settled himself into a furry heap. He laid his head on her lap with a sigh of content that made her smile. His head was heavy, but she liked the weight of him. She wondered very much why he had slept for so long.

"I guess we're not taking your friend home?" Uncle Samuel murmured.

For a split second, Rage thought he meant Anabel. "Oh, L-L-Logan!" she stammered stupidly when she figured it out. "Um. He . . . his . . . parents are coming to get him." The hesitation had been odd enough to make her uncle give her another quizzical look. "They're his foster parents," she explained.

"He's an orphan?"

"Sort of," Rage said. They drove the rest of the way back to Winnoway without speaking. By the time the car pulled up outside the front door, it was pitch dark even though it wasn't that late. Uncle Samuel used a little flashlight on his key ring to fit the key into the front lock.

It was deliciously warm inside the house because the fire had been banked up, but the warmth that flowed through Rage as she shed her coat had nothing to do with the temperature. Tonight she would dream-travel to Valley with Billy again. She was determined that this time they would go straight to the wizard's castle.

The phone rang as they entered the kitchen, and Uncle Samuel nodded at Rage to answer it while he unpacked the groceries he had brought. She switched off the answering machine, noting that no one had left any messages, before picking up the receiver. To her dismay, the person on the other end of the line was Mrs. Somersby.

"Is this the Winnoway residence?" Mrs. Somersby demanded.

"Ah, no. Yes," Rage said after a brief pause, during which no sensible thought came to her.

"Either it is or it isn't," Mrs. Somersby snapped. "Is this Rebecca Winnoway?"

"Yes," Rage said.

Her voice must have sounded odd because her uncle looked over. Rage forced a vague smile, willing him to go out into the hall so that she could tell Mrs. Somersby that he wasn't there. "Um, the reception is very bad. I can hardly hear you. Who did you want?"

"I would like to speak to your uncle!" Mrs. Somersby shouted as Uncle Samuel bent to put the vegetables in the bottom compartment of the fridge.

"No one of that name is here," Rage said, keeping her voice low and hoping that the fridge hum would stop him hearing what she was saying. "I'm sorry." She hung up quickly, setting the receiver at a slight angle so that anyone calling would get a busy tone. She had no doubt that Mrs. Somersby would call back. She was that sort of woman.

"Who was it?" her uncle asked, straightening up and closing the fridge.

"Too hard to hear but I think it was a wrong number," Rage said. "What are we having for dinner? I'm starving." It was not true, but she wanted to steer the conversation away from the phone call.

Fortunately, her question about food was the right one, and Uncle Samuel started talking about making an omelet. Rage fiddled with the radio, wanting the distraction, but tonight it was only giving out white noise. It looked as if the latest round of storms was closing in sooner than predicted.

It was only when the omelet had been made and divided neatly in two that Rage saw her uncle's face and realized that his mind was as far away as hers. The little appetite she had possessed withered at the thought that he might be thinking about how he could get out of his promise to take care of her at Winnoway. Despair gave her the courage to ask something that had been bothering her.

"Do you think they'll still move Mam to Leary with the roads being so dangerous?"

"I spoke to the doctors this morning, and they say the weight of the vehicle will make it stable enough for the journey. Your mam is not the only patient being relocated."

He rose suddenly and carried his barely touched plate of food to the sink. Rage knew she ought to stop, but she couldn't. "Will we be able to go to Leary to see her?"

"Depends on the weather," her uncle said distantly. "I have to go and do some work. Don't stay up too late." He noticed the phone was not properly in its cradle and straightened it as he passed. Rage held her breath, but to her relief it didn't ring.

He had gone out the door before she registered that he had not said good night. Billy gave a whine, and she looked down at him with a rush of affection. "I know *you* care," she said softly. Billy wagged his long, toffee-colored tail and pawed lightly at her leg, communicating his own impatience for the night to come.

Rage finished her meal and carried her plate to the sink. She decided to do her homework in bed. Nothing was guaranteed to send her to sleep faster. Her uncle would think it odd that she had gone to bed so early on a Friday night, but suddenly she didn't care.

Just as she reached the door, the phone rang. She froze, but the fear that her uncle would hear and come made her pick it up. "Hello?" she said warily.

"Hi, Rage. It's me, Logan." His voice sounded diffident, and she wondered if he was remembering the last time he had called. "Are you okay? You sounded funny when you answered the phone."

"I'm glad it's you," Rage said sincerely.

"Why? Who were you expecting?"

"Mrs. Somersby," Rage said, and Logan groaned in sympathy. "She's trying to tell my uncle about that program."

"So what?"

"I'm afraid he would want to have me stay in town."

"Would that be so bad?" He sounded cool.

"Logan, I think he'll leave if he doesn't have to take care of me. Then what will happen to Billy and the farm? And he *has* to stay because I have to make him understand that Mam needs to see him to get well."

"You really believe that?"

"I do," Rage said. "Anyway, how come you're calling? Is everything okay with you?"

"Everything's fine. I mean, Mrs. Do-gooder made tripe for dinner if you can imagine, and they're still treating me like a genius, which I could get used to," he said lightly. "The thing is, I still can't stop thinking about those things that came after us. I just don't get it that no one else has seen them."

Rage licked her lips and made a decision. "Look, I want to tell you something that might be connected to those creatures but not on the phone. On Monday at school I'll—"

"You mean Wednesday. We have Monday and Tuesday off this week for the teachers to get their act together, remember?"

Rage groaned. "The teacher study days are *this* week? I forgot!"

"So it'll be Wednesday before you get to spill your secrets. Unless you want to give me a hint?"

"I . . . I can't," Rage said.

There was a long pause. "Okay," Logan said with such a jarring cheerfulness that she thought he must be offended. "So what are you doing for the long weekend?"

"I guess I'll do homework and read and . . . you know. Visit Mam on Sunday before she gets moved to Leary." Rage felt depressed all over again at the thought of Mam being taken so far away.

"I guess we couldn't catch up on Sunday? Maybe we could practice our rehearsal parts."

"My uncle will be with me the whole time," Rage said.

"Okay." Logan sounded suddenly distracted. Maybe one of his foster parents had come into the room where the phone was.

Rage said goodbye, then hung up and stared at the phone for a bit before deciding to pull the plug slightly out of the jack. That way the answering machine would continue to show a green light, and her uncle would only notice the phone was not working if he tried to make a call, and he hardly ever did that. Going down the hall, she made a mental note to remind her uncle about the teacher study days. With a little thrill, it suddenly occurred to her that she could suggest that with Monday and Tuesday off, they could actually follow the ambulance to Leary and visit with Mam in her new hospital. They could stay overnight in a cheap hotel and then come back the next day.

By the time she was in bed with her hair and teeth brushed, the storm had built to a crescendo, the wind howling like a wounded animal. Rage thought that there was probably no need for her to have disabled the phone since the weather was likely to do it for her. She opened her schoolbooks and started reading her notes, meaning to work until she started to feel sleepy. She looked at Billy. He had curled himself up beside her, but his eyes were open and watchful. "You'd better try to sleep," Rage told him seriously. He closed his eyes and pretended to sleep. She gave a short laugh, then returned her gaze to her book.

When at last she switched out the light, she fixed Gilbert in her mind as clearly as she could while imagining herself and Billy in winter attire.

Rage was standing on the side of a misty, snow-covered slope. She was clad, as she had imagined, in warm jeans, good snow boots, and a thick, fur-lined jacket with a drawstring hood. She even wore mittens and a scarf. The familiar slight tug at her shoulders told her that she was wearing a backpack. Billy was standing a little distance away, grimacing at his boot-shod feet. But there was no sign of Gilbert or of the wizard's castle. Nor did the country look familiar to her. Through drifting skeins of mist, she could see nothing but anonymous, snow-covered hills.

"I wonder where we are this time," she sighed.

"It doesn't smell like Valley," Billy admitted.

"What does Valley smell like?" Rage asked, wondering if it was possible for a whole land to smell of anything in particular.

"Magic," Billy said simply. Rage felt goose bumps rise on her skin that had nothing to do with the cold. "Maybe it's a dream place, like that playground where you first brought me," he added.

"Maybe." Rage wondered if thinking about clothing had disrupted her focusing thoughts on Gilbert.

"Let's walk," Billy suggested. "I have a feeling about this place."

Rage stared at him. Then she shrugged. "All right, we'll walk. But tell me what happened when I disappeared from Valley."

"As soon as you disappeared, I warned Mr. Walker and Gilbert that I'd probably vanish soon when I woke in our world. But Gilbert said he could put a spell on me to keep me asleep in our world for a little longer, so I could come up to the castle. Before I could say a word, he wriggled his fingers at me. From then on, although I did not wake here, I kept falling asleep there. I was there for three days after you left."

"*Three days!*" Rage cried. "So you went to the castle?"

Billy nodded. "It wasn't really a castle, though. It was

just a big house with a sort of little room on top."

"It looked huge," Rage said, but she hadn't seen it properly.

"It changes size," Billy said. "Gilbert muddled an illusion spell, and the wizard said it could stay that way until Gilbert figured out how to fix it."

"That's pretty tough," Rage said indignantly.

Billy shook his head. "From what Mr. Walker said, I think it was more that the wizard didn't mind how the castle was, but Gilbert feels guilty about what he did. It *was* pretty confusing. That first night in the castle, I went to bed in this grand chamber all hung with tapestries and woke on a rush bed in a little one-room shack. Then the next day it was just a small mansion."

"Did you have a chance to see the wizard's papers?"

Billy gave her a look. "I saw them, but I can't read."

Rage sighed in frustration. "So what happened then? Did Gilbert say anything more about why the wizard or Elle went through the door?"

Billy frowned. "He just said no one should do anything until you came back. But Mr. Walker said we ought to go through because you could dream your way to them. Nomadiel agreed, but Mr. Walker shouted at her that she wasn't going anywhere except back to Fork. I don't know what happened then because I fell asleep when they were arguing, and when I woke up, the witch Mother was there and Mr. Walker was insisting that she take Nomadiel back to Fork." Billy's eyes widened. "*That* was what I was trying to remember! The witch Mother said that the wizard wrote in his notes that he had to go through the winter door because it was the work of *another* wizard."

"Did Rue have any idea why Elle went through?"

"It's hard to remember exactly because I kept falling asleep," Billy said. He thought for a moment, then he shook his head. "She did say the expedition had to set out soon because the wizard wouldn't be able to close the gate alone. She said that eight had to pass through the winter door from Valley, but the only ones she was sure of were Mr. Walker, one of the witch men, and Puck, because she had seen them going through in her vision."

"Puck!" Rage echoed in surprise.

Billy nodded. "He came to the castle with Rue. You could see from his reaction that she had not told him before they came that he was to go through the winter door."

"The wizard, Elle, Mr. Walker, Puck, and one of the witch men makes five, then there will be you and me. I suppose Gilbert must be the eighth?" Rage calculated.

But Billy shook his head. "Not you. The witch Mother said that although you were supposed to help shut the winter door, you weren't to go through it."

"But I don't understand. I thought *I* had to go to the wizard. . . ." Her voice trailed off because she realized that the witch Mother had not said that. "Did you tell them about me dreaming of the firecat?"

"I tried to but I fell asleep, and when I tried again later, I woke up."

Rage frowned. "I wonder if the firecat did something to stop us talking about it."

"Like last time," Billy agreed. "It would be just like it to not want anyone talking about it." Abruptly Billy stiffened and looked around with a strange expression. "I know where we are," he said in a soft voice.

Rage looked around. They had reached the top of the

hill they had been climbing. Below them lay a flat, long plateau covered in snow, bare except for one or two dead trees rising up above the whiteness.

"It's the dam near Winnoway," Billy said, and then Rage saw it, too. The flat plateau was the frozen surface of the dam, covered over in snow, and they were making their way down the hills on the opposite side of the dam to Winnoway Farm. The higher mountains that they had been looking at from the other side of the hill were the rest of the range.

"We're near the bramble gate," Billy reminded her.

"Where it used to be," Rage said.

"Maybe it's still there if this is a dream," Billy pointed out, looking excited.

Rage felt her pulse quicken as Billy took the lead, cutting across the face of the hills around the dam. Once they had reached the side closest to Winnoway, they climbed up and over the ridge to where the hills folded and curved away under a pristine white blanket of snow. Billy sniffed the air and then entered the secretive fold between two hills where they had once been led by the firecat to the bramble gate. Snow was mounded over the blackberry clumps, but Billy wove through them until they reached the wall of brambles where there had once been a gateway to another world.

Rage stopped dead at the sight of the arched gateway cut through the brambles. She felt the thrilling fizz of magic against her cheeks and neck. The foliage about the opening was frosted with white, and the spiderwebs that sewed the leaves together were strung with glinting ice beads. The opening was blocked by long, impossibly slender spikes of ice that hung from the very top of the archway to the snow mounded beneath it.

"It's a dream bramble gate," Billy murmured. "I wonder what would happen if we went through."

Rage sucked in a breath of icy air. Was *this* the meaning of Rue's cryptic words? Maybe they were meant to reach whatever lay on the other side of the winter door by some other means than through the winter door.

"What are you doing?" Billy asked.

Rage had drawn closer to the bramble gate. The feel of the magic was strong enough to make her skin itch, and her ears felt as if they were about to pop. "I think we should try it," she said. "The witch Mother told me that the way to close the winter door was between me and the wizard. If I'm not to go through the winter door, it must be that I'm meant to get to the world beyond it in some other way."

"Maybe this won't lead us to the same place," Billy said.

"I think it will," Rage said. She took a deep breath and shouted, "Firecat! I know you're here!"

But there was no answer.

"It doesn't matter," Rage said. "The firecat said it had a way to get me to the wizard, and I'm sure this was it. Let's go."

Billy reached out at the last minute and caught hold of her mittened hand. She looked back at him in surprise. He shrugged. "We don't want to get separated."

She smiled and squeezed his hand. "Together, then," she said. She reached out to push at the icicles, expecting them to snap, but they were surprisingly strong. She pushed harder, then she let go of Billy's hand and pushed with both hands.

"Let me try," Billy said. He shoved at the icicles with his strong shoulder. But not even one icicle cracked. Billy took off his mittens and touched the bars of ice. Then he looked at Rage. "Maybe the dream is reflecting the fact that the wizard didn't get rid of the door but only blocked it," Billy said. "If it were closed, I couldn't have smelled my way here."

"But this is a dream door," Rage murmured. She stopped because the mist about them had thickened so much that she could no longer see Billy. "Billy?" Her voice sounded flat and small, as if the mist had sucked the power out of it.

"I'm here," Billy said, but he sounded strange, too, and farther away than he ought to sound.

"We'd better hold hands again," Rage said, trying to see him.

"Rage?" Billy called, as if he hadn't heard her.

Her heart speeded up. "Billy?" Her voice sounded frightened.

No answer.

"Billy!" she screamed. For a moment, the mist thinned, and there was no sign of the bramble gate and no sign of Billy. There were only snowy hills and dark shapes that she hoped were trees or bushes. But she couldn't help thinking of the creatures that had chased her and Logan, and as if her thought had conjured them up, she heard a low growling.

Her heart almost leapt out of her chest at the knowledge that this time she would have to face them without Logan. Then to her astonishment, she saw Logan standing in front of her looking bewildered.

"Rage?" He was squinting as though he could hardly see her.

"Logan—" she began, then they both heard the growling again.

"Oh Jesus, this is a nightmare," Logan groaned.

Rage didn't know what it was, but they had to get away. She pictured the playground, and just like that, they were both there. But it was night again, and she sensed the nightmare beasts wouldn't be far behind them. Logan was staring about in a dazed fashion. Rage wondered where Billy was, and abruptly he appeared at her side.

He stared at Logan and then smiled sweetly at him. "I remember you. You smell of biscuits."

Logan's mouth dropped open, and he switched his green gaze to Rage. "What kind of dream is this?"

"Sssstupid ragewinnoway," a voice hissed.

Rage's heart leapt. "Firecat! I'm so glad you have come back," she cried quickly, searching for the confusion of air that would reveal the presence of the firecat. But there was nothing. "Listen, I'm really sorry I was so rude to you before. Won't you tell me your message?"

"Wizard needing help," the firecat spat. "Maybe too late for him now. Your fault!"

"Firecat, did you go into Elle's dreams and tell her that the wizard needed help?"

"Sssstupid elle not helping wizard," the firecat snarled. Rage could see it was on the other side of the swings.

"Is Elle all right? Where is she now?"

"Don't know. Don't care," the firecat retorted.

Rage thought of what Billy had told her. "Did your master go to see the other wizard? The one who lives on the far side of the winter door?"

"Ragewinnoway musst coming!" the firecat howled. There was a spluttering of light like a wet firecracker and then a soft, popping sound. Then silence.

"It's gone," Billy said.

"This is a hell of a dream," Logan said, staring from Rage to Billy.

On impulse, Rage pointed a finger at him. "Wake, Logan!" And just like that, he disappeared.

Rage felt a surge of elation at her power. Maybe if she had such power, she could call Mam to her. She could tell Mam about Uncle Samuel. Surely a dream wouldn't hurt her.

Rage . . .

She gasped because it was Mam's voice. Had she called her by thinking about her?

"Rage?" Billy asked, and his voice was sharp with concern.

"Billy, I can hear Mam! She's here!" Rage saw a flash of pity in Billy's eyes and anger coursed through her. "I *did* hear her, and why couldn't I have brought her here just as I brought you and Logan? I'm sure he wasn't just a dream."

"He smelled real," Billy said doubtfully. "But—"

Rage . . .

It was Mam's voice again, but how thin it sounded. Rage turned toward it and began to run.

"Rage, be careful, this is not the real playground. . . ." Billy's voice followed her, sharp with alarm, but the sense of his words was lost in her desperation to find Mam.

Rage? The voice called again, and now it was no more than a whisper of sound.

"Mam!" Rage called back in despair. "Mam, where are you? I can't find you!"

Billy's voice behind her rang out. "Wait! I can't smell her! Do you hear me, Rage? *I can't smell her!*"

Rage stopped in confusion, knowing it couldn't be her mother if Billy couldn't smell her. Then it was snowing heavily again. Snow slithered down her neck when she looked down to see that her boots were sunk to the ankles in a fresh fall of powder snow.

"Billy?" she called, looking around. A wind-driven flurry of snowflakes blinded her. She stepped forward and found that there was nothing under her feet. . . .

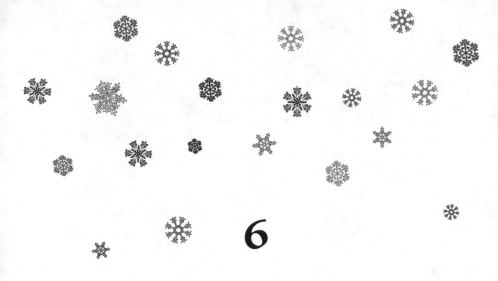

6

"Billy!" Rage gasped.

She reached out to switch on the bedside lamp and there he was, blinking at her, one silky, toffee-colored ear curled endearingly back on itself. "Billy, were you with me at the bramble gate and the playground or was that only a dream?"

He pawed at her leg to signal *yes*.

"And you saw Logan and smelled the firecat?" He scratched at her again.

Rage let out a long breath of air and lay back against the pillows. That meant the firecat really had come to her and told her that the wizard needed help. And from what the firecat had said, she was certain the firecat had convinced Elle to go through the winter door after him. But what had become of Elle if the firecat was still seeking help for its master?

Rage wondered what she ought to do. Even if she could have made herself fall asleep again at once, there was no point in trying to dream herself to Valley, since the witch Mother had said she was not to pass through the winter door. Her thoughts shifted to Logan and the amazing fact that she had summoned him to her in his dreams. She couldn't help smiling at the memory of the look on his face when Billy told him he smelled of biscuits. It was heady to think she could call anyone to her in their dreams. She could even call Mrs. Somersby and give her a good fright. But she couldn't do that, no matter how tempting, because Mam always said the only good use for power was to do good.

Outside, thunder rumbled. Rage climbed out of bed and drew the curtains. The sky between the clouds was a pale blue rather than the black she saw when she awoke to the alarm on weekdays. The sheds and fence and the tree that were normally her view were almost obscured by snow. She had not seen the yard in the daylight since the previous weekend, and it was a shock to see how much snow had fallen.

The sound of an engine spluttering to life cut through the tangle of her thoughts. She threw off the blanket and ran to the window, to see the taillights of her uncle's car casting reddish smears of light on the fresh fallen snow as it pulled away. Rage ran out of the bedroom and down the hall, but by the time she wrenched open the front door, the car had vanished from sight. Instead, she saw heavy black clouds mounding on the horizon; this was the storm the thunder had heralded. Closing the door against the wind, Rage returned to her bedroom and dressed. She went along to the kitchen and found a note in her uncle's blocky handwriting. "Will be back late."

Rage wondered why he hadn't at least waited until she had got up. There was no smell of toast or coffee, so he had gone without eating, too. She turned to the phone and found that the plug had been pushed back in. What if Mrs. Somersby had rung and spoken to her uncle! What if he had gone to town to arrange to have her taken in by a family?

Billy whined and pushed his nose against her leg, his eyes worried. Rage chided herself for jumping to conclusions. She and Billy sat together in the big chair by the fire, Rage nibbling at honey toast and thinking about her dream.

All at once she knew exactly what to do.

"Let's go look at where the bramble gate was," she said aloud to Billy.

He cocked his head, and she decided to interpret this as a shrug.

It was almost lunchtime by the time they set out. Rage packed an old rucksack with a lunch for herself, a thermos of hot chocolate, and water and dog biscuits for Billy. Rage left a note alongside her uncle's saying that they had gone out for a walk. Then, just in case he *hadn't* got a call from Mrs. Somersby, she pulled out the plug to the answering machine. Dark clouds were unraveling in great thick strands as she and Billy came out of the house. They had not gone more than a few steps before the clouds parted to allow a bit of thin sunlight through. There was no warmth in it, but Rage felt her spirits lift at the way the snow sparkled.

Thunder rumbled as they passed through the yard gate into the paddocks. Rage ignored it, knowing the storm would be several hours in coming. If it did catch them, they could take refuge in the hikers' hut at the far end of the dam until it was over. The wan sunlight soon vanished, but Rage's spirits remained high. It was just good to be outside doing something rather than sitting huddled in front of a fire. Billy looked up at her and barked. His eyes caught the light, and Rage could see that he was enjoying himself, too.

When they reached the highest hill on Winnoway Farm, Rage stopped and looked at the land stretched all around them. Trees, bushes, paths, and most fences became gentle, unfamiliar curves beneath the snow. A half-buried farm gate marked the last Winnoway fence, and crossing it, Rage was struck by how the pristine snow gentled the ragged and unkempt dam area.

Rage and Billy toiled up the last hill before the one that overlooked the dam. It was very steep, so they were both panting. As they crested the hill, a bitter wind clawed at Rage's face. Looking back, she was dismayed to see a mist rising from the folds in the hills like a miasma. Worse, the storm was almost overhead. She walked more quickly then, leaning into the wind along the top of the hill toward the final hill they would have to climb. It was a little easier at one point because a section of the path lay clear of the snow, and someone—Uncle Samuel, she supposed—had sprinkled it with gravel.

Time passed, and Rage felt that they had been climbing for hours. Half the time she was on her hands and knees because her feet kept slipping out from under her. It was even harder for Billy because he was staying close by her so that she could hold on to him. It seemed forever before they had gained the crest and started down the other side.

Rage blew through her mitten tips to warm her fingers, which had grown numb with cold. Her nose felt numb, and her toes, too, and no wonder. She had the wrong clothes on, and she had not even had the sense to put on a knitted cap. She just hadn't expected it to be so very cold. Billy's footpads must be frozen, too. Certainly his eyes were streaming with cold, just like hers. He hadn't whimpered once, but animals bore a lot more pain than humans before they would show it. A dog's pain is a dog's pain, as Bear had once said.

A misstep sent Rage pitching forward. Fortunately, the hill had flattened out, and she fell only a short way before landing hard and sliding to a halt. Winded, she picked herself up with Billy's help. His coat was heavy and wet, and some of the strands had matted into icicles. Then it began to snow even harder.

The only safe thing to do now was to find the hikers' hut. Rage groped for Billy's collar and they went on down. It was more awkward for them both with Rage holding his collar, but she was comforted by his nearness and hoped he felt the same. She could not help but think of the storm in Valley that had caused her to feel so dreadfully bleak and hopeless.

They finally reached a flat place where they could stand upright without slipping. Rage let go of Billy and sank to her knees. She just *had* to rest for a moment. She no longer felt so cold, but she was very tired, and it was even a struggle to keep her eyes open. Billy growled at her and worried at her sleeve with his teeth until she gave in and got to her feet, and they went on. She was tired enough now that even the fact that the wind was growing stronger did not dismay her. Dimly she registered thunder overhead, but it was as if her mind was numbed as well as her body. For a time, her teeth chattered hard enough to make her jaw ache, but that passed, too. She fell any number of times. Without Billy to nudge and pull her upright, she would have lain there and fallen asleep. Indeed, the longer she walked, the more alluring sleep seemed.

At last and incredibly, they reached the bottom of the hill. Again she fell, this time because she had trodden too hard, not expecting the jarring suddenness of flat ground. Billy bit her on the hand hard enough to startle her into the realization that she was sitting there with the snow melting under her and seeping into her clothes.

Rage struggled to rise, but her legs wouldn't seem to work. She slid her fingers under Billy's collar and he surged forward, hauling her to her feet. She used her free hand to rub at her face and eyes. She could feel neither and understood that if they did not find shelter soon, she would freeze to death. If she did, Billy would freeze, too, because he would never leave her. Leaning down carefully so as not to overbalance, she put her face next to Billy's ears and shouted, "We need to find shelter quickly, Billy. Sniff out the hut. The hikers' hut."

Billy barked, a flat, hollow thump of sound against the roaring vibration of the storm. Rage braced herself when he pulled forward. His strength alone drew them at first, but as her legs moved, the exertion warmed her slightly. She was so stiff that she fell again and again. Gradually a fatigue rolled over her so great and compelling as to make her wish that Billy would leave her. Then she could lay her head upon snow that felt suddenly as warm and softly inviting as her own lilac pillow, and sleep. The next time she fell, she closed her eyes, thinking that she would just have a little nap before she went on. She would go after Billy in just a moment.

Rage woke and sat up, heart pounding at the knowledge that she had almost gone to sleep in the snow. Struggling to her feet, Rage found that she was still stiff but no longer numb. The momentary lapse seemed to have done her good. She went a few steps forward and was startled to find that she was not at the bottom of the slope but on a jutting-out section that offered a little plateau. She frowned, feeling certain that she and Billy had reached the dam level before she fell. Or had she dreamed that?

She began to descend the dark slope carefully, straining her eyes to see the bottom. It was so easy to get confused in the snow and wind. If it hadn't been for Billy's help, goodness knows where she would have wound up!

And where was Billy, anyway? Worrying about him kept Rage toiling downhill when it seemed that the slope must be endless. Her legs were aching abominably by the time she finally reached flat ground. It was clearer here, not that being able to see helped much, because nothing was the least bit familiar. She seemed to be in a narrow canyon between hills rather than in a valley. Since the canyon went out of sight in both directions, there was not even any way to suggest which direction she ought to walk to find the hikers' hut. She opened her mouth, took a deep breath, and shouted Billy's name.

Her blood froze when her only answer was the long, ululating howling of a wolf. Rage might have panicked, but she noticed a single, fitful light, like a flashlight with a bad battery, a little way down the canyon. Hoping it was her uncle, she broke into a slow, stumbling run.

"Hello! I'm here!" she shouted.

The light stopped, then it began to bob toward her. Only when the light was close did she realize that it was not a flashlight but a torch like those they had lit in the hut in Deepwood. She stopped, confused, then she saw who was carrying it and her mouth dropped open.

It was Mr. Walker.

"However did you get *here?*" Rage gasped incredulously. She wanted to throw her arms about him, but instead of smiling, he was glaring at her suspiciously.

"What are you? Some sort of phantom sent out to deceive us?"

Rage wanted to laugh at the melodrama of his words. However, the look on his sharp little face was serious, and his free hand was resting so purposefully on a small silver sword that she sensed he knew how to use it. "Mr. Walker, it's me! Rage! Did you come here to find me?"

His face cleared. "Rage! It really *is* you. But how did you get here before us?"

"I . . . I was here all along. How did *you* get here?"

"We came through the winter door, of course."

Rage was too confounded to speak.

The little dog-man twitched his huge soft ears and demanded, "Have you hit your head?"

It was like a repeat of their arrival in Valley through the bramble gate. Mr. Walker had done nothing but scold her and tell her she had been knocked senseless, because it had taken her so long to understand that the dogs and goat had been transformed. "Mr. Walker, listen to me. I have just been out walking with Billy in the hills around Winnoway looking for the bramble gate. But it started snowing hard and the wind got so strong. Anyhow, I fell and Billy must have thought I was hurt and ran off to get help. The next thing, I see your light and now you're telling me that you came here through the winter door."

Mr. Walker stared at her. "This is not the world of Winnoway Farm where once we all lived with the Cold Man. If it were so, I would have smelled it. This is the land on the other side of the winter door, which we have named Bleak." His sharp little eyes widened.

"But how did I get here?" Rage asked softly.

"I do not know," Mr. Walker said. "But I think we had better go to the others and let them know that you have come. In stories it is always a bad thing for expeditions in dangerous places to split up."

Rage had no idea what had happened, but it was easier to imagine she had been magically transported to the world beyond the winter door than that Mr. Walker had passed through it and ended up in *her* world. She noticed that Mr. Walker was looking around uneasily, and remembered the wolf call. "What is it? Can you smell another animal?"

"Not an animal. Something else. Perhaps it is coming from the settlement."

"A settlement?"

"You can't see it from here," Mr. Walker said. "It is farther down that way." He pointed back the way he had come, then he took her arm and began to walk with her in that direction.

"What kind of settlement?"

"A human settlement, from the smell."

"Don't you know?" Rage asked.

"We intended to enter the village at once, but at the last minute we changed our minds. You see, something smelled . . . not wrong, but not right exactly. Thaddeus said we ought to camp and go into the settlement in the morning. He found us this cave to sleep in."

Thaddeus was the witch Mother's friend. He was the renegade keeper who had rescued some sprites when she was rescuing Elle and Billy from the High Keeper's prison tower. She wanted to ask who else had gone through the winter door, but she thought of something else.

"Have you picked up Elle's scent?"

Mr. Walker's face fell into somber lines. "We have found traces of it closer to the village, but she is not there now. That's another of the reasons we don't want to rush in." He changed the subject suddenly in his characteristic way. "I heard you calling Billy just now," he said. "I thought I must be imagining it."

"Is that why you came out of the cave?"

"I came out because there was a ground tremor. Didn't you feel it? There have been several since our arrival. Then you called out. I thought I was imagining that someone was calling Billy's name until I saw your face. Where is he?"

"I don't know," Rage said. "Maybe he's back there while I'm here." Her heart twisted at the thought of Billy wondering what had happened to her. "Who else came through the winter door besides you and Thaddeus?"

The little dog-man was angling away from the canyon now and moving toward a pile of broken boulders topped with snow.

"Puck, but Billy would have told you about him?" Rage nodded as Mr. Walker led her around a big boulder. There was a cave opening behind it. Rage wondered at the coincidence of a good cave in just the right place at just the right time.

Never trust coincidence, a strange voice spoke in her mind. "Who else came through with you?" Rage asked.

"No one," Mr. Walker said.

"But Billy told me that eight were supposed to go through. If I count you three and Elle and the wizard, that's only five. Even if you count me, there would still be two missing. Unless Billy *did* come through—"

"I would have smelled him," Mr. Walker said. "If he comes, he will make six, but only if he comes through the winter door. We are not to count you because you did not come through the winter door."

The cave was quite small but warm and well lit because a fire crackled in a shallow pit at the center of it. Thaddeus, a big, curly-haired witch man, was seated cross-legged by the fire, his cloak lying stretched out beside him to dry. Puck was perched atop a boulder on the other side of the fire, frowning disconsolately into it and flexing his wings. Like all wild things, he wore only a few scraps of tattered cloth because he didn't feel the cold. He noticed Rage and Mr. Walker, and his exclamation alerted Thaddeus, who jumped to his feet, dropping his hand to a long-bladed sword at his side.

Then Puck's face cleared and he bowed low. "Child Rage! How good it is to see you! Though I understand that it is less time for you than for us in Valley. How came you here?"

"She doesn't know," Mr. Walker said.

Rage sat by the fire and told her story again. When she had finished, Thaddeus pressed a bowl of hot berry juice into her hands. She gladly drank, although the warmth of it did not reach the chill she felt deep inside.

"I cannot think how you came here, unless the storm you mention has opened a rift to this world, through which you managed to stumble," Thaddeus said, looking interested.

"It would be a pretty big coincidence," Rage said doubtfully.

"I think it matters less how any of us came here than what we do now that we are here," Puck said heavily.

"The sooner we close this door, the sooner we can go home."

"Perhaps you are correct," Thaddeus said with faint reluctance. "Nevertheless, this is a puzzle that I will work at in the alcoves of my mind."

"There will be many of those, most filled with bats and worms," Puck said rudely.

"Now, now, little man," Thaddeus said, laughing. But the sound of his laughter rang strangely hollow in the cave.

"How is it that Gilbert didn't come?" Rage asked.

"He meant to, but an hour before we were to pass through, he tripped down a stairwell and broke his leg," Mr. Walker said, exasperated. "He is now convinced that the expedition will fail because of his clumsiness, even though the witch Mother said that he mustn't be meant to go through."

"I think you are right that we must forget about who else might come and proceed as we best can," Thaddeus said firmly. "I would suggest that we all try to get some sleep now, for tomorrow looms large, and it will require all our wits and will to accomplish our task here."

"*I* do not need sleep," Puck retorted, giving the big man a look of open dislike.

"Then you will make a perfect watch," Thaddeus told Puck smoothly. "Especially since you do not feel the cold. Summon us if you see aught to trouble you."

Puck gave him a cold look before flapping his wings and flying gracefully out the entrance.

When he had gone out of sight, Thaddeus smiled at Rage. "Poor little fellow thinks I am his rival for his beloved mistress's affections, when he ought to know she adores him." He opened his mouth in a cavernous yawn. "I daresay it is rude of me when you have only just arrived, Child Rage, but I must sleep." So saying, he rolled himself up in his cloak and lay down close enough to the flames that his eyebrows would be singed if a spark flew. Within seconds, he was snoring loudly.

"Oh, for Bear's sake," Mr. Walker snapped, giving the sleeping man an affronted look. He reminded Rage so much of the snappy little Chihuahua he had once been that she couldn't help reaching out and hugging him. He stiffened, then hugged her back. The strength of his small arms was a reminder that Mr. Walker was far more now than he had once been.

"Prince Walker," she said softly as she let him go. His eyes darkened with sorrow, and she regretted her words immediately, knowing they must remind him of his wife. Yet now that they had been said, there was no unsaying them. "I am so sorry about Kelpie," she said, using the name Princess Feluffeen had called herself.

Mr. Walker swallowed as if he were choking down his grief, then he said in a strangled voice, "I will find this wizard that sent a fell winter of death and despair to us, and I will revenge myself." Rage found her skin prickling into goose bumps at the intensity of his oath.

He drew his cloak about him as Thaddeus had done. The gesture warned her not to ask any more questions that would open up another wound. The death of Princess Feluffeen seemed to be the reason for Mr. Walker's harsh manner with his daughter, though how it could be her fault that her mother had died, Rage did not know.

There was a faint ground tremor, but it lasted only a moment.

"Perhaps we should lie down and rest, and sleep, too, if sleep will come in such a place as this," Mr. Walker murmured. He glanced one more time at Thaddeus, whose face looked younger in sleep, then he lay down with his back to Rage and the fire both.

Rage tried to stretch out and was startled to discover that she was wearing her knapsack. She slipped it off and stared at it in surprise. It was not her cheap rucksack with its rusted buckles, but a small, light, nylon backpack with a multitude of useful-looking pockets and Velcro fastenings. She opened it and found her own solid thermos inside, as well as a squashed package of sandwiches. She didn't feel hungry, but she unscrewed the lid of the thermos and poured herself a mug of hot cocoa, marveling at the steam rising from its surface.

The hot drink comforted Rage in some elemental way, perhaps because it reminded her of better days with Mam. Gradually all the mysteries and puzzlements and anxieties buzzing about her faded, or seemed so trivial that she need not concern herself about them. She lay down by the fire, using her arms as a pillow, and slept.

She dreamed of a snowstorm. Billy was pulling and barking frantically at her in the dream, but his barks were barely audible over the wild screams of the wind, which was like no wind she had ever experienced. The dream shifted and she dreamed of her uncle, wandering lost in the same furious storm. That shifted into a dream of Mam, also wandering lost in the storm.

If only they would all meet, Rage thought confusedly. The sound of the wind was so feral that she began to think of the storm as a great, dark beast.

She longed for Billy, but he did not come. She thought of Logan, and the next thing, she was stumbling into him.

"Why do I keep dreaming about you?" Logan demanded, not noticing the wildness of the storm buffeting them. Again he was wearing pajamas. Rage tried to speak, but the storm seemed to have blown all the words out of her, making her no more than a tunnel through which it might bluster and moan.

"Rage! Talk to me," Logan said, his confusion turning to anxiety. "What's the matter?"

"I'm lost," Rage whispered. "Billy is lost, too." The thought of Billy being lost brought tears to her eyes, and she grasped at his pajama front. "Logan, you have to tell Billy I'm all right. Promise me!"

"Rage!"

Rage woke with a gasp to find Mr. Walker looking into her face. "Get up, someone is coming."

She staggered to her feet, dazed with sleep and dreams. Thaddeus was standing with a hand on his sword, head tilted to listen. Puck was nowhere to be seen, which meant that he must be outside. But if someone was coming, why hadn't he given a signal?

Rage listened, but she could only hear the sound of the storm outside at first. It sounded like the howling gale of her dreams, but then she realized there was an intermittent whistling sound as well.

"Puck," Mr. Walker said.

The small, winged man appeared at the door to the cave, walking rather than flying. Behind him came Nomadiel, bedraggled and exhausted. Rally was clutching her shoulder under her hood.

"What are you two doing here?" Mr. Walker demanded.

Nomadiel gave a little shaky bow. "Father."

"I said, what are you doing here?" Mr. Walker strode across the cave to glare down at her. "I forbade you to come here."

"You can't forbid me," Nomadiel said. "The witch Mother said that I was supposed to come. Both Rally and me."

"And when did *this* notion come to her?" Puck demanded, his voice almost as chilly as Mr. Walker's.

The small girl looked taken aback, but she lifted her chin and said, "I was going to sneak through the winter door with Rally, but the Mother was there waiting, and Gilbert as well. She said that she had been waiting for two who were yet to pass through, and that it was obviously us. She made Gilbert let us go through."

"Two . . . ," Thaddeus murmured, and they all turned to him. "One to go."

"She should have said three."

Nomadiel shrugged. "*She* must be the eighth." She was looking at Rage resentfully.

"Do not speak of Rage Winnoway as *she* in such a disrespectful voice," Mr. Walker said angrily.

"Of course not!" Nomadiel lashed back. "I mustn't say anything about your precious Rage Winnoway, the one person in all the worlds that you love since my mother died!"

Mr. Walker's face whitened with shock, and then his face became stony. "Do not speak to me of matters that are beyond your years and wisdom, daughter," he said in a lifeless voice. He looked at Puck. "I will keep watch now."

No one spoke as he walked out, then everyone turned back to Nomadiel, who was now ash-pale and trembling. She said defensively, "I did not mean to say that. I just—" She bit her lip, fighting tears.

"If the witch Mother said we are meant to come, then it is foolish to cry out against it," Rally opined in a ripe, sonorous tone.

"He is right," Thaddeus agreed, but the look he gave Nomadiel was not warm.

Rage would have liked to ask why Nomadiel had wanted to come through the winter door. It was clear that she would have done so whether or not Rue had approved.

"It is as dark as night still, but day has come," Puck announced. "We should leave this place and go to the village now."

"I will go in first, alone, as we decided last night," Thaddeus said in a voice that brooked no argument. Puck snorted under his breath. It did not take the witch man long to comb his hair, drink some water, and don his coat and hat. There was another earth tremor as Thaddeus turned to Rally. "Will you come with me?"

"No!" Nomadiel cried, but Rally was already winging to the witch man's shoulder.

"I must," the crow told her. "If anything goes wrong, I can fly back with a warning."

"Clever bird," Thaddeus said with a smile. Then he left, saying that they would return within an hour, and everyone ought to be ready to move.

When Thaddeus was gone, Puck seemed to brighten as he set about preparing a breakfast from their packs. Rage contributed her own thermos and sandwiches. Nomadiel sipped suspiciously at the still-warm cocoa, and the first hint of a smile Rage had ever seen lifted the lips of Mr. Walker's daughter. It was a smile of such surpassing sweetness that Rage was reminded of Nomadiel's mother. It was so sad to think of Kelpie dying and leaving her daughter to Mr. Walker, who had become so strangely harsh.

"If neither of them return within the hour, we will have to go in after them," Mr. Walker said.

"We might as well, because if they take him prisoner, you can be sure that they will soon be back for the rest of us," Puck said.

Within half an hour, Rally returned, coming to land on the boulder where Puck was sitting. Mr. Walker strode over as Puck slid to the ground.

"What happened?" Nomadiel asked Rally eagerly.

"All doors are barred and the few small windows tightly shuttered in the settlement. The witch man pounded at one door. It opened, and the woman inside was dressed and smelled of breakfast. A man came out and told us to go away. He said strangers were not welcome. Thaddeus answered that he was a traveler in need of shelter. The man told him that there was a sleeping place for travelers at the end of the settlement, so we went there. The people did not want us to come, but Thaddeus insisted. When I spoke, they stared at me. I think that animals in this world do not talk. Indeed, I have not seen a single sign of bird or beast here."

"What about Elle and the wizard?" Nomadiel urged. "Did the witch man ask about them?"

The crow ruffled its dark feathers and ignored the interruption. "The witch man said he had friends coming who would also want shelter, but the man said there was no room. Then he tried to make the witch man leave. When Thaddeus refused, the man demanded to be paid for lodgings. He wanted metal. Luckily, Thaddeus had some to give, then he sent me to fetch the rest of you.

He didn't dare leave in case the man barred the door to us all."

"Let's go," Mr. Walker said impatiently. He looked at his daughter. "You will remain here."

"No," Rally said. "Thaddeus told me that if you ordered Noma to stay, I was to say that it would be safer for us to remain together. He said to remind you that in stories, expeditions that part always come to harm."

Mr. Walker scowled at hearing his own oft-repeated words quoted against him, but finally he nodded, twitching his soft ears. He turned to his daughter and said coldly, "Stay close and do not speak when we enter this village. Do not hamper us with more than your presence."

This was so cruel that Rage drew in a breath, but Nomadiel merely responded with a nod, head lowered. Rage wondered if she was hiding fury or hurt, and determined to talk to Mr. Walker about the way he treated his daughter the very next moment they were alone.

"At least you are more sensibly attired this time, Rage Winnoway," Puck said as they left the cave.

Rage was too distracted to try to pay much attention because now that she had come outside, she saw that it really was as dark as the middle of the night though day must long have dawned.

"I *really* don't like this place," Puck muttered as they set out.

The settlement turned out to be an unprepossessing huddle of single-story, slab-roofed, gray-sided cottages set against a stretch of gray cliff too steep for snow to settle on. Windows were shuttered and doors barred just as Rally had said, but there were a few poles with lamps swinging from hooks, and these shed enough light to see.

Except for these and the yellowish smoke coming from the smokestacks of the huts, it would have been easy to imagine the settlement was deserted.

"It doesn't look very inviting," Nomadiel murmured.

Mr. Walker gave her a hard look, but whatever he might have said was forgotten as a cloaked Thaddeus appeared.

The witch man was carrying a small lantern like the ones hanging from the poles, and his face was so serious that Rage felt he must have some terrible news to impart. But he only said, "They have agreed that we can stay here, but we will have to be careful because I don't think it would take much for them to ask us to leave." He spoke in a dull monotone and his eyes urged them to caution, so they followed him back through the settlement to a hut with a pale door. Thaddeus knocked. The door opened a crack and a wan face peeped out, the eyes huge and gray. Then a slight boy opened the door to let them in. His face showed no emotion and his movements were measured. He led them along a hall to a room where an older man and woman sat on a bench, their hands folded and their eyes blank. The boy stopped before them and bowed, then he stepped aside.

The old man addressed Thaddeus. "These are your travel companions?"

Thaddeus nodded.

The old man looked at each of them expressionlessly before nodding to the boy, who gestured for them to follow. Rage thought it odd that he showed no surprise at Puck, who wore little more than a cloak to hide his wings. But perhaps there were such strange things in this world as to make all of them seem ordinary. The boy then escorted them along another short passage to a low-roofed room with beds along one wall, as in a dormitory. A table and stools were set up before a small hearth. A tiny yellow fire burned there, but it was still very cold in the room.

Moving closer to the fire, Rage had a pang of longing for the bright fire in the cave where they had spent the previous night. When the boy opened the door to depart, Thaddeus asked him about food. Another door opened on the other side of the hall, and Rage had a clear view of a big public room where men and women sat drinking from mugs, eating stew from bowls, and smoking long, thin pipes. It was like watching a scene with the sound switched off, for no one spoke loudly or laughed or even rattled a mug. The expressions on the faces of the drinkers were as flat as those of the old man and the boy.

"What is wrong with these people?" Mr. Walker asked after the boy had gone.

"I don't know," Thaddeus said, coming to sit by the fire. "But I think it is better that we do not let anyone know we are outworlders just yet. They seem worried about strangers. If anything has happened to the wizard or Elle, it is very likely to be known that they came from another world. We need to fit in, and learn as much as we can without giving anything away."

"How can we fit in?" Mr. Walker snapped. "Look at us!"

"Given their lack of reaction and the few bits of information I have managed to pry out of them, it seems like there are many different kinds of creatures here besides humans, mostly living in their own settlements."

The earth trembled again. They all looked up at the roof uneasily, but not so much as a fall of dust resulted.

"I *really* don't like this place," Puck repeated.

"There are no windows in this room," Mr. Walker said, pacing about.

"There is a small one, over there." Thaddeus pointed toward the other end of the room. "That is how I sent Rally to get you." He nodded to where the bird now sat, preening himself gravely.

"Did Elle or the wizard come through here?" Mr. Walker asked impatiently.

"I didn't want to begin by asking too many questions, especially not big ones. There is a little maid bringing food and drink who might talk if coaxed. That is why I asked for food, aside from the fact that you might be hungry. I have already learned from the maid that the ruler here calls himself the Stormlord and lives in a fortress."

"His name makes him sound like he might be behind the storms coming through the winter door," Rage said.

"That is what I thought," Thaddeus admitted. "So we must be careful. We don't want one of these blank-faced villagers reporting to him that friends of the wizard have come looking for him. If our wizard did go to the Stormlord, then there is a chance that he is now being held prisoner."

"But how could the wizard be held against his will?" Nomadiel asked.

"He was imprisoned by the firecat," Puck said. "Besides, if this Stormlord is behind the winter door, then he must have a wizard working for him."

"But why send storms to Valley?" Nomadiel asked.

"Perhaps it is the beginning of an invasion," Thaddeus said.

"I've just been thinking," Rage murmured. "If the wizard went to see this Stormlord, then Elle would have done the same thing."

"Not without finding out about the Stormlord first," Mr. Walker said. Rage opened her mouth to say that Elle would have rushed in, but Mr. Walker was saying, "She has been here. I can smell her."

Nomadiel nodded her own confirmation, which seemed to disconcert her father.

"All right. That's important to know," Thaddeus said. "But it's all the more reason for us to be careful. We need to find out about this Stormlord. If it turns out that he had nothing to do with making the winter door, we can ask for his help. It might even be that he saw our wizard and Elle and sent them somewhere else."

"Where do these people think we came from?" Rage asked curiously.

"No one asks any questions. That is what made *me* wary about asking questions. The little maid assumes I came from another settlement."

"We could pretend that we have come to pay our respects to this Stormlord," Nomadiel said.

"Perhaps, but the maid behaved oddly when she spoke of the Stormlord, so do not make any specific reference to him. Perhaps they are so grim because he is a tyrant."

"They don't smell scared," Mr. Walker said.

"They don't smell of anything," Nomadiel said. "Except that boy. He smelled of a tiny bit of curiosity."

There was a knock at the door and Thaddeus went to open it. A girl with mousy brown hair scraped into a tight plait that ran down her back stood there. Her expression was bland, but her eyes were bright and inquisitive. "You wanted food?"

"My companions are hungry," Thaddeus said. He made a gesture and the girl entered. Her eyes darted about before returning to the floor. Thaddeus had her recite the choices, then ordered olvish stew, milbread, and a jug of brew.

He dismissed the girl, but as she moved to the door, he nodded pointedly to Mr. Walker.

"Uh. Wait, girl," Mr. Walker said. The girl gave him a startled look, and he quickly modified his own voice and expression. "Perhaps you can settle our argument." The girl waited, saying nothing, and Mr. Walker continued. "My friend here says this settlement is not far from the Stormlord's fortress, but *I* think we are still some distance away."

"Usually those going to Stormkeep are summoned," the girl said.

"We are not summoned there," Thaddeus said hastily. "It is merely a game my companion and I play in guessing distances to pass time as we journey about."

"A game," the girl echoed blankly. "Well, Sorrow is a day's walk from the fortress of the Stormlord, if the black wind does not blow, or the gray rain fall, or if the Stormlord does not send one of his storms to purify us."

Thaddeus nodded triumphantly to Mr. Walker and casually dismissed the girl. Once he had closed the door, he signaled them to stay quiet and pressed his ear to the door. Then he straightened and said softly, "I don't think she would listen, but it is better to be careful."

"Sorrow," Puck murmured. "I wonder if its closeness to this fortress is not the reason for the name."

"I don't like the sound of a ruler wanting to purify anyone," Rage said.

"He sends storms," Rally croaked pointedly.

"We should not jump to conclusions," Thaddeus warned. "She and the others here may *believe* the

Stormlord sends storms, but it might not be true. Or if it is, he might have some reason."

"What do you suppose she meant by saying that people are usually summoned to Stormkeep?" Rage asked.

"Where there is someone with power, there are always soldiers to enforce their power," Mr. Walker said bleakly. A look of pity crossed Nomadiel's face.

"Rage?" Thaddeus said. "When the girl returns with the food, see if you can learn anything from her about Elle. But be careful. A person who will gossip might be more than merely inquisitive."

There was another knock on the door. Rage answered it this time. It was the maid bearing a laden tray. Thaddeus had drawn the others away. Now he called out in a peremptory voice for Rage to help lay the table, his tone suggesting that Rage was also a servant. The girl gave her a shy look and passed her a loaf of heavy, grayish bread and a knife.

Slicing bread while the other girl ladled out bowls of an unappetizing grayish stew with a vinegary smell, Rage let their eyes meet again. There was warmth in the other girl's eyes, though she did not smile. "You must live far from here for your masters to so freely name Stormkeep," the girl whispered. "Some say the black wind listens for the sound of that name and reports the speaker to its master."

"They say that in our village, too," Rage lied.

"Your masters are foolish."

"Perhaps they are brave," Rage murmured, and was unprepared for the burning look the other girl gave her. Unable to decipher it, Rage added a shrug, as if it had been a joke. Then she said, "It is said in our village that those who travel from place to place lose themselves, and it may be that my masters have lost wise fear."

"I suppose they are paying your parents well," the maid said.

Not understanding, Rage judged it safer to change the subject. "I . . . I met a woman in another village where my masters stayed. A woman with ears somewhat like the little man's over there. She had golden hair over her body and seemed to me to be unlike anyone I had ever met before. She was coming toward Stormkeep."

"She came here," the girl murmured, casting a quick look over her shoulder at the others. "But we must not speak of her."

"I suppose it is always better to mind one's own business," Rage said.

The maid leaned closer and said in a barely audible voice, "It's not safe to speak of her. She asked when the sun would rise!" Rage tried to look shocked, but she must have failed because the maid added, "Do you not know that this is how summerland rebels greet one another?"

"You think she was a summerland rebel?" Rage asked, struggling not to reveal how lost she was.

"What else could she be?" the maid asked eagerly. "And do you know, the earth began to shudder and groan the day she came!"

Rage stared at the girl, trying to understand what she was being told.

"That will do," Thaddeus called.

Rage started as sharply as did the maid, which was just as well. They completed laying the table in silence. When the girl had gone, Rage told the others what had been said.

"Rebels?" Nomadiel asked, puzzled. "Perhaps they oppose the Stormlord."

"I wish I'd asked outright if Elle went to Stormkeep," Rage said. "I didn't really learn anything useful."

"It was *good* that you did not show too much interest in her," Thaddeus disagreed. "Especially if something Elle said made her seem aligned with people rebelling against the Stormlord."

"What do we do now?" Nomadiel asked.

"I'd like to take a look at Stormkeep," Thaddeus said.

"Just make sure that its lord does not have a look at you, or maybe you will find yourself summoned," Puck sneered.

"Good thought," Thaddeus said promptly. "I had better take someone with me, just in case I am spotted. Master Puck, *you* can easily slip away to warn the others if there is any trouble."

Rage thought the little fairy man would argue, but he merely grunted. In the end, Mr. Walker went as well. He pointed out that if Elle or the wizard were about, he would be able to smell them, thereby saving the threesome the need to expose themselves by asking questions.

Left alone with Nomadiel, Rage thought to see if the little girl could be brought to talk about her father. But as if she guessed Rage's intent, the small girl immediately went and lay on the farthest bed, turning her back. Rage paced for a while before lying down, too. She drifted back into the dream of wandering in a storm, which continued until she was roused by a knock at the door. Rage answered it, her heart thumping, but it was only the maid, come to clear away the dishes. Rage helped her and asked when day would come.

The other girl gave her a shocked look. "Day is only a summerlander fairy tale, but the telling of it will rouse the wrath of the Stormlord."

After the maid had gone, Rage went to the small window and unlatched it, staring out into the relentless darkness. "Could it be that day does not come in this world?" she whispered.

"Perhaps the wizard who made the winter door keeps day from coming," Rally said from behind her.

Rage turned and looked into the crow's eyes. "Then the summerland rebels . . ."

"Would be rebelling against him," Rally concluded.

Rage nodded. "If the Stormlord gets angry at someone talking about day, then he must be working with the wizard who stops it from coming. But what sort of people would want the sun never to rise and winter to rule?" Rage asked.

"Those whose own souls are bleak and cold and dark," Rally said.

There was a thump at the door. It swung open to reveal Thaddeus, Puck, and Mr. Walker. Rage opened her mouth to speak but Thaddeus shook his head. A moment later the maid appeared with a tray of hot drinks. Nomadiel sat up and yawned theatrically.

"Stormkeep is a good step from here," Thaddeus said when they were alone again. "It is an impregnable fortress built on a great, freestanding pillar of stone rising from an abyss. There is a narrow stone bridge to the mainland that goes over the abyss and also over a glacier that runs across this icy land and over the edge into the abyss. There is no other approach."

"Are there walls about the fortress?" Nomadiel asked.

"Of course," Mr. Walker said. "High as three willow seat towers atop one another, they run straight up from the edges of the stone pillar, so the fortress is a sort of extension of it," Mr. Walker murmured.

"If we wanted to get in, would there be no choice but to pretend to be a servant or something?" Rage said.

"Impossible," Thaddeus said. "We stopped in a tavern to drink, ask questions, and listen to gossip. Seems like no one but those who are summoned go into Stormkeep. The interesting thing is that when they come out, they are changed."

"Changed how?"

"They are what the settlers call 'aligned,'" Mr. Walker put in.

"But other people must go to the fortress," Nomadiel objected. "What about those working there? Maids and cooks and cleaners and guards? What about whoever brings supplies? And who escorts the people who are summoned into the keep?"

"No one lives there but the Stormlord. He is served in all capacities by things called gray fliers," Thaddeus said. "It is they who do the escorting."

"One man told us that summerlanders needed alignment," Puck said.

"Alignment is a punishment, then," Rage said. She told them what the maid had said.

"It can't be too terrible, though, because there were a couple of people in the tavern pointed out to us as having been aligned. They looked fine other than being a little more grim than the rest," Thaddeus said.

"Did you ask if there was a wizard creating the storms?" Rally inquired.

"No one spoke of any wizard," Thaddeus answered. "But a wizard might not necessarily want anyone to know he exists. Or maybe he is a prisoner being forced to do the Stormlord's bidding. In which case the Stormlord might not want to advertise his presence."

"What are we to do, then?" Rage asked.

"Well," Thaddeus said, "it seems to me that there is only one way to enter Stormkeep and that is openly and by the front door."

"You *are* mad," Puck said cheerfully. "Shall we send a letter to announce that we are coming so that they can prepare the method of execution in advance?"

"I did not say that we would enter that way, only that it was the sole way to enter," Thaddeus said. He looked at Rage. "I wonder if you are right, though, about this place being a world of night."

"There are such lands in fairy tales but usually they are under some sort of evil enchantment," Mr. Walker murmured.

"The sun must have risen here once or how else could the summerlanders speak of it?" Puck said.

"Maybe it never rose but they *want* to believe it could," Nomadiel said slowly. "Wouldn't you want to believe that sunlight and summer existed somewhere or even once upon a time? Maybe these summerlanders'd rather believe and fight for something beautiful than accept the way things are, even if in their hearts they don't think there really could be anything else."

Thaddeus gave her a long look, then he said, "Even if you are right, the notion of sun and daylight have to have come from somewhere. If these summerlanders have never seen the sun, how could they have a word for it?"

Before anyone could answer, Rage felt the tugging sensation of her flesh calling her dream-traveling self back. She fell into darkness.

And woke to pain.

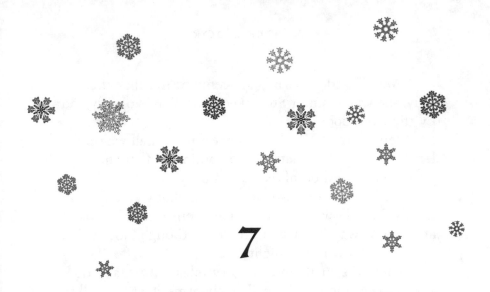

7

Rage groaned. Her hands, feet, and face burned as if they were on fire. She would have screamed, but her throat ached as if she had already yelled herself hoarse. Somewhere she could hear a deep, muffled howling.

She felt the same soft, wet warmth on her face that had wakened her. Heartened, she forced her eyelids apart, but it was too dark to see anything. Nevertheless, a breath of hot air told her that someone was leaning over her. The soft wetness brushed her again. A tongue! And when she felt fur tickling her cheek, she knew that it was Billy licking her face.

"What happened?" she croaked, trying to rise. There were blankets over her, heavy and peculiarly stiff. She tried again to sit but had no strength left. Billy nuzzled the front of her jacket, caught hold of it, and dragged her upright. She flopped forward when he let go. She stretched her hands out and found Billy's soft form. She held on to him with one arm and put the other back to hold herself up. Her fingers brushed cold, damp wood.

Where on earth was she?

Rage listened to the booming howl of storm winds outside. Then she knew exactly where she must be: the hikers' hut in her world! Her last memory was of struggling through the snow and falling. She must have hit her head and, while unconscious, dream-traveled to the world of Bleak. Meanwhile, Billy had dragged her to the hikers' hut, got the door open somehow, and pulled the fire blankets over her.

Rage pulled Billy close, whispering, "You saved my life."

She massaged life back into her stiff limbs and then got clumsily to her feet, realizing that she was still wearing her pack. Billy had not been able to undo the buckles with his teeth, of course. No wonder she had been lying so awkwardly. Shrugging the pack off, she felt in the side pocket for the matches in plastic and the stump of candle she kept there. It took three matches before she managed to light the candlewick, and then she took out her thermos. It was eerie to find it full of the hot chocolate she had drunk already in another world. She drank half a mug and poured a bit in the lid for Billy to lap up. Then she gave Billy some dog biscuits and ate one of the sandwiches.

There was no telling how long the raging storm would last. Rage paced for a while longer, but eventually she grew tired and got back under the thermal blankets with Billy. He fell asleep almost at once, head in her lap. She kissed him gently and thought what a fool she had been to set off, knowing a bad storm was approaching. Hadn't Mam warned her a million times how dangerous the cold could be? She had been so set on discovering if the bramble gate was still there that she had been deaf to common sense.

She wished Billy could talk to her because she would have liked to hear what he thought about what had happened in Bleak. He was sure to have some clever, unusual idea about what had become of Elle and the wizard. Thinking about Bleak was rather like having been forced to put a book down halfway through. Part of Rage was longing to pick it up and read some more. But she was also anxious about her uncle. What if he returned and found her note? He would be frantic. She could only pray he had been trapped in town by the storm. She worried for a while, then she snuffed out the candle carefully and slept.

A sound brought her back to wakefulness. It was Billy, scratching at the door. She hobbled to it and opened its tiny shutter. The storm had passed and the sky was clear, but it was dark. She must have been unconscious for ages. She closed the shutter and opened the door. Snow piled up against it slid into the hut. The world beyond was a dazzling silver-and-black landscape. Rage's skin prickled at the thought of walking through the moonlit world.

"Billy," she said, "let's go home."

Billy gave a wriggling, puppy-like leap that made her laugh. She went back into the hut, pushed her thermos and the remaining sandwiches into her pack, and buckled it closed. She shoveled the snow impatiently out of the hut and dragged the door closed, and then they set off. The snow was so deep that she sank up to her hips in it, but it was not hard-packed, so she could move quite easily. She marveled that so much snow had fallen in just a few hours.

Billy raced ahead, plowing a narrow furrow through the powder snow and then circling back in his own excitement. Rage thought the moonlit landscape the loveliest sight she had ever seen, but she had little energy for anything but walking. At first, brushing through the powder had been easy, but there was enough of a drag that her legs began to ache. Worse, she noticed more dark clouds on the horizon.

Once they had climbed the hill above the dam, Rage stopped to rest for a bit, feeding the rest of the sandwiches to Billy and drinking the cocoa herself. She wiped her forehead and winced to find a sore place on her temple. Fingering it, she found a sizable bump with some grazing. She must have hit her head, then. Knowing that made her feel slightly better. At least she hadn't just stupidly lain down to sleep. Of course, she would not have fallen at all if she had sensibly stayed at home.

The moon was setting as they came over the rise and saw the roof of Winnoway. And not a moment too soon, for there was a rumble of thunder, and the gathering clouds merged, plunging the world back into darkness. Rage ran the last bit of the way, relieved to see that there were no lights on. That meant her uncle must have stayed the night in town.

When Rage got inside the house, she realized how ravenously hungry she was. Despite the chocolate and sandwiches, she felt as if she had not eaten for days. Annoyingly, the fire was completely out, but it did not take long to start another. She stuck some frozen pies in the oven and went to get warm in a bath. Undressing, she inspected her hands and feet and was relieved to find that the only damage was a few chilblains that reddened and itched as she climbed into the water.

Sinking up to her neck in hot, soapy water, she gave a sigh of contentment. She slipped right under to wet her hair and lie still, enjoying the feeling of being warm all over. When she surfaced, Billy was peering anxiously at her. She laughed and sat up to wash her hair, then she immersed herself again to wash off the suds. She would have liked to soak longer, but she was too hungry and tired. Toweling vigorously, she dressed in warm flannel pajamas and Mam's old red fleece dressing gown and padded back to her bedroom to don some thick socks. Then she rescued the pies from the oven, and she and Billy ate them in front of the stove with relish.

She told Billy all that had happened in Bleak, then she thought again how lucky it was that she and Billy were safe and Uncle Samuel need never know what had happened. She wondered if he had called, and hoped he would manage to get back in time to take her down to the hospital for a visit with Mam. Luckily, they were not supposed to move her until later in the afternoon. Belatedly, Rage remembered that she had pulled the phone line out of the jack. She got up to connect it and was startled to find it was pushed in already.

Rage frowned and wondered if she hadn't completely pulled it out, or had just imagined doing it. Then she shrugged and checked the answering machine. To her relief, there were no messages from either Mrs. Somersby or her uncle, but there was one missed call. She checked the clock. It was just past eight, and that was pretty early for a Sunday morning, but she was too impatient to wait. Maybe it had been her uncle calling from a hotel. Rage dialed three numbers and listened warily, hoping that the redial sequence would not connect her to Mrs. Somersby.

A phone began to ring, and a moment later a woman's voice said, "Hello, Margery Stiles here."

Rage blinked. Stiles was the last name of Logan's foster parents. That meant Logan must have been the last caller. "Uh, I know it's pretty early but . . . I was wondering if I can talk to Logan. We go to school together and—"

"Oh! You must be Rage," Mrs. Stiles interrupted. "I hope you don't mind if I call you that? It's just that Logan does."

"N-n-no," Rage stammered, startled to hear that Logan would refer to her in conversation with his foster parents. It hadn't sounded as if he talked much to them at all, but maybe the whole move and possibility of a new school had broken down some barriers between them.

"Rage," Mrs. Stiles was saying, "I should like very much to meet you. Since Logan has been . . . well, he has been so much *happier* lately, and I believe it is at least in part due to you."

Rage didn't know what to say. "Thank you," she said at last, feeling embarrassed and awkward.

"You must come to dinner sometime soon. Or perhaps for lunch. I know you live out of town and this winter is making travel so difficult. Sometimes I do feel that spring will never come, but of course it must." She gave a light laugh. "Oh, listen to me rabbiting on and you want to speak to Logan. I should have said right away that he is out. In fact, he was gone already when I went in this morning. I would have been worried that he had gone back to his old wandering ways—my husband used to call him our lone wolf—but he's a good lad, and lately he has really settled down. Anyway, I will let him know you called as soon as he comes in."

"It doesn't matter, I'll see him Monday at school."

"You mean Wednesday, don't you?" Mrs. Stiles laughed. "Because today and tomorrow are holidays, aren't they?"

Rage had forgotten about the days off again, but what was Mrs. Stiles talking about, saying today was a holiday? Sundays were always holidays. "Oh yes," Rage said vaguely, not wanting to prolong the conversation. Mrs. Stiles was nice but pretty talkative. "Well, maybe he can call tonight."

They said goodbye. Rage hung up and added a big log of hardwood to the stove, then flopped into the chair. The storm outside had grown in strength, and the lights were dimming every few minutes—an indicator that the power would soon fail. Rage got up and switched on the radio. If it was storming this badly now, there was every chance her uncle would cancel the hospital visit. At first, there was only a lot of white noise. She twitched the dial minutely, fishing for the elusive signal.

". . . worst storms to hit since . . ." The sound faded out and in again. ". . . the minister will meet with other ministers, town officials, and emergency services personnel to discuss strategies . . ." The voice dissolved into static and Rage thought that it must be a pretty drastic storm if all of those official-sounding people were going to meet on a Sunday. She gave up on the radio and went back to the fire. The log had begun to catch, but rather than risk the fire going out again, she decided to really make sure before closing the flue. She had half hoped her uncle would be home before she went to bed, but when the power went out, she decided it was time. She shut the flue and wrote a brief note by candlelight telling Uncle Samuel that she had gone to bed, to stop him waking her when he came home and dragging her back from Bleak.

She left the note by the phone, on top of her uncle's, and pushed her earlier note into her pocket. Then she carried the candle through to her bedroom. The heater was out, but she would be warm enough with Billy sleeping beside her. She patted the bed and let him get comfortable, then she reached across to blow out the candle. She looked at the clock beside her bed, which showed the day as well as time.

It read *Monday*!

Rage gasped, her mind whirling. If today was Monday, then she hadn't just slept a few hours in the hut before Billy woke her. She must have been unconscious all of Saturday and Saturday night and most of Sunday and Sunday night! She must have concussed herself when she fell. No wonder Billy had gone crazy when she finally got up and spoke to him.

But what had happened to her uncle? Was it possible the amount of snow that had fallen had really made the roads impassable and he had ended up staying Saturday and Sunday nights in town? But why hadn't he called? The answering machine had been on. Unless the phones had been down. But if that was so, how had Logan got through?

Monday. Rage swallowed a sudden, hard lump in her throat. Uncle Samuel would have gone to the hospital alone to explain that Rage wouldn't be able to come after all, because of the weather. Tears burned in her eyes at the idea of the doctors telling Mam that she hadn't come. For once, she hoped her mother had been too dazed and sleepy to understand properly. Mam must be in Leary Hospital now.

She lay back against the pillow, but now she was so upset that she was afraid she wouldn't be able to sleep at all. She closed her eyes and imagined Nomadiel and Rally, Mr. Walker, Thaddeus, and Puck. She pictured the big, bare room they had been given at the settlement of Sorrow, trying to see every detail in her mind's eye. She saw herself and Billy dressed for winter, and wearing well-filled rucksacks. In the moment before she fell asleep, she wondered if they had found any sign of Elle yet.

Rage opened her eyes and found she and Billy were standing side by side in a tiny room. It was lit by a single candle carried by one of two filthy youths who gaped at them in shock.

"Demons!" one of them said in a frightened voice, his voice squeaking at the end. He was probably younger than Rage, though he carried a knife in his spare hand and looked as if he knew how to use it.

"We ought to kill them before they enchant us," the other hissed.

Rage wondered how they could extricate themselves from the mess she had landed them in! Billy was sniffing the air, a curious expression on his face.

"They are not demons," said a familiar voice behind them. Rage gave a cry of delight and whirled to face Elle.

"I thought I could smell you, but your scent has changed!" Billy said. He flung his arms about the tall, smiling dog-woman.

Elle laughed and pounded his back. "You smell different, too, Billy Thunder. You have grown, and not just in stature!" She turned to Rage, who gaped. Elle wore grubby trousers and a filthy sweater, and had smears of dirt on her face and on the tips of her pointed ears. Her golden hair, once very short, now hung below her waist. It was matted and carelessly pulled back in a rough ponytail, but it caught the candlelight like a spider web of spun gold and made the perfect foil for her impossible, radiant beauty. How had she become so beautiful without really changing? Rage wondered incredulously.

"You have grown, too, darling heart," Elle said, her deep-set almond eyes tender. She gathered Rage into her arms and held her tightly. Rage clung to her, her eyes filling with tears. Dimly she was aware that the earth was quaking again.

"Oh, Elle, I missed you so much," she whispered, feeling the dog-woman's muscles beneath the loose clothes.

"I missed you, too. Both of you, though I have been happy in Valley," Elle said, releasing them both. From the corner of her eye, Rage noticed that the two boys were regarding them with wonder.

"These are summerlanders, too, Lady Elle?" one of them asked reverently.

"They are my friends," Elle said firmly. She looked back to Rage. "You dream-traveled here?"

Rage nodded.

Elle shook her head. "Rue spoke of this power that let you visit her at the heart lake, but I did not know that Billy Thunder had it, too."

"I brought him with me," Rage said. "I was trying to bring us to Mr. Walker and the others, but I thought of you just before I fell asleep."

"You mean to say that Mr. Walker is here?" Elle asked eagerly.

Rage nodded. "When I was with them last, they had

got your scent, but I guess they haven't found you yet."

Elle's eyes flashed with amusement. "Nor will they find me unless I choose it. Which I do, now that I know who seeks me." Elle turned to the boy who had spoken. "Lod, go and find if other strangers have been seen in any of the settlements about Null." Rage broke in to explain that they had been staying in Sorrow. "That makes it even easier," Elle said. She turned back to the boy. "Go to Sorrow and seek them out. One will be a small man with ears like mine, and there will be a faun, too. A man with goat's horns and legs—"

"Gilbert didn't come," Rage interrupted again, to explain that he had broken his leg and had been unable to come through the winter door.

Elle shook her head. "Poor Gilbert. Well, then find the small man and bring him and his companions to me. But be careful, we do not wish the Stormlord to know what we are about. We have yet to learn who informs upon those taken by his gray fliers."

"I obey, Lady Elle," the boy said, his eyes shining with adoration. He turned and slipped through a rough door behind Elle.

"The Stormlord!" Billy said. "Rage talked about him. Does a wizard serve him?"

Elle glanced at Rage. "I have wondered that, but so far I have heard no one talk of a wizard." The boy that had not been sent away had drawn closer as Elle spoke, his face slack with devotion. Catching sight of him, Elle laughed, and ruffled his hair affectionately. Her laughter was truly lovely, especially in this dark place.

"How did you meet these boys?" Billy asked.

"I had no idea if it was early evening or late when I reached the settlement of Hollow. So I asked when the sun would rise, and everyone reacted as if I had sworn. I realized that I had made some sort of mistake, and left. Fortunately, as it happens, because I am told the gray fliers came for me."

"Who or what are gray fliers?" Billy asked curiously.

"Winged creatures who serve the Stormlord," Elle said. "I have not managed to see any of them up close, but they smell of nothing, so I think that they might be some sort of machines."

"And these boys?" Rage asked.

"They are summerlanders. Their leader, Shona, came to me in the next settlement I found myself in. She explained that only summerlander rebels spoke of the sun rising, and then only to identify themselves to one another. She said that she knew I was a great warrior from the summerlands, come to free Null from eternal night. That is what the inhabitants of this place call it: *Null*. The summerlanders believe that it is the Stormlord who makes sure it is always night here and always winter."

Billy sniffed the air. "Where are we now? It smells like we are underground."

"Your nose is still keen, little brother. We are in a chamber at the end of a tunnel, which runs from the outskirts of the settlement of Sorrow to the edge of a cliff. The window there faces the great pillar upon which is built the fortress of Stormkeep. We have to keep it closed because gray fliers patrol the cliff. They don't seem to have any sense of smell, but their hearing is keen." Elle pointed to the door behind her. "This door was built to keep out the dampness and stink of the earth in the tunnel. Unfortunately, the only way to get back to Sorrow is to crawl along the tunnel."

"Why are you here?" Billy asked.

"I wanted to see if I could smell if our wizard was there, but unfortunately the distance is too great."

"You haven't found any sign of him, then?"

"No, but that may not mean anything, for it was the wizard himself who showed me a spell to hide my scent."

"Can I see Stormkeep?" Billy asked.

In answer, Elle led him to a slit in the wall. She opened the shutter and motioned everyone to silence. Billy leaned forward and peered through the opening. He stepped back after a long moment, his expression grave. Elle motioned to Rage, who looked out, too. There was a mist rising from the abyss into which the window opened; through it she could see the great pillar of stone upon which Stormkeep was built. Exactly as Thaddeus and Mr. Walker had described, its towering outer walls merged seamlessly with the pillar, leaving not even the slightest ledge where one might walk. The top of the battlements was far away, but she could see fire torches set along the top of the wall, revealing sharp, toothlike crenellations. Last of all, faintly, she saw the stone bridge—thin and insubstantial as a spiderweb—that was the only means of reaching the fortress.

"It is a grim place," Elle said after she had closed the shutter. "Well, we must return to the others." She ought to have been downcast, but she merely gave a philosophical smile. It was so dazzling that Rage did not wonder that the rebels worshipped her. Just being around her made you feel more hopeful.

"Others?" Billy asked curiously.

"Shona and some of her followers await us in Sorrow. If Lod has moved swiftly enough, Mr. Walker and the others might also be there by the time we arrive." Elle went to the door and opened it.

Rage noticed the remaining boy staring at her and wondered if the Stormlord forbade smiling and laughter as well as sunlight.

Elle dropped to her knees and crawled into the sour-smelling tunnel. The boy gestured that Rage should go next. She nodded, took a deep breath, and crawled in after Elle, praying that there would not be any tremors.

"Who else came . . . ?" Elle's voice was muffled.

"Thaddeus, Puck, Nomadiel, and Rally," Rage gasped, her hands and knees numb from crawling.

"Noma and Rally, too! I would not have guessed they would come. But that is nine, counting the wizard and me. Rue said that only eight were to come."

"Billy and I don't count because we didn't come through the door," Rage panted. "That makes seven that have come through, which means there is one other to come from Valley."

The sheer physical effort of crawling made it impossible to go on talking. When they were all finally out, Elle closed a trap over the tunnel and led them through a door into the chilly night. Rage saw that they were just outside the settlement of Sorrow. There was no need to hide because not a soul was visible. They entered another building and were surrounded at once by a crowd of solemn, pale people, mostly teenagers or little children.

"Greetings, Lady Elle," said an older girl. She bowed deeply and then the others did the same, even the little ones.

"Do not bow to me, Shona," Elle said gently. "You are the leader here, and your followers should be in their homes. It is dangerous to gather like this."

"I told them, Lady, but they wished to see you," Shona said. Rage realized with a shock that this girl was the leader of the summerlanders. "They needed to see that you had not abandoned us."

"You must have the courage to believe," Elle said.

"I *do* believe. Does not the very earth shudder in anticipation of the sun rising since your arrival?" The girl made a gesture. Quickly, and in almost complete silence, all the people slipped away. Many reached out to touch Elle in passing.

"Who are they?" Shona asked, nodding at Rage and Billy.

"Old friends," Elle said. "Now, let us have some food before we talk further."

Shona nodded to the boy who had been in the tunnel hut and directed them to a circle of seats. "Lod came back and said he was to seek out other strangers. They are friends, too?"

"They are," Elle said. "Let me introduce you to Rage Winnoway and Billy Thunder."

The girl nodded to them in turn. "I am pleased to greet you, fortunate dwellers of the summerlands." She turned back to Elle. "Your quest was successful? You smelled the presence of the wizard who is your ally?"

"I could not smell him," Elle said. She reached out and laid a hand on the girl's slumped shoulder. "You are tired. Go home and sleep. It is harder to be brave and to have hope when you are weary."

The girl nodded and rose obediently. As she was leaving, the boy returned with several young people bearing covered dishes of food. It turned out to be the same dull stew Rage had eaten before, and she decided that she was not hungry. But Elle and Billy ate heartily while Rage told them again all that had transpired on her previous visit to Null.

"So, you vanish from here when you wake there, and when you dream-travel here, you appear just as you did in the tunnel hut, leaving your proper body behind?" Elle murmured. "An amazing ability, for you look and feel perfectly real. But how did you come here?"

"I was thinking about you when I fell asleep," Rage said.

Elle shook her head. "Then it is only a matter of disciplining your mind to focus very intently on whom you want to come to for you to master this power." She fell silent, then she rose suddenly. "I must think about what you have said." Rage must have shown her surprise, for the dog-woman gave her a smile. "I am somewhat better able to see the use in thinking these days. Indeed, I am quite addicted to it. I also want to see if there is any word of the others before we discuss this further."

"She is different," Billy said softly to Rage when Elle had gone. "She smells, I don't know, brighter?" He shook his head in his characteristic annoyance at being unable to find a human word to describe some nuance of dog-life.

Now that Elle had gone, the boy and the other children who had brought the food crept closer. "Will you tell us of the summerlands?" a boy asked.

"Have you ever seen the sun?" Billy asked curiously.

The children shook their heads as one. "The olders say there is no such thing, and that the sun has never shone here," the boy said. "But I think they lie out of fear."

"You think they are afraid of the sun?" Rage asked.

"Not of the sun, but of talking about it," said a curly-haired moppet. "That's what makes the fliers come take you to the keep."

"To be aligned?" Rage asked.

"They look the same as before they are taken," the girl said. "But they are different inside. They don't talk about the sun or the summerlands anymore."

"Perhaps they are afraid to talk about those things in case they are taken prisoner again," Billy suggested gently.

But the girl shook her head. "They don't *want* to talk about such things. They don't care about them anymore."

"What happens to them inside Stormkeep?" Billy asked.

"We don't know," the older boy said. "They don't remember anything."

"What does the sun look like?" asked an older girl gravely.

Billy looked at her and Rage saw pity in his soft brown eyes. "It is a hot, bright light, only very big and very far away. It rises in the sky and lights the world like a giant lantern, and all flowers open their petals and turn their faces to drink its warmth."

Rage stared at him, touched by his gentleness, and by the poetry of his words.

"Then there *are* flowers," the little girl declared, and she made a ferocious face at the boy beside her. "I told you!"

"Does the sun make the sky blue?" asked another boy.

"How could it do that?" said the older boy who had been in the tunnel hut. "The sky would be white with all of that brightness."

"Sometimes it is almost white, but sometimes the sky is blue, too," Billy said. "Other times it is red as blood and then still other times it is yellow like the palest candlelight."

"I have dreamed of flowers," the little girl said. "I have dreamed of how warm it will be when the Lady Elle defeats the Stormlord."

Rage wondered uneasily what Elle had actually told these people. After all, their task was not to bring sunlight to this world but to find the wizard and close the winter door. But perhaps like Mr. Walker, Elle now had her own plans. One thing was certain: if she had told these people she would help them, then she would not go until she had done so.

Billy went on talking to the children. They drank in his stories of sunlight and warm beaches and butterflies and rainbows. Rage felt sick at the thought that these children might be taken inside Stormkeep to who knew what fate.

"What are you thinking about, Rage?" Billy asked suddenly. An older boy was shooing the children away with the empty plates.

"I was thinking about what will happen to these children. Elle can't make the sun shine here."

"Maybe the wizard can if . . ." Billy's eyes widened. "Rage, I know what Elle wants you to do!"

"She didn't ask me to do anything."

"She didn't, but she will. She is going to ask you to dream-travel inside Stormkeep!"

"Could you do it?" Elle had returned.

Rage ignored the fear that rose in her throat. "I *think* I could dream myself to the wizard."

"I will go, too," Billy volunteered. Rage felt a fierce

love for him because he did not tell her that she could not go, that it was too dangerous or she was too young.

"I can go," Rage said. "But first I have to wake up in my own world and go back to sleep again. And time passes faster here than there."

Elle nodded. "I have considered that, but we have no choice. You have seen Stormkeep. We must learn if the wizard is there before we consider trying to get inside to save him."

The door burst open behind her and both Rage and Billy jumped to their feet. It was the boy Lod. Behind him were Thaddeus and Nomadiel with Rally on her shoulder.

"Where is Mr. Walker?" Billy asked eagerly.

Only then, when Nomadiel and the boy stepped aside, did they see that Thaddeus was carrying Mr. Walker, hanging limp and dreadfully still in his arms.

"What happened?" Rage cried as Thaddeus lay Mr. Walker carefully on the nearest bench seat. The dog-man's face was clammy pale except for bright spots of color high on his cheeks.

"He would not rest nor eat though I told him that I could smell sickness growing in him," Nomadiel said. Her eyes were dry but diamond-hard in her heart-shaped face.

"But what happened to him?" Rage asked her. "He can't just have gotten sick."

"Well, he did!" Nomadiel snapped. There was a brittleness to her that was not far from tears. "Just as my mother did!"

Rage recoiled from the fury and despair in the girl's voice and turned back to Mr. Walker. Elle was kneeling at his side now, her hand on his brow. She called his name softly. After an endless moment, the little man's eyes fluttered and then opened a slit.

"You . . . ," he breathed.

"Yes, it is me," Elle said lightly, smiling down at him. "Don't think you are going to get out of helping us to close the winter door by getting sick!"

His lips curved slightly, and Rage wondered if there was anyone in any world who would not smile at Elle. But the smile faded almost at once, as if the effort of maintaining it was too great. "I'm sorry," Mr. Walker whispered.

"Don't dare talk like that," Elle said with soft mock sternness. "As if you are making a farewell speech! I won't have it." She turned to Lod. "Go and see if there is not something we can give him for a fever." Then she looked back at Mr. Walker. "As for you, rest and get well, for we have need of you."

Mr. Walker closed his eyes and seemed to lapse back into unconsciousness.

"You must save him!" Nomadiel cried. Then, without waiting for an answer, she turned to Rage. "Where did you go when you vanished? It's your fault he got sick! You made him lose heart."

"I awoke back in my world," Rage said gently, pitying the girl. "It turned out that I had been asleep the whole time I was here after all. I didn't know because I had fallen and knocked myself out. When I slept again in my world, I tried to will myself to you and Mr. Walker, but I thought of Elle for a moment, and . . ." She waved her hand at Elle.

Puck glared at Elle. "You might have waited for us, and then we would not have wasted so much time looking for you! We ought to have gone through all together."

Elle only gathered him up and hugged him. He seemed to enjoy it despite his scowls. "I am glad to see you, for your bad temper is like a warm fire in this wearyingly bland world where no one seems to feel anything very much, and if they do, they are soon taken away."

"Is it only summerlanders who are taken?" Billy asked as she set Puck down.

"Mostly," Elle said. She turned her attention now to Nomadiel and held out her hand solemnly. Nomadiel blushed as she laid her own small hand in it.

"I am very glad to see you, Lady," she said.

"And I you, Noma, though these are difficult days," Elle said very seriously. "We will have need of your courage on this quest." She bowed her head gracefully to Rally, who stood on Nomadiel's shoulder blinking at her. "And we will have need of your wisdom, too, Master Crow."

The bird gave a pleased squawk and preened slightly. "I am at your service, Lady Elle," he said.

Elle nodded and rose to face Thaddeus. "It is good to see you again, witch man, though I am surprised your lady spared you." Puck snorted rudely. "I wish I had realized sooner who was seeking me. When I heard that a big, grim-faced man was asking questions, I thought it must be some agent of the Stormlord. Indeed, I was planning to capture you because you were the first person I had heard of who might be capable of answering questions about the keep."

"Grim-faced!" Thaddeus echoed indignantly. "I could hardly go about smiling like a great fool here, could I?"

"True," Elle conceded, grinning. "You have met my summerlander friend?" She nodded at the door through which Lod had gone in search of fever medicine.

"*He* is a summerlander?" Thaddeus asked incredulously. "Why, he is no more than a child."

"Almost all of the rebels are young or very young, including their leader," Elle said. "I do not know why, but they are as brave and determined as any adult warrior could be."

"Well, that may be," Thaddeus said, looking unconvinced. "The lad said only that the Lady Elle wanted to see us. So we came at once. But how did you get mixed up with summerland rebels anyway?"

"It is they who decided to mix themselves up with me," Elle said, gesturing to them to sit. "Their leader declared that she knew that I was a great summerland warrior who had come to free this world from endless night. It seems there is some legend here to that effect, and the fact that the earth tremors here seemed to have begun about the time I arrived doesn't help."

"You were not stupid enough to let them believe that you were their legendary warrior come to unveil the sun, I hope," Puck said sourly.

Elle laughed. "I make no promises that I will not keep, little man," she said. "Now, let us talk seriously. Rage has told me quite a lot, but you must add what you have learned since her departure."

"Not much," Thaddeus confessed apologetically. "When we could find no way to confirm that the wizard was here, we put our efforts into finding you." He added that the only thing they had heard about the wizard was a rather vague rumor of an old man visiting Stormkeep, but when they investigated, the description did not sound like the wizard.

"The man who told us of him did not smell of lies,"

Nomadiel added earnestly. Rage noticed that her eyes hardly left Elle's face as she spoke, as if all hope lay in the lovely dog-woman's face, which perhaps was true.

"Perhaps he did not lie," Elle murmured thoughtfully. "The wizard would have known how to prevent anyone marking him as a stranger. I have been unable to find proof that he is here, either, but the fact that the people here believe the master of the keep visits his wrath upon them in the form of storms makes me certain that our wizard would at least have gone to Stormkeep, even if he went somewhere else afterward."

"You have a plan?" Nomadiel asked, her eyes alight.

Elle nodded. "The bones of one, at least. It is a two-fold plan. Rage will be drawn back to her world again when she wakes. Next time when she sleeps, she will dream-travel to the wizard. If he is in Stormkeep, then he will most likely be a prisoner. It may be that Rage will be unable to break the iron circles that will bind him, but at least she will be able to speak to him."

"Iron circles?" Rage echoed blankly.

"Everyone knows that iron stops magic," Nomadiel said scornfully.

"Remember the bracelets the High Keeper made girls wear to stop them becoming witch folk?" Thaddeus said.

"I remember, but the wizard was trapped in an hour-glass when I was here last, and he couldn't do magic then . . ."

"The circles do not have to be about his hands. They can also be either side of him or above and below him," Nomadiel said.

"The hourglass was capped at both ends with iron circles," Billy said softly to Rage. "He could manage to reach your dreams as he did because the iron wasn't actually around his wrists."

"I think this plan is madness," Puck announced. "What if the wizard is dead? What if she dream-travels herself under the ground?"

Rage's skin rose into gooseflesh, but Elle merely shook her head. "He is not dead."

"What if the Stormlord's pet wizard is waiting?"

"I am not sure there is a wizard in Stormkeep, but—" Elle began.

"An alarm clock!" Rage broke in. "I can set it so that I will only sleep a little while. That way I won't be there long enough for anyone to notice me."

Elle nodded her approval. "A good thought. So Rage will wake, then sleep again as soon as she can manage it, and then she and Billy will return to tell us what they discovered. Our wizard might also be restored to us by then."

"Puck is right," Thaddeus protested. "The danger to Rage will be great. You cannot count upon the Stormlord not noticing an intruder, even if she is only there for a short while."

"That is true, witch man," Elle replied. "But I will send a message to him announcing that I mean to send one of my minions inside his supposedly impregnable keep to reveal my power. If he captures Rage, he will want to question her about me."

"You can't know that," Puck said.

"He would be a fool if he did otherwise, and I do not think the master of this place is a fool. Yet there is a risk," Elle admitted. "And Rage has already agreed to take it."

"It is a better plan than sending Rally or me flying over the walls to see if the wizard is there," Puck said grudgingly, giving Thaddeus a black look.

"You would have been spotted and shot from the air by arrows, for the watch-walks about the walls are manned by gray fliers," Elle said.

"And if Rage cannot release the wizard so that he can effect his own escape?" Rally asked.

"I have some thoughts on that, but I am not ready to utter them yet," Elle said calmly. "Rage, how long do you think before you will wake?"

Rage thought of how tired she had been after her long walk to the dam and back. "I'm afraid it might be a while yet."

Thaddeus let out a low cry. "I have something that won't help you wake in your own world, but it might help you sleep, if you can carry it there with you." He reached into his pocket and pulled out a small pouch. "Sleep dust. The best thing about it is that you won't sleep for long."

Rage did not know if things could shift with her dream form, but it would be marvelous if she did have the sleep dust with her when she woke because they would not have to wait to return to Null.

"All right, now we must compose a letter for the Stormlord, and think on how it might be delivered," Elle said briskly. She looked at Nomadiel. "Since I cannot write, you will have to do it for me." She rose and Nomadiel followed her.

As they reached the door, Rage had an idea. "Elle, what made you come here so suddenly from Valley? Isn't it because you dreamed of the firecat?" she cried. Rage felt herself flush as everyone stared at her, including a puzzled-looking Elle. "I'm sorry I yelled," Rage said, feeling foolish. "I just thought talking about the firecat might make me wake up, because every other time I've tried to tell anyone about it, I've woken up."

"A pity it did not work," Elle said. "But how did you know that I had dreamed of the firecat?"

"You saying that the wizard wasn't dead made me think of it. Because how could you know that unless the firecat had come to you again?"

Elle laughed. "It is true that the wretched creature plagues my dreams, demanding that I seek out its master, but it can offer no help except to insist that he is here somewhere. For some reason, the firecat is terrified of entering this world. What did it tell *you*?"

Rage felt the blood in her cheeks drain away. "It said that the wizard was in trouble. But I wouldn't listen. I thought it was a dream."

"So that is why it came to me! I did wonder. Well, you shouldn't trouble yourself about it," Elle said.

Nomadiel suddenly gave a little scream and everyone turned to her in startled alarm. "He disappeared right in front of my eyes!"

"Who did?" Thaddeus asked.

"That boy. That Billy Thunder."

Rage swung round, but even as she did so, she experienced the pulling sensation of waking.

She woke to find Billy gnawing her fingertips gently.

"It's all right! I'm awake!" Rage sat up and gave him a hug, marveling that for once her mind was quite clear about what had been happening. It was pitch dark and she looked at the clock. It read five o'clock. She had been asleep for a long time. She was wide awake, but if she *had* managed to bring back the sleep dust, she could use it and go right back to sleep. She dug into her pocket but it was empty. She would just have to wait until she was sleepy.

The bedroom was icy cold, which meant the power was out again, but the stove would still be hot. Rage climbed over Billy, who wagged his tail and got down, too. She patted him and told him to be quiet so as not to wake her uncle.

If he had come back.

Rage pulled on her robe and went through the house to the extension. The door was open, which meant he had not come in. Just the same, she went to the front door and opened it to make sure the car was not in the driveway. Billy slipped past her and padded away around the side of the house. It was too cold to wait for him to come back, so Rage shut the door and went back to the bedroom. She dressed in jeans, two sweaters, and her old zebra-head slippers.

She went to the kitchen, flicking the light switch as she entered. Nothing happened. She checked the fuse box by the back door but it was fine, so the power was out. She opened the flue to the stove and fed in some more wood. She had used the last in the wood box, so she went to get some more from the outside stack, dragging on the old coat hanging on the back of the door as she went though it.

Once the wood box was replenished, Rage scrambled eggs and made tea. Only when she sat down to drink it did she let herself think about what might be happening in Null. She worried most about Mr. Walker, and whether he had recovered. Elle had seemed certain that he would. But something had been wrong with the little dog-man, even before he had gone through the winter door.

Disliking the somber turn of her thoughts, Rage decided that the quickest way to get sleepy would be to tire herself out, so she went to chop some wood. Then she dusted and swept and lit candles around the house, feeling like a seventeenth-century maid. She even mopped the kitchen floor. Then, with nothing else to do, she got out her homework. Spreading it on the floor beside the stove, she immersed herself in reading, but thoughts about her uncle kept creeping in to distract her. Why hadn't he called?

He iss having accident! whispered the firecat inside her mind.

"What do you want?" Rage snapped aloud, but there was no answer. The firecat voice was merely the voice of her own gnawing doubts and fears.

Billy scratched at the door and she let him inside and fed him, then she forced herself back to her homework. For a time, she managed to concentrate. Finally, she threw the book aside. "Oh, Billy, I can't bear this waiting," she cried.

As if in response, the power suddenly came on. At the same time, the phone began to ring. Rage froze in surprise, then she scrambled to her feet and ran across the room. Instinct made her hesitate to lift the receiver. She heard her voice on the answering machine greeting the caller, then came the voice of Mrs. Somersby asking for Uncle Samuel. To her horror, she heard the older woman say that she was sorry to have missed their meeting, but that she looked forward to discussing the program with him as soon as was convenient. Then she hung up.

Rage felt sick.

Why would Uncle Samuel agree to a meeting if he

wasn't planning to get rid of the responsibility of looking after Rage? Perhaps he had guessed that she had been trying to keep him from learning about it.

She calmed down, telling herself she didn't really know what had happened. Going restlessly to the window, she peered out. It had begun snowing lightly again. There was mist rising that gave the white landscape a strange, ghostly look, as if everything in the world were dissolving.

Rage thought about her uncle and found herself going back through the house to the extension. The last few nights at home, he had gone to his room early, saying he had work to do. It had not occurred to her before to wonder what work he meant. She went to the desk. All his books and papers were as they had been except for two notebooks that had been set aside. She took up one of them. It was new, while the one under it was battered like all the others that her uncle had brought from the jungle.

Rage flipped through the new notebook. It fell open at a point where the writing broke off halfway down the page.

It has been some time since I have felt so restless. I think I must soon consider moving on again. I have done as much as I can be expected to do here. One cannot always see everything to the end. Someone else will take on where I leave off. There are so many things that torment me when I am not engaged in a project. I must see if I can get funding for some research into

The scrawled writing ended at this point, and Rage closed the book, biting her lip and wishing she had never opened it. It was one thing to suspect that her uncle wanted to leave and another to see it in his handwriting. The diary note and the call from Mrs. Somersby were proof that her uncle *was* intending to leave. Rage carefully put the notebooks as she had found them and left the little study, closing the heavy extension door behind her. As she walked back to the kitchen, her legs felt wooden, and only when she sat down did she discover that tears were rolling unchecked down her cheeks.

Billy sat up and licked at her face. She fended him off gently and stroked him until he lay back down, then she lay down beside him, hooking one arm around him and cuddling close. It was warm in the kitchen, but the chill inside her would not go away. Tears kept falling and falling until Billy's fur and the pillow under her were both sodden. At last, she began to feel sleepy, and wearily she summoned up a mental image of the wizard as she had last seen him.

But instead of being transported to the wizard, she found herself in a dream of mist again, wandering and hearing her uncle calling out her name. She saw him and went closer. For a moment, he didn't see her, but then his eyes widened and she realized that he was staring at her.

"Rage?"

"Why do you always go away when people need you?" she asked.

"This is a dream," her uncle said, and he dissolved into snow and mist.

Rage made herself think of the wizard. To her relief, she felt the pulling sensation in her middle that she now associated with dream-traveling.

Rage and Billy were standing in a vast, silent, round room with mirror-smooth black flagstones underfoot. Before them, an old man sat slumped on a stone bench, oblivious to their presence. Rage made a motion warning Billy not to speak. The sole source of light was a cluster of lanterns suspended from a long chain in the center of the enormous chamber, but their light made little impression on the dark. Turning back to the old man, Rage knew that she would not have recognized the wizard if she had not expected to see him. His mouth hung open, his chin resting on his chest, and his once sleek ponytail of silver gray hair lay lank and tangled on his shoulders. His unkempt black beard was streaked with dull gray.

Swallowing her reluctance, Rage walked over to the wizard and bent down to look into his face. The wizard wore the same jeans and T-shirt he had worn at their last meeting, but over them was a heavy, hooded cloak, and he had a thick scarf about his neck. His hair and face were spotlessly clean, as were his hands, clasped together loosely in his lap. Rage thought that whatever his captor had subjected him to, the old man had not been physically neglected.

The wizard stirred. Rage became aware of a humming sound. She wondered if they had set off some sort of alarm, but no one shouted out to them to stop. The silence seemed deeper than ever as Billy pointed to the wizard's bound hands. A steel cord ran from the chain between the manacles, over the wizard's lap, and behind him to a big metal disk embedded in the black stone. Rage bent closer. The chain was welded, which meant there was no way they could free the wizard.

Rage thought she heard a noise and glanced around.

The smokiness in the air had cleared a little, and she saw that it was not a round chamber but a circular tower. She and Billy were standing partway up the tower on a wide stone ramp that ran in a flat spiral around the walls. In the middle of the tower was only empty space. Rage went warily to the edge of the ramp to look down. It was about ten turns to the bottom, and there seemed to be nothing down there but the end of the ramp and, presumably, a door out. Looking up, she saw that the ramp continued circling as far as her eye could reach. Feeling slightly dizzy, Rage backed away from the edge. She stumbled, and Billy gasped. The sound became an alarming susurrus of gasps that filled the air about them. But still there was no outcry.

Rage looked up once more. This could not be Storm-keep, for she would have seen such a tower from the hidden tunnel. She was about to turn back to the wizard when she noticed the most horrible thing of all: hundreds and hundreds of metal wheels were embedded along the curving ramp. Seated at the base of each, on a bench like the wizard's, were people, many small enough to be little people or children.

Billy touched her and then his nose and then he shook his head. He did it again and she tried to understand what he was trying to tell her. That he couldn't smell something, but what? He pointed to the people and then repeated his pantomime. Now Rage looked around, and the eerie silence of the place struck her. Not one out of the hundreds of people spoke or moved. If she had not been able to see the wizard's chest lifting and falling, she might have thought all of them dead. Rage turned back to the wizard and stumbled again. She looked down at her feet in puzzlement and saw that she was wearing her zebra-head slippers! She shrugged off her dismay and turned to the wizard. She shook him gently. At first, he did not respond. Then, just as she was wondering if a spell hadn't been laid on him, the wizard opened his eyes. They were so like her uncle Samuel's eyes that it took her breath away.

Rage swallowed a lump in her throat and shook his shoulder a little more firmly. "It's me, Rage Winnoway," she whispered. Her words seemed to fly out in a thousand hissing echoes. But gradually the rustling fell into silence. Still there was no outcry, though the hum continued.

The old man was staring at her incredulously. "You *are* real!" he mumbled. Even his mumble set up an echo that went on forever.

"Hush," Rage whispered as softly as she could.

"Don't worry about the noise," the wizard rasped. "No one listens."

Rage came closer. "I will free you from the manacles if you can tell me how."

He shook his head. "Why are you here?"

"We came to close the winter door," Rage said, trying to ignore the echoes.

"There *is* no way to close the winter door! Didn't the firecat warn you and the others as I commanded?"

Rage stared. *That* had been the warning the firecat had been meant to deliver? "There *must* be a way to close it," she protested. "Rue used soul magic and she said there was."

"She squanders her life for a glimpse of our dwindling tomorrows," he mumbled. His eyes began to droop again, and Rage wanted to shake him.

"Where is this tower and who imprisoned you here?

Was it the Stormlord? Does he have a wizard to do his bidding?"

"I am tired," the wizard said, giving her a dim look. "Let me sleep."

Rage shook him angrily and his eyes opened. "I won't stop bothering you until you tell me what you dreamed that made you come through the winter door without waiting for the others."

He gave a feeble shrug. "Wizards are wizard business."

"You dreamed of the other wizard, then? The one who made the winter door? Does he serve the Stormlord?"

The wizard said nothing. "If you don't care about yourself, then answer me for the sake of Valley," Rage said loudly.

The wizard roused at last. "I failed as anyone would have done. The best thing you can do is to leave this hellish place." His eyes filled with tears. "You cannot know how the memory of Valley haunts me."

Rage almost shouted in her frustration. "Look, I told you that the witch Mother says it *is* possible to close the door. Why would she say that if it weren't true?"

"She misread the vision," the wizard said bleakly. "There is no hope. We are all doomed. Better to forget the sun and laughter and light."

Rage felt like slapping him, despite the fact that he was an adult.

"Who stopped the sun rising here?" Billy spoke for the first time, his voice gentle.

The wizard's bleared gaze shifted to him. "No one stopped the sun, lad. This was a world created without it."

"But the rebels believe—" Billy began.

"They are wrong," the wizard said. "They speak of

visions brought by their ancestors who stumbled here from other lands."

"The people in the settlements think the Stormlord stops the sun rising. They think he sends storms to punish them," Rage insisted, calmer for Billy stepping in and helping.

"The Stormlord cares nothing for them. It is they who cause the storms," the wizard said flatly. He slumped back. "People always create their own misery."

"What do you mean?"

The wizard only shook his head, and Rage dropped to her knees before him again. "I thought that you were wrong for running away to leave Grandfather Adam grieving and longing for you, but this is worse. It's *not* brave to give up and die. It's cowardly!"

The wizard began to laugh. Rage backed away warily. "Someone will hear."

"The Stormlord knows that you are here in his tower. In his fortress. He knew it the moment you came."

Rage and Billy exchanged an alarmed glance. Then Billy said to the wizard, "Won't you help us to help you? We only came here to free you."

The wizard's laugh was harsh, the veins in his throat standing out like cords. "I would have to kill myself to save myself. I have wanted to die but that is not permitted."

A wave of sadness flowed through Rage. She and Billy had wasted their time coming here. But what did it matter if the wizard was right? They were all doomed, now or later, when the deadly winter from Null flowed into Valley and then into her world.

Billy touched her arm, and she noticed that the

vibrating noise had increased in volume. He was grimacing as if it hurt him.

"Is it an alarm?" she asked softly.

The wizard reached out and caught at Rage's sweater. "Do you hear that? *You* did it, and if you don't leave now, you will find you can't go." When Rage did not move, the wizard threw himself forward against his bonds. "Go while you have the chance!"

"We can't leave here until I wake," Rage said.

The wizard's eyes widened, and Rage thought it was because of what she was saying, then she realized he was looking *past* her. Billy was now looking beyond her, too, his expression one of blank horror.

"Turn," said a voice behind her with the abrasive hiss of sand over sand.

8

Above the edge of the platform, the shape of a tall, lean human hovered on great, whirring transparent wings. It was impossible to tell if it was male or female because its long limbs and body were encased in pale shimmering armor. Its head was hidden in a helmet cut into myriad sections, reminding her of the eye of a fly. It carried a gleaming lance tipped with a glass spike and capped at the base in gray stone.

"What is it?" Rage whispered.

"A gray flier," the wizard rasped. "I warned you to go and now it is too late."

"Silence." The flying creature's voice was the rattling whir of a cicada.

Billy flinched.

"Walk," it ordered, jabbing its lance to the upward ramp.

Before they could react, another creature exactly like it flew out of the dark void at the center of the tower and landed on the platform behind them. It was impossible to tell the two apart as they turned their helmets to one another. Then one of them turned to the wizard and touched the metal plate in the wall behind him with the blunt end of its lance. There was a flash of blinding light, and the wizard gave a hoarse scream and fell heavily to his knees. He was still manacled, but the sinuous metal cord that had been fixed to the wall had been severed. The wizard retched and groaned.

"What did you do to him?" Billy demanded, moving to help the old man. Two identical blades flashed out to rest with delicate peril against the front of his jacket.

"Back," one of the creatures buzzed. "No communication."

Rage kept herself from screaming, frightened one of them would stab Billy, but the effort of staying silent made her heart hammer.

Billy backed off. "I just wanted to help him."

"Walk," the fliers said in unison. The air reverberated with the echoes of their buzzing voices.

Rage exchanged a swift, frightened glance with Billy as one of the fliers hauled the wizard to his feet. The wizard staggered.

"Where are you taking us?" Billy said, using an aggressive tone so unlike his usual gentle one that Rage guessed that he was trying to draw the creatures' attention.

One of the fliers gestured upward again. Billy obeyed, turning to walk up the ramp, and Rage did the same. When Billy glanced at her, she took the chance to signal her puzzlement at their being taken to the top of the tower. "Maybe their master lives up there," he murmured.

"Silence," commanded the flier behind them, lifting its lance. "No communication."

Rage dared not say anything more. She looked back at the wizard shambling along like a sleepwalker and again felt an unwanted stab of pity for him. He might have failed his responsibilities and neglected those who cared for him, but as far as she knew, he had never knowingly set out to hurt anyone.

She tripped in her zebra slippers and wished that the alarm in her world would hurry up and go off. She wasn't sure you could die while dream-traveling, but she didn't want to test it out. Then her heart sank as she remembered that she had not set the alarm! She told herself it didn't matter. Her uncle might come home, or the phone might ring, or she might just wake at any second. For the wizard's sake, she must be careful to let the Stormlord—to whom she assumed they were being taken—understand that the wizard had nothing to do with their activities, for when she and Billy vanished, he would be left to bear the brunt of the Stormlord's displeasure.

Stumbling again in her oversize slippers, she wished uselessly that she were more sensibly dressed. It was going to be hard to get the master of Stormkeep to take her seriously, dressed as she was. She had not looked at the other prisoners, but when they passed a small child, Rage wondered what the poor little mite had done. The child seemed to her not so much asleep as sunk into some evil dream. Was this "aligning," then? They passed a young woman, and it struck Rage that the prisoners bore deep-etched lines of despair, no matter their age. The vibrating hum did not cease, though it had dropped in volume when the gray fliers appeared.

The ramp ended at an open doorway. Rage followed Billy through, her heart thumping. She was startled to find that they were in a snowy, cobbled courtyard. It was night, and it took her a moment to realize that what she had taken for a tower was actually a hole cut down into the stone pillar upon which the fortress had been built. *That* was why she had not seen it.

The walls of the fortress rose smoothly on all sides. The only light was shed by torches flaring dully blue above, throwing leaping shadows to the cobbles below. As they began to cross the courtyard, Rage noticed rank upon rank of gleaming gray fliers standing motionless in perfect grid formation. Rage remembered that Elle thought they might be machines.

Two fliers standing in the arched doorway stood aside at once and allowed the other two fliers to herd their three prisoners through. Not a word was exchanged. The fliers directed them along a passage. Like the houses in the settlement, it had no ornamentation. Rage wondered if the Stormlord was human.

They entered an enormous rectangular room, passing more battalions of winged warriors to arrive at the sole piece of furniture—a plain black chair. It ought to have looked absurd in all that space, but somehow it did not. A man sat upon it, clad in a great mass of rich gray cloaks and wrappings. His stooped posture and slumped shoulders made him seem old, and his face was dreadfully white and wasted. He looked so full of despair that Rage wondered if he was not the Stormlord but another prisoner that had been made to suffer unthinkably.

Then Rage gasped. Behind the black chair, to one side, was a great, sleeping pack of the giant beasts that had chased her and Logan: neither pigs nor wolves, she saw now, but something of both. They were hard to look at because their shapes seemed to shimmer from one thing to another and then to something else.

"Stop," buzzed the flier behind Billy and Rage, although they had already stopped.

The wizard shuffled to a halt beside them.

"What do you smell?" Rage whispered to Billy, nodding toward the man on the black seat.

"Emptiness," he whispered back. "Same as those people in the tower."

"No communication," warned the winged creature at their side.

"Why are you here?" asked the man on the black chair. His eyes had been closed, but now he opened them partway, almost as if he were too exhausted to bother opening them all the way. His pupils were very black and shining, yet lifeless. They reminded Rage of the polished eyes of a stuffed animal in a museum.

"Are you the master of this place?" she asked. This strange, chilly man was so unlike the evil tyrant she had been expecting that she was confused.

"There is no master here but despair," he answered. "Why have you come?"

"We wanted to see this wizard," Rage said, making up her mind to tell the truth, hoping they could find out what was going on. "We want to close the winter door."

"The winter door will remain open," the man said.

"But it mustn't!" Rage cried. "It is causing terrible harm to other worlds. Why would you want it to stay open?"

"I want nothing," the man said drearily.

"Then who does want it open?" There was no response to this. "You say you want nothing but that's not true," Rage said. "You wanted the wizard to be your prisoner."

"I did not ask him to come to Null, or to Stormkeep," the man said. "Nor do I desire him as a prisoner. It is his own desires that keep him here. When he is no longer tormented by them, he will be free to leave."

"You mean you are keeping him here because he wants to close the winter door?" Rage asked, confused.

"He cannot close it," the man said. "Now tell me what your mistress desires here. This Lady Elle."

Rage's heart leapt, for it seemed that Elle had sent her letter after all. Without warning, one of the winged creatures lashed out with the blunt end of his spear, and Rage fell to her knees. "Answer the Stormlord," it commanded.

Billy stepped forward to help her, but again a lance flashed out to block his way.

"No communication!" the flier chittered.

Rage was dizzy from what had been some sort of electrical shock.

"I *wasn't* communicating," Billy protested. "I was just trying to help her up."

"Touching is communication where humans are concerned," the Stormlord announced dully. "And for these creatures who serve me, it is an intimate thing to touch another even in the most casual way."

"Can't you tell them that I didn't mean anything by it?" Billy asked.

"Did you not?" he asked. Billy blushed. "Why has your mistress invaded my realm?"

"None of us are invaders," Rage said indignantly. "We just want to close the winter door."

"Wanting is forbidden," the Stormlord said. "Null was created to offer a sanctuary for those who want nothing. Those who invade do so at their peril."

"What about the people in the settlements? They didn't invade," Billy said.

"Their ancestors invaded. I closed the gaps by which they came here and suffered them to remain because they were aligned to this world. It was a mistake, for they bred and their offspring were infested with desire. I see now that there is only one answer to all those worlds beyond this one where creatures yearn."

"What answer?" Rage asked with terrible foreboding.

"The winter door will remain open until all worlds are as Null."

"This horrible, black, sick place!" Rage cried. "No one could be happy here." Clearly the Stormlord was himself a wizard.

"This place does not require happiness," the Stormlord said implacably. "That is its virtue. There is no hope of joy or brightness, and in time those who dwell here cease to long for such things. Eventually all worlds will be as this one, and no one anywhere will yearn for anything."

"Why would you want to hurt other worlds?" Billy asked.

"I want nothing, save to be free of yearning. But this will never happen while there are other worlds full of beings to yearn and invade and damage this world with their wanting and hungering. The door is open and so will it remain until all share the peace of this world."

"This isn't peace!" Rage said. "This is a nightmare! And why did you keep the wizard a prisoner?"

"I have told you that it was the wizard's desire to be free from the pain of longing that drew him here. Just as it calls to you."

"Wh-what do you mean?" Rage stammered. "I came here—"

"Seeking an end to pain," the man said. "The machine felt it when you were near and so did I. There is only one way to end pain, and that is to want nothing."

"But . . . that would be death!" Rage said.

"Death is merely oblivion. This world offers another way. To live, and yet to be free from desire. You came here for that reason."

"I . . . I . . ." Rage faltered to a stop. She felt uneasily that the man was uttering a truth, albeit a twisted one.

"She didn't come here for this black, cold emptiness," Billy said firmly. "Nor did I."

"No, you came here because of what you desire, boy, and yet that desire can never be fulfilled. In your heart, you know it already." Billy paled. The Stormlord continued. "For the last time, tell me why your mistress came here. She is not a wizard, or I would have sensed it. But she has some great power that is unknown to me, with which she disrupts Null."

Rage thought of the earth tremors, and the maid's assertion that they had begun when Elle arrived. Was that what he meant? "You will have to ask *her* about the source of her power," she said. "You don't imagine that we who serve her would know such things, do you?"

The Stormlord stared at her for a long moment. "Very well. You will remain here until your mistress comes to seek you. Then she will answer my questions."

"What are you going to do with us?" Billy asked.

"You will be aligned, and this wizard will be re-aligned, for it is clear that your appearance has caused him to regress. The machine felt it, and so did I. That is why I commanded that the link be broken. He will need realignment before he can be reconnected." He seemed to look closely at Billy for a moment. "It will take longer for you because there is only a very little darkness in you yet. It will have to be coaxed to life if it is to grow."

"You are a hateful man," Rage cried, too angry to be afraid. "You like hurting people, and you *want* them to be sad and miserable or you would never have made such a horrible, ugly world. And what about all those other people you have chained up in your tower. Do they all want nothing? Even the children?"

"I see that you come from a world that deludes itself that children are innocent, by which you mean witless slaves with no ability to affect or be affected by the worlds they occupy," the Stormlord said with hollow humor. "I do not make that mistake. The children of the invaders are more difficult to align because they have not experienced enough pain. They must be made to know it without having experienced it. They will have to remain here for many years before they can be allowed to leave this place."

"You must be mad!" Rage said. The ground under their feet pitched violently and then gave a long shudder. It was the strongest earth tremor they had yet experienced.

"Why does your mistress attack Null when she claims to desire a parley?" The Stormlord's dull monotone did not alter, and yet it seemed to Rage that his eyes had grown more densely black.

"No one is attacking you," Billy said before Rage could stop him. "And you are wrong about yearning only leading to pain. Not everyone wants to be free from it. Maybe yearning is actually more important than having what you want."

The floor trembled under their feet again, and this time the Stormlord rose to his feet. Now that he was not slumped in his chair, Rage saw that he was very tall. "So that is your trick, lad?" he said to Billy. "You think to strike at my world by accepting pain and embracing it?" He made a signal and again the winged creature struck out with its lance. Billy cried out and fell convulsing to the ground, blood dripping from his nose. Stepping forward, Rage groped in her pocket for a handkerchief. Instead, she encountered something soft. It was the pouch of sleep dust Thaddeus had given her! She did not know how it had come into her pocket, but she pushed her hand into the pouch, scooping up some of the fine, silky dust, and hurled it into the face of the Stormlord.

He swayed and his eyes rolled back in their sockets as he collapsed at their feet. The fliers didn't comprehend what had happened, and Billy was up and snatching the lance from the one that had hurt him. Instead of using the sharp tip, he batted at the creature with the gray end, using it as a club. There was a stunning explosion of light, and the flier fell beside its master. The other fliers did not move, although several of them were beginning to rock back and forth and flutter their wings.

"They must be linked to the Stormlord somehow, but the dust doesn't last long," Rage said, wondering what she had set in motion.

"It doesn't matter," Billy said. "You have given us the chance to get the wizard out of here, so let's try. Do you have any of the dust left?"

Rage nodded. "What are you doing?"

Billy hoisted the unconscious Stormlord across his shoulders. "You can use the dust on him to keep him asleep, and then we'll use him to stop the fliers from doing anything. Bring the wizard."

Rage looked warily at the ranks of fliers about the room, all rocking and fluttering their wings, and prayed that they would not be able to act until their master awoke. Billy was already heading for the door, so Rage caught hold of the wizard and dragged him after her.

The ranks of fliers outside were standing quite still, but it was unnerving as Rage and Billy passed those gleaming, many-mirrored faces. As soon as they had passed out of their sight, Billy began to run slowly. Rage pulled the wizard along as fast as she could. They had just reached the courtyard archway when the Stormlord began to stir. Rage threw another handful of the dust in his face and he was still. Now the fliers in the courtyard barred their way, regarding them passively.

Rage looked around and saw a small door to one side of the arch. "Let's go through here," she whispered.

Billy nodded, and Rage felt the hair on her neck stir, for as they made their way to the small door, several of the fliers turned their heads to watch them go.

"Uh-oh," Billy said. The doorway only led to the bottom of a set of stairs. "We'd better go up," he said. "Maybe we can find another way to the main gate."

They climbed slowly because the staircase was narrow and curved, and an unconscious man and a sleepwalker hampered them. They came to the end of the stairs and to another door. It led them onto the watchwalk that ran along behind the crenellations of the walls of Stormkeep. There were gray fliers stationed along it, armed with lances, and they all turned toward them.

"Now what?" Rage groaned as some of the fliers began to draw nearer, lifting their lances.

"There is only one way out of this," Billy murmured determinedly. He stepped boldly away from the turret door, forcing Rage to move out along the battlements. She glanced over the wall and felt sick. Another tremor shook the fortress and she clutched at the wall, but Billy shouted, "See what power our mistress has? Your master should have known better than to hold her servants as prisoners. You must let us go, lest she smash this place to rubble."

"What are you doing?" Rage whispered.

"I command you to carry us to the settlement below, where our mistress awaits us, then I will release your master," Billy went on, ignoring her.

"Release Stormlord now," the nearest creature responded in its dry, clicking voice.

"First take this girl and the man with her down to the settlement, then I will release your master, and you can take me down."

"I won't leave you," Rage said. "All we have to do is wait until we wake!"

"There is no time," Billy said softly. "These things are starting to smell violent. Go, Rage Winnoway, whose name is also Courage. I will make them bring me down with the Stormlord!"

Rage prayed he could hold them off with the threat of harming their master. "Billy, he was wrong, there is no darkness in you."

"Take them down now," Billy said loudly. One of the flying creatures swooped at Rage, and as its cold, hard hands closed about her, he added, "If you drop her or harm her or the wizard, I will throw your master into the abyss."

Rage couldn't imagine Billy doing such a thing, but

she hoped the flier clasping her under its arm believed him. It reached for the wizard and tucked him under its other arm. The flier's wings whirred and they rose in the air, clearing the wall. There was no time to say anything to Billy because the moment they were clear, the flier turned and dived straight down! Rage would have screamed if she could have found the breath for it, but in what seemed like seconds, the creature banked its wings, and they were gliding to land not far from the outer rim of a settlement.

The flier released them and took off again immediately.

Rage heard someone calling her name, but her eyes were riveted to the flier as it soared back up to Stormkeep. Once it vanished over the wall of the fortress, she hoped to see it reappear with Billy and the Stormlord in its arms. Instead, a tiny figure climbed onto the top of the wall.

"What is happening?" the wizard asked in a groggy voice.

"Billy is up there," Rage whispered, clasping her hands together so hard that they hurt. *What was he doing and where was the Stormlord?*

Billy was falling.

Rage screamed and dropped to her knees, pleading with the fates to wake her so that she could wake Billy before he hit the ground. But she did not wake. Billy fell and fell, down the gleaming black walls and into the abyss. Rage was only dimly aware of hands lifting her to her feet.

"No," Rage whispered, closing her eyes, but the ghastly sight of Billy falling seemed to go on and on against the inside of her eyelids. The ground shuddered as if it shared her grief. Then someone was cupping her face with warm hands, and she opened tear-blurred eyes to see Elle's face.

"*Billy,*" Rage gasped.

"Hush, darling heart, I saw it, too," Elle said, her face raw with grief. "Come away now. There is nothing you can do here."

The wind had grown bitter, and the snow fell so thickly that each breath was choked with it. Rage let herself be led back into the settlement, into the summer-land meetinghouse where Thaddeus was waiting. He took one look at Rage's face and grew pale. Elle explained swiftly what had happened.

"He died because of me," the wizard rasped, and there were tears on his cheeks. "First his mother and now the boy."

"If anyone is to blame, it is me, for it was my idea that he and Rage go to Stormkeep," Elle said. "But what is the use of trying to lay blame? It will not change what has happened." Elle took the wizard by the shoulders and shook him once, softly but insistently. "You did not kill him, my friend. Billy Thunder chose to save you and Rage, and it was a deed both bravely and brightly done. You must not diminish his actions by assuming responsibility for them. He sought to free you because he knew that we could not close the winter door without you." She looked at Rage. "And he saved you because he could never see *you* hurt, whom he loves above all others."

"If only we hadn't tried to get out," Rage sobbed. "We could have just waited and kept the Stormlord talking, but the gray flier hurt Billy, and I . . . I threw the sleep dust without thinking it through—"

"You spoke with the Stormlord?" Elle broke in.

Rage nodded. "He said this world had been created as a sanctuary for him, and that the people and other creatures here came here through gaps. He said he closed the gaps at first and let the people stay because they were aligned. I suppose he meant that they were like him. But then they had children who dreamed of flowers and sunlight and blue skies and wanted them. That's what he hates most of all and why he means to leave the winter door open."

"Yearning," the wizard murmured. "He built this world to offer nothing so that he could kill yearning in himself. But the world is flawed because *wanting* to end pain and *wanting* not to yearn are themselves desires. Such a paradox would naturally create gaps. But a door is not a gap. . . ." He frowned in thought.

Rage could not speak, as fresh grief at Billy's loss flowed through her.

"Hush," Elle said, touching her cheek. "You must try to sleep now. You are exhausted and overwrought with sorrow. Sleep has healing properties."

"I wish I could wake," Rage sobbed.

"I am sorry," the wizard said brokenly.

Rage bit back the desire to agree. "It wasn't your fault," she said huskily. "Billy always knew what he was doing, even when he suffered for it." She thought of him jumping through the night gate after her, condemning himself to a life as a dog, rather than as a person who could reason, imagine, and decide his own destiny.

"It's so unfair," Mr. Walker said. Rage looked over to see the hollow-eyed little man levering himself up on his bed. "Life is seldom as just as the stories would have it."

"All of you must get away from this place," the wizard said. "The purpose of this world is to force all who dwell here to the end of their darkest desires."

Rage opened her mouth, but at last, and too late for Billy, she felt the inexorable pull and the world spun away.

She resisted waking, wanting to drift forever in the place between waking and sleeping so that she would not wake to the pain of an existence without Billy's sweetness and kindness and his true, steadfast love. In all her life, there had been no one else whose love she could trust so well. Mam was slipping further and further away, and her uncle wanted to leave. Perhaps he had already gone. Even Logan was going away. Without Billy, she would be alone.

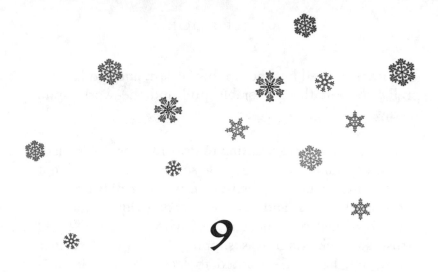

9

It was terribly cold and dark. The coldness became a kind of numbness in which Rage couldn't remember Billy's face, nor the feel of his arms about her. It was like losing him a second time, but even the pain of losing him was fading away. Rage thought of the deadness of the Stormlord's face and understood that *this* was what was inside him. She roused then, knowing she did not want to die, because alive she at least would have the joy of remembering Billy and their lives together. She tried to wake, but the falling had its own pull and she could not break free. Fear came and was sucked away, leaving a gray emptiness. Rage felt herself begin to fade.

Suddenly a terrific starburst of pain filled with shocking heat and color struck her. She reached out and clung to the pain, knowing it was a lifeline back to her body. She clawed her way up, climbing the pain, feeling it more fiercely and welcoming it. Then, just as suddenly, there was no resistance, and she was slammed back into her flesh with such force that she woke gasping and aching all over. It was difficult to open her eyes, as if she had not made it all the way back into her body, but she forced her eyelids apart.

Logan Ryder was peering anxiously into her face.

Rage screamed.

Logan jumped back, a look of such comical fright on his face that Rage started to laugh hysterically. Sitting up, she realized that she was lying by the fire and not in her bed. There was no Billy beside her, which opened the wound of sorrow.

"Oh, Billy," she said brokenly, and began to cry.

"Jeez," Logan murmured, sitting heavily on the nearest chair. "Is this the way you always wake up?"

"You don't understand," Rage wept.

"I guess not," Logan admitted. "I tell you, Rage, getting to know you has been some roller-coaster ride. First there are those things that chased us, then I'm in the middle of a dream about hiking in the hills, and all of a sudden I'm dreaming I'm in that playground opposite the school and there's you and this boy I never saw before but he thinks he knows me. You keep calling him Billy, like your dog. Then we hear those werepigs howling, and you and the boy Billy start talking all of this crazy stuff. Then you tell me to wake up and just like that, I do. That was weird enough.

"I tried to call you the next day, but there was no answer. Then Mrs. Do-gooder tells me the power is out all over the area because of the storms, so I think that's it. But then last night I dream of you again and this time you're lost in a storm. So I start feeling like maybe the dreams are some kind of message and you really are in trouble. I called and called but no answer, and I think what the hell, the storms have stopped for now, so I hike out of town and boost this trail bike from a guy I know and come up here. It was a hellish ride and I nearly wiped out about ten times, but I finally get here. There's no light but I hammer like crazy at the door, then I come round the house tapping on the windows.

"All of a sudden Billy Thunder leaps through the curtain and bashes against the glass so hard it's a wonder he didn't smash it. I swear I nearly had a heart attack. He was barking like a maniac, and I thought at first he must be rabid, but then I saw his tail was wagging, and he runs to the door, and you're not gonna believe this but he flips the latch from the inside and lets me in! Like Lassie or Flipper or something, and then he's dragging at my leg. He herds me in here and you're laying there like . . . Well, I come over and you weren't breathing. I shook you and I called your name and finally, I got scared, and I slapped you. I guess you'll have a bruise, but you groaned and started breathing. It was still hard to wake you, but then you do wake and scream and laugh and start crying all in about five seconds."

Rage was staring at him with open-mouthed astonishment. She had never heard him say so many words all together before! Then something in his amazing monologue penetrated her astonishment.

"You said *Billy* . . . jumped at the window?" Rage whispered, hardly daring to move. Dimly she was aware that her cheek was throbbing.

Logan nodded. Then he turned and looked around. "He was here just a second ago. Hang on." He got up just as Billy hurtled through the kitchen door and ran straight at Rage like a catapult. He knocked her back and licked her face frantically, whining and barking and huffing. Rage hugged him and kissed him, weeping and laughing.

"Wow," said Logan, who was still standing. "This is too much. If you go on like this every time you see one another, I don't know how you have the energy to do anything else in a day."

Rage started to laugh. She laughed so hard her stomach hurt, but she couldn't stop. Logan ended up laughing, too, though he still looked confused. At last, Rage managed to gasp to a halt, and then she looked back at Billy, who had not taken his eyes off her face, and sobered abruptly.

"You're alive," she told him, and she wrapped her arms around his neck and began to cry again. Not the wild tempest of tears she had first shed out of sheer joy and relief, but quiet, desperate tears, because she really had thought he had died. Hard tears, Mam always called tears like that because they felt like stones melting in you and running out.

Logan came and knelt on the ground beside them. "Rage . . . ," he said helplessly, reaching out to pat her shoulder awkwardly. "I . . . what's wrong? Can I help you?"

Rage looked at him through puffy eyes and felt a wave of affection for him. No, not just of affection. Because he had come, and because he had been scared for her, and because it must have been him who woke Billy in time. He had saved Billy's life, and it sounded as if he had saved her life as well, because for a while there she hadn't wanted to live. It chilled her to admit that to herself, because maybe that was how Mam felt.

"You *have* helped, Logan," she said huskily. More tears threatened then, but she blinked hard and wouldn't let them fall. "I guess you'd better try to call your foster parents to let them know where you are."

He nodded. "Yeah. I'll tell them I came up with your uncle and that the storm means I have to stay the night. They'll have a fit if I tell them about the motorbike. Where *is* your uncle?" he added. "Is it going to be okay with him that I stay?"

Rage licked her lips. "He went off early yesterday morning and he didn't come home last night or tonight, and he didn't call, either."

"Maybe he couldn't call because of the blackouts, and he couldn't make it up here."

"You made it!"

"Yes, but I was on a trail bike with snow spikes. Parts of the road were so narrow that only a bike could have come through."

"Maybe he called," Rage said, but there was no con-viction in her voice. "You phone your parents and I'll make us something to eat. I guess you're hungry?"

"Does a dog bark?" Logan asked, and Billy gave a bark that made them both laugh. "He's a pretty smart dog, isn't he?" He went to the phone. "Hey, they could make a television show of him. Billy Thunder, Dog Wonder."

Rage looked at Billy and said softly, "You are a won-der, Billy, and I love you so much it hurts, so never, *never* do that again." Billy licked her right on the mouth. "Yuck," she said, and went to fill the kettle, trying to get her thoughts in order.

She heard Logan give a self-conscious cough and realized he must have got through to his house. "Uh, it's me, Mrs. Stiles. I'm at Rage Winnoway's place. . . ." He stopped and listened. "She did? Oh yes, well, I called her again from town, and she said her uncle was in Hopeton, so I met up with him and he brought me up. Yeah, well, he was going to bring me down but it's pretty bad weather. He thinks I ought to stay the night. . . ." Another pause. "He's next door at the moment, but I can get him to call when he comes back. Oh. Okay, then. Well, I'll call you in the morning. Yeah, okay. Thanks. No, that's okay. Yes. Thank you. I have to go now. Okay." He gave Rage a look of exaggerated desperation and she smothered a laugh.

"Okay, I will. Yes, I better go. Okay. Bye." He hung up and rolled his eyes at Rage. "Boy, can she talk! She said you called yesterday."

"I called because I figured out that you called. She invited me to dinner sometime."

Logan looked pleased but embarrassed. Then his expression became thoughtful. "Look, Rage, do you have asthma or some sort of heart thing, because you were really not breathing, and when you started to wake up, you gave this great gasp like someone had been strangling you."

Very seriously, Rage said, "Logan, I'm fine, but I have to tell you that I don't know if the Logan Ryder method of resuscitation will catch on."

He gave her a lopsided grin. "The truth is, I was so mad to think that my first-ever pal was going to cut out on me that I let you have it. So remember, there is no way out once you have me as a friend. It's a lifetime thing."

"Friendship forever," she said, and felt warmed by the words. She turned to the sink and started getting out tea things. She made toast and opened a can of baked beans. She fed Billy, who ate hungrily. He did not take his eyes off her. She longed to be able to talk to him about all that had happened, but in this form, he could only listen.

Over beans on toast that tasted delicious after the bland fare of Null, she found herself telling Logan about her uncle's notebook entry.

"So he really is leaving. I can't believe he would just go without even leaving a note for you," Logan said. "I know he took off years back, but he's not a kid now."

"A man doesn't have to be any more responsible than a child," Rage said.

"I know that better than anyone," Logan said. "Just the same, your uncle Samuel didn't seem the type to run out on you. But what do I know?"

Rage laughed because he had slipped into the comical voice he had adopted when he had read the play.

Over tinned pears and ice cream, they fell into a silence, which Logan finally broke by asking Rage if she believed you could dream things that were going to happen.

"You think I might get lost in a snowstorm?" she asked, smiling.

But he didn't smile back. "It seemed so real, Rage. I really felt like it was more than just a dream."

"I think you *can* dream real things," Rage said slowly.

Logan turned to look into the fire, where the flames were now leaping against the sooty glass. "Have you ever heard of astral travel?"

To Rage's relief, the phone rang. "Don't answer it," she said quickly. "It might be Mrs. Somersby."

"What if it's your uncle calling? Or my foster parents. I didn't give them the number, but they could easily look it up in the phone book and call just to check with your uncle."

"We'll hear who it is when the answering machine—"

Rage began, then she stopped because the tape of her voice had ended. Mrs. Johnson was saying that she and Mr. Johnson were staying in town as he had suffered a mild attack. Could Rage be a dear and feed the fish, and they would call in the next few days. "My love to you both," Mrs. Johnson ended, and hung up.

"Your next-doors?" Logan ventured. Rage nodded and took their plates to the sink to wash. Logan came over and took the tea towel from the rack to dry. "You know, I didn't tell you something yet. I didn't know how to." Rage looked at him. "When I was coming up here, I saw some of those things that chased us." Rage's pulse quickened. Had the Stormlord sent them after her? Her thoughts must have shown on her face because Logan said, "Rage, do you know something you haven't told me about those things?"

Rage looked over at Billy. "What do you think? Will I tell Logan everything?"

Billy got up, walked over, reached up, and pawed decisively at her leg. Then he returned to the fire. Rage took a deep breath. "All right." She let out a long breath and peeled off the pink latex gloves, hanging them over the edge of the sink. Logan was staring dumbfounded at Billy.

"That was amazing. How did you train him to do that?"

"I didn't train him to do anything. That's part of what I'm going to tell you. Let's sit down."

Logan laid down the tea towel with an almost ritual air, then they both went to sit back by the fire. He took the chair and Rage curled up on the floor beside Billy, who settled his gaze on Logan. "It's a long story," she warned.

"I haven't got any appointments."

Rage sighed. "I guess I'm stalling a bit because now that I come to it, I'm kind of nervous about telling you."

"Telling me what?"

"Something you're going to find hard to believe."

"I have a very broad mind," Logan promised.

"Maybe," Rage murmured. She took a deep breath and began to speak.

The first thing Logan said when Rage finished was, "So you're saying that *was* you in my dream?"

"I'm saying that was you in *my* dream," Rage said. "The part of you that travels in dreams, I mean."

Logan nodded at Billy. "And he was in the dream, only he wasn't a dog?"

"I told you, I called him into my dream just as I called you. And Billy can be human shaped when we dream-travel if I think of him that way."

"Could you make me a tiger?"

"Logan, Billy *was* a human for a while, that's why he can be that shape as well as a dog."

"This is pretty out-there stuff."

"I know." Rage was disappointed.

"The most far-out-there thing is that I actually believe you," he continued, speaking more to himself than to her. "I mean, I want to believe you because it means there really is magic, and monsters and great quests and other worlds. Also, I don't think you're a nut or a liar who would make up such a far-fetched story and try to say it was real."

Rage wasn't sure that came out to unqualified belief.

Logan went on shyly, "Besides everything else, I want to believe it because in your story I come out as a bit of a hero." He reached out and patted Billy. "I saved him, in your story."

Rage nodded, feeling herself flush. She had not told Logan that he had saved her as well because it meant admitting that for one awful, shameful moment she hadn't wanted to live.

"No wonder those monsters didn't faze you after that black city and that evil head keeper."

"He wasn't really evil," Rage felt compelled to say. "And Fork isn't black anymore. Now it's—"

"It's in love with Elle."

"In love?" Rage gaped a little at him. "I didn't say that."

Logan seemed not to hear her. "It must have fallen in love with her when she was helping it to fight the winter. She sounds pretty stunning. I wish I could meet her."

Logan suddenly sat bolt upright. "Wow, I've just had a thought! If you can take Billy Thunder dream-traveling, maybe you can take me!"

Rage blinked at him. "I could, I think," she admitted. "But I don't know if I should. You see, I thought the wizard gave me the power but—"

"He might still have done," Logan broke in eagerly. "He didn't actually tell you he didn't, did he? Anyway, maybe you had the power all along but you just didn't know it. Maybe your father was a wizard and you have wizard blood in you! You said you didn't know who he is."

Rage flinched. "I don't *want* to know who he is. It doesn't matter to me. Anyway, you're talking like this is a story in a book. I don't have wizard blood. If I did, I would have been dream-traveling all along."

"Maybe not. This firecat thing could have been a sort

of—what's the word? A catalyst." He looked impressed with himself.

Rage couldn't help but laugh. "It's a catalyst, all right, but it never makes anything good happen."

"Well, what does it matter, anyway, how you got the power? You're going to use it to go back to Null. I mean, you have to, right?"

"Maybe I don't have to," Rage said slowly. "The wizard can tell Elle and the others everything I heard. . . ."

"But you're supposed to be there for them to be able to shut the winter door? That's what the witch queen said, right?"

"Witch *Mother*," Rage murmured.

"Whatever. She said you were part of it."

"There were supposed to be eight other than me, but there were only seven, so—"

"Maybe I am the eighth!" Logan looked elated. "I'll go! I'll fight alongside Elle and Thaddeus and the others. They'll need everybody they can get if they are going to storm the castle."

"It's a fortress, Logan, and no one's going to storm it. There's no need, now that the wizard is free."

"Yes, but they have to get the Stormlord out, too, so they can make him close the door. He's the key, isn't he?"

"I don't know how we can close the door. The wizard says there is no way."

"The witch Mother said there is a way, and besides, you have to go back so they can find out that Billy didn't die."

"Logan, I *can't* take you. I've only ever taken Billy, and if I try to take the three of us, it might go wrong. We might all end up somewhere else."

There was a silence, and outside the wind howled.

Logan straightened up. "Okay, I'll stay here. Someone should be here to watch over you two sleeping beauties. But you have to go."

"I know," Rage said. "But after what almost happened to Billy, I guess I'm scared."

"You'd be dumb if you weren't," Logan said. "But I bet that Elle will have figured out a plan by now, her and the wizard."

"I hope so." She took a deep breath. "I guess we'd all better stay in Uncle Samuel's room tonight. It's solid brick, and if those things come again, they won't be able to break in. We'd better push the wardrobe against the window. And we should take in a thermos of drink and something for you to eat, too. And candles and something to read. . . . Oh. Sorry, Logan."

He gave her a lopsided grin. "I'll practice. Maybe I'll surprise you."

Rage gave him an impulsive hug. "After this is over, I promise I *will* take you dream-traveling if I can."

"It's a date," Logan said lightly, then he flushed. "I mean, I didn't mean . . ."

"Come on," Rage said.

It took them an hour to get the extension ready. Logan had a mattress with piles of bedding, a portable radio, and candles. Billy and Rage would sleep on Uncle Samuel's bed. They had a thermos of hot coffee, sandwiches, biscuits, and a couple of apples. Finally, they banked up the fire in the kitchen. Then they sat talking in front of it, because there was no point in lying down to sleep if they were wide awake. But Rage didn't think it would be too long before she slept because she was already drained by all the emotions she had experienced.

Logan still had lots of questions to ask about Fork and magic in Valley, and about her great-uncle being a wizard. "It's pretty amazing to think he just became a wizard and made his own world," Logan said. Then he grinned. "I wonder what would happen if I told the school careers advisor that I want to be a wizard when I grow up."

Rage laughed. "I never really asked him how he did it because, well, I guess I was too busy blaming him for what happened to Mam."

"It wasn't really his fault, though," Logan pointed out.

Rage nodded. "I know that now. I suppose I knew it all along, but I wanted there to be someone to blame. Because if there wasn't, then it was Mam's fault, or Grandfather Adam's fault."

"I think *fault* is just the wrong word," Logan said thoughtfully. "I wanted to blame my father for what he did, too, but just lately I've been thinking that maybe he just couldn't do any better."

"It's so strange, but when I saw the wizard chained to that wall, I felt . . . sorry for him, and I realized that he was blaming himself for what happened to Mam and Uncle Samuel. I told him that he was a coward for giving up. . . ." Her voice trailed off as she remembered the strength of her own desire not to wake.

"You know, I think that feeling bad about everything he had done was why he was connected to that machine," Logan said thoughtfully. "I think it feeds off negative feelings, and being aligned means being made to feel hopeless about everything. And you know what? I think that all those people connected to the machine are not just being made to feel bad so that they fit in, in Null.

I think that the machine uses their negative feelings for power. And those quakes? I bet the summerlanders are right and that they *are* being caused by Elle, because it doesn't sound like she has negative feelings at all."

Rage stared at him, feeling the truth of his words. "But why make a machine like that?"

Logan shrugged. "Maybe it started out just being a machine to make people feel sad so they'd fit in, but he realized that their bad feelings were a source of power. And the summerlanders were a problem, so he decided to break them and then connect *them* to his machine as well."

Rage nodded. Maybe she had been too close and everything was all muddled up with fears and feelings to see these things herself.

"I suppose after that it was like they always say in history class," Logan went on. "Power corrupted him, and he figured why not use the winter door to make all the worlds like his."

"Do you think he used the power to *make* the winter door?" Rage said.

Billy whined and gave a bark. Logan gave him a sympathetic look. "It must be hard for him when you're here, him wanting to talk and only being able to bark."

"He has a much better sense of smell as a dog than he does when he is human shaped, and he can see really well and run faster. . . ." Rage stopped, wondering why she was saying those things. "I just mean he is good as a dog, too. Good in other ways."

"Yeah, but I was only saying he might have some good ideas right now but he can't say them."

Billy sighed again.

"I wonder what the Stormlord meant when he said

there was a darkness in him," Rage said.

Logan glanced at Billy. They stared at one another for a long moment. Then Logan nodded, as if some understanding had passed between them. Rage waited for him to say something, but he only patted Billy and said again that it must be hard. Rage had the feeling that she had missed something important, but she was really feeling tired now and told Logan so.

Rage banked the fire with wood, closed the flue, and switched out the lights, then Logan opened the front door and they stood in the doorway as Billy went out, watching the relentless wind lift powder snow into brief eddies. Neither moon nor stars showed, so the light cast from the hall light lay as bright as a shaft of gold. The light would be visible for miles in this darkness.

"There's a gun," she said softly.

Logan stared at her. "What?"

"My uncle has a gun in his room. It's on the top of the wardrobe and the bullets are in the desk drawer. If those things come tonight, you might need it. You could shoot in the air."

"You think they're after you?"

"I don't see how. I'm pretty sure the Stormlord doesn't know I was dream-traveling, but they do seem to be hanging around Winnoway."

"Are you sure the things are his?"

"Whose else could they be? But I don't think he sent them after me in particular. I think they just wander through the winter door and then they come here. I think they come with the bad weather."

"It's incredible to think there are these openings where you can just step through into another world, if you only know where they are." His eyes widened. "Hey, maybe that's where all the people who have disappeared went."

"I wondered about that, too," Rage said. "Maybe that's why the police never find so many of them. Anyway, I was going to say that the Stormlord might have sent those things here after me, because he would've been pretty angry when he woke up."

"To be honest, it's hard to imagine the guy you described getting angry," Logan said. "Seems more like he'd just be relieved you were gone. But if he was mad, he'd be mad at Elle because he thinks she's your boss."

He was right. The Stormlord had sounded interested in Elle. He had kept asking about her, as if he didn't believe she only wanted to close the winter door. And if what Logan had suggested about the tremors was right, maybe it really *was* Elle's sunny, confident nature that was hurting his world.

Once they were in the extension bedroom, Rage showed Logan how to bolt the door to the main part of the house, in case he needed to go out to the bathroom.

"It's like an air-raid shelter," Logan said, looking around. "I wonder why your grandfather built this. It doesn't fit the rest of the house."

Rage had never wondered about the extension before. "Maybe he thought another war would come," she said lightly. She took off her zebra slippers, reminding herself firmly to picture herself and Billy in sensible attire this time. She climbed into bed feeling suddenly shy, even though she was not in her pajamas.

Logan paced around the small room a few times with his hands in his pockets before self-consciously sitting down on his mattress. Billy was drowsing on the end of Rage's bed.

"One of the best things about being an animal is that

they can live in the moment," Rage murmured, leaning down to stroke him. "They don't think so much about the future and worry so much about the past because they know that it won't help."

"I know what you mean," Logan said, settling more comfortably back on his pillows. "We waste so much energy and time thinking about everything except the moment we are in, and so in a way it's like we don't even notice we're alive."

Rage turned on her side. "I'm glad you're here, Logan."

"I'm glad, too," Logan said. "I wonder where your uncle is," he said after a while.

Rage wondered also. Uncle Samuel hadn't called, even though the answering machine had been on, and the power as well, for most of the time. That made it less likely that he had just been delayed because of the roads. If he hadn't called by morning, she would telephone the police.

"Listen," Logan said. Rage started and realized she had been on the verge of falling asleep. "It's the wind," he went on. "It's stopped." He got up and went into the study to peer out the strip of window above the crate. "It's snowing again. A real whiteout."

Rage heard the words as if from a great distance, and she barely remembered to imagine herself and Billy dressed warmly as she slid into sleep.

Rage and Billy were standing on a snow-covered hill in a cold, windless night filled with softly falling snow.

"I was so glad to see you when I woke up," Rage said, giving Billy a hard hug. "I was so scared when you fell."

"Me too," Billy said seriously. "But I was more scared when I couldn't wake you. I thought something must have happened to you. Logan was great. He saved my life by waking me." He hesitated. "I think he might have saved your life, too, Rage, because you started to smell of death. It was horrible, and I ran out because I couldn't bear it, and he . . . well, he woke you."

"I think I almost did die, Billy," Rage confessed in a low voice. "I didn't want to be in a world without you." She was embarrassed to admit that she had been the same sort of coward she had accused Mam of being. "Then I tried to wake up but I couldn't come back to my body. Then Logan hit me. . . ."

"He *hit* you?" Billy echoed, the hint of a growl in his voice.

"He didn't mean to do it, but it's lucky he did because the slap let me find my way back to my body."

"I like the smell of him," Billy said at last, looking strangely sad.

Rage looked around. "I wonder where we are. Can you smell if we're in Null again?"

"It's not Null or Valley. Rage, I don't think the Stormlord sent those wolf things after you because I don't think he controls them. Otherwise, why didn't they stop you when we took him hostage? They just sat there watching us leave."

"Maybe they couldn't act after the Stormlord was unconscious. Like the gray fliers."

"They didn't behave like the stunned fliers did. They were watching us, but it was like they were not interested in what we were doing."

"Then where did they come from?"

Billy shrugged. "Maybe they came here from some-where else, like the other settlers. Then they went to Valley through the winter door."

"But why did they chase me and Logan and come to the farm? And how would they get inside the fortress?" Rage asked.

"I don't know," Billy admitted. "But there's some-thing else. I was thinking about those gaps you and Logan were talking about when I was a dog. Remember how the wizard said there was something wrong about the winter door?" Rage nodded. "What if it *began* as a gap, then the firecat conjured a way to hold it open."

"But wouldn't the wizard have figured that out?"

"Maybe he was so busy thinking about the other wiz-ard that he didn't look at it properly," Billy said.

Rage frowned. If Billy was right, it would explain why the firecat would have claimed to have made the gate. "But how could the wizard have contacted the fire-cat with those iron manacles around his wrists?"

"Maybe the firecat came to him of its own accord in a dream? Or maybe the fact that the firecat is connected to the wizard sort of got around the iron blocking his magic."

"Maybe," Rage said. "Why do you think it didn't tell me what the wizard said?"

"Because it wanted him saved," Billy said. "That could explain why it came to you rather than going to Rue. She might have been able to tell it was lying."

Billy looked around. "Maybe you'd better try to take us to Null."

Rage was deciding whom to use as a focus for her dream-traveling when she heard a voice crying out. She could tell from the look on Billy's face that this time he heard it, too.

"I've heard it before," Rage murmured, trying to make out what it was saying. "I thought it was the voice of the wizard, but it can't be since he's free now. Can you smell anything?"

Something howled in the distance.

"Maybe you'd better get us away from here," Billy advised. He reached out to take Rage's hand in a firm grasp. She closed her eyes and summoned up Nomadiel's small face. The snowy landscape dissolved and the voice called again. This time she heard clearly what it was saying.

Help . . .

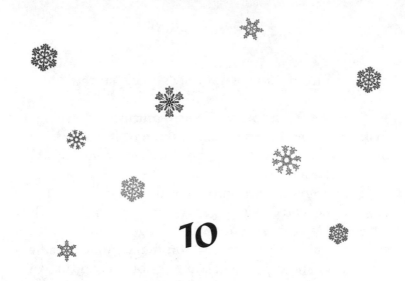

10

Rage and Billy were in the same room from which Rage had vanished after Billy fell from the wall of Stormkeep. Puck and Thaddeus were even standing in much the same positions.

"You!" said the witch man incredulously, staring at Billy. "I thought—we believed you had been killed when you fell!"

"I would have been if a friend in our world had not woken me in time," Billy said soberly. "How long have we been gone?"

"You disappeared four days ago," Puck said.

"Only a few hours have passed in our world," Rage said in disbelief.

"Where are the others?" Billy asked.

"Elle is visiting the other settlements, and the wizard sleeps in an antechamber. He is weak from his long confinement, but he is improving daily."

"Does he still say that there is no way to close the winter door?" Rage asked.

Thaddeus frowned. "He says the winter door is not

tuned to a maker because it was merely formed inside a random tear in the flawed fabric of this world."

"You were right, then," Rage said to Billy.

"Why is Elle visiting the other settlements?" Billy asked.

"She wants to talk to all the other sorts of people here, even those who are not summerlanders," Thaddeus said. "She wants to lead a force against Stormkeep to see if they can free the prisoners in the hidden tower. She believes that the machine is strengthening the Stormlord somehow."

"She says that if we cannot close the door, then we must stop the Stormlord from making his fell storms," Puck said.

"But how will they get into Stormkeep?" Billy asked.

"She means to lure a gray flier down, capture it, and force it to carry her inside the fortress. Everyone will be waiting outside for her to open the gates," Thaddeus said.

"Where are Nomadiel, Rally, and Mr. Walker?" Rage asked.

The witch man and Puck exchanged a look that filled Rage with apprehension. Then Puck said, "Nomadiel went out with Rally the night you vanished. She left a note saying that she was going back through the winter door to ask the advice of the witch Mother. Only she didn't get to the winter door."

"What happened?"

"She and Rally were taken by the gray fliers," Thaddeus said. "Prince Walker saw them attack."

"The fliers took all three of them?" Rage asked, appalled.

"Not Mr. Walker. We do not know why, for there

were more than enough fliers to take him as well, by his account," Thaddeus said.

"Where is he now?" Billy asked worriedly.

"He came back to tell us what happened, half mad with despair, and at length he ran out again. We followed, but we could not catch up to him before he reached the bridge to Stormkeep. We thought that the gray fliers would come and take him, or kill him, but they did nothing."

"Nothing?" Rage said in disbelief. "But . . . where is he now?"

"He is still at the gates of Stormkeep."

"You just left him there?" Rage demanded.

"Puck and I tried to get him," Thaddeus said, "but the gray fliers swooped on us. They no longer come into the settlement, but they attack anyone who ventures outside. Puck's wing was torn and he fell, but I managed to get him back inside."

"No need to boast," Puck snapped, but there was less real anger in his voice than before. "I would have recovered and saved myself if you hadn't interfered."

"If the gray fliers attack anyone leaving a settlement, how did Elle leave?" Billy asked.

"She left to tour the other settlements right after you vanished, Rage. No flier tried to stop her or her summerlander followers, but we do not know why."

"What do the other settlers say about what has been happening?"

"Nothing," Thaddeus said. "They are like the Stormlord. They don't want to feel anything. But some of them can't help themselves because their children are summerlanders. The woman who has looked after the wizard is one. She also gave Mr. Walker fever medicine, though I fear his madness will have undone any good it did him."

"We have to help him," Billy said to Rage.

The inner door opened and the wizard entered slowly. Rage was startled to see how thin and frail he was. In Stormkeep, he had been so swathed in cloaks and shawls that it had been impossible to tell.

"I thought I heard you," the wizard said in a thin voice. "Billy Thunder, I am more glad than I can say to see that you are safe. I take it you woke in time."

"I was woken by a friend, sir," Billy said. His nose twitched, and Rage wondered what he could smell on the old man.

The wizard hobbled to sit by a small fire in a hearth that had been set up to one side of the chilly room. "I have been thinking about why Prince Walker was not taken with Noma and Rally, and it has come to me that if Elle is right about the machine drawing power from the despair of those linked to it, then it may be that Prince Walker is serving a similar role by lamenting at the gate to Stormkeep; I mean, he is feeding its master his despair." He lifted salt-and-pepper brows above piercing Winnoway amber eyes.

"I think you are right," Billy said.

The wizard smiled at him. Then he looked at Rage. "Despair is a power, you see. Was it not you who once told me that sorrow is a contagious disease that can be passed from generation to generation?"

Rage felt herself flush, then pale.

"You were right," the wizard said softly. "But the rightness of your accusation only served to deepen the hurts caused by my actions, because your words ate into me and crippled my strength. They made me feel that there was nothing but to give myself to guilt and regret.

The words you said generated deeper despair. I do not blame you, child. It was I who allowed them to do this.

"Strangely, coming so close to seeking the oblivion offered by this world, I see that although what you said was true, it was not the only truth or all of the truth. Pain does cause pain and sorrow causes sorrow, but to accept it and allow oneself to be crippled by it is a choice one makes. One can also choose not to be shaped by pain and sorrow, given or experienced, but to grow because of them and then leave them behind. Yet such a choice requires courage."

Rage was trembling because the truth of all the wizard was saying was like a knife gliding into her. For hadn't she even begun to see that she could no longer blame the wizard for what his brother had done to her mother and Uncle Samuel, and what they in turn had done to her? She felt humbled by the way Nomadiel had gone on believing in her fierce, proud little way that she deserved to be loved by her father. And she thought how Billy had gone on loving his mother, no matter how she hurt or rejected him. He had not despaired nor held the pain close, allowing it to gnaw at him. He had let go of it and passed on only his steadfast love. That was the highest kind of courage.

Rage looked into the wizard's lined face and drew herself up. "You are right. I said the things I did to you in Valley because I wanted to hurt you because I had been hurt. Forgive me."

The wizard's amber eyes grew bright. "Forgive *me*," he said.

"Maybe we can forgive one another," Rage said, and brushed aside her own shyness to step forward and put her arms around the wizard. How wonderful it was to be hugged back so tightly, as if she was precious and worth living for. And how strangely easy to let go of anger and resentment and bitterness.

The ground shuddered. Rage and the wizard drew back in startlement.

"Can't you do something about Mr. Walker using magic, sir?" Billy asked.

"I have too little strength to work a spell that would transport him," the wizard said regretfully. "Especially when he does not will it."

Rage had an idea. "Do you have enough power to make me invisible?"

"My dear Rage, invisibility is no small thing. But because it is you, and we are connected by blood, I may be able to make you extremely hard to see, which is almost as good as invisibility. But I won't be able to hold the spell for long."

"I will go to him," Rage said, feeling that anything could be possible now. The world shuddered again. Rage wondered with a little thrill if *she* had caused that tremor. She hoped so.

"I'll go, too," Billy said.

But the wizard shook his head. "I will not be able to hide you as well as Rage." He looked at her. "But perhaps you should think on it a little. Prince Walker is small but if he fights you, it is likely that you will both fall into the abyss spanned by the bridge. Or he might call the attention of the gray fliers."

"I don't mean to force him," Rage said. "I am sure that he will come away willingly once he realizes that he is helping the Stormlord."

The wizard looked at Rage. "Can you wait until the Lady Elle returns? My strength grows with each hour that passes. By tomorrow, I will be capable of much more than I am now."

"I would wait, but Mr. Walker has been out for three days."

"Very well. When will you go?"

"*Now*," Rage said decisively, and her pulse began to race at her own audacity. "Do you have a coat that will fit Mr. Walker, and something I can carry a hot drink in?"

In a short time, she was padding along a snowy street. Billy and Thaddeus were with her and would wait at the edge of the settlement until she returned. Rage hugged Billy hard. Then she turned to say goodbye to Thaddeus, who held out his hand. She thought he meant her to shake it, but instead, she found it held another of the small pouches of sleep dust.

"Just in case Prince Walker is unable to listen to reason," he said. "He will be easier to carry if he sleeps."

"Thank you," Rage said, putting the soft pouch into her pocket.

She turned and began to walk away from the buildings. Ahead, the glacier glowed white, and the stone bridge to Stormkeep looked as insubstantial as a thread stretching out across the black abyss. The torches that had lit the fortress crenellations had been extinguished, so Stormkeep was no more than a vague dark shape. Rage expected to hear the chittering clamor of gray fliers, but she heard nothing save the snow crunching under her boots. When she reached the stone bridge, she hesitated. Not only was it very narrow, but there were no rails. It also curved steeply up. Once she was standing on it, she could not see the other side.

Rage forced herself to step onto the bridge, and at once she shivered, for the glacier gave off an icy aura.

She took a deep breath, fixed her eyes ahead, and began to walk. When she was about to pass over the edge of the glacier where it fell into the abyss, she made the mistake of looking down. Her head spun as she saw the white, glittering icefall plunging into blackness. She dragged her eyes back to the bridge and went on. She had taken only a few steps before it grew windier in blustering surges. If Rage took one wrong step, she would fall, and the chances of Logan waking her at that moment were very slim.

When she came to the midway point of the bridge, she was surprised that she could see the end of it: the great black doors to Stormkeep. But there was no sign of Mr. Walker. It was not until she had her feet on the broad platform of stone leading to the doors that she noticed a dark shape on the ground. She ran to where Mr. Walker lay half buried under snow, his face pressed against the pitiless gate.

"Mr. Walker," Rage whispered, kneeling beside him and setting down the flask so that she could pull him around to her.

He was blue with cold, with a crust of ice over his face and long, furled ears. She unwrapped the cloak Thaddeus had given her and put it around the little dog-man. Then she unstopped the flask and poured a tiny amount of the steaming soup into his mouth. It trickled out at once, but he began to cough. The coughing did not stop. It built to a jagged, phlegm-clogged spasm that made her fear it would draw unwanted attention. At last the spasm ended, leaving Mr. Walker gasping.

"Mr. Walker," Rage whispered urgently. "Prince Walker!" He did not move. "Mr. Walker, you must wake up and come with me, for Nomadiel's sake."

Brown eyes as dull as pond stones opened. "Nomadiel is gone. It is my fault," he croaked.

"No. She chose to go," Rage said firmly.

"She is a child."

"Yes, but still she chose to go and try to get help because she has great courage."

"I have been a bad father."

"Maybe you have," Rage said softly. "I don't suppose you could help it if you were. But I don't think she hates you for it or even blames you. She loves you, which is why she deserves for you to be better to her from now on."

"It's too late—"

"It's never too late!" Rage said. "How could it be too late for you to love her and be a father to her? You must give up grieving for Kelpie and become a father to her daughter and yours."

"I cannot forget her," Mr. Walker said brokenly. "I loved her so much."

"I didn't say to forget her. You've spent too much time thinking about her dead instead of remembering her alive. You have to stop hurting yourself and Nomadiel because she died. Kelpie would be so sad to see how the two of you are."

"Nomadiel is better off without me."

"That's not true," Rage said fiercely, wondering if her mother had thought this, and maybe her uncle, too. "How can it possibly be better not to have a father? She loves you, and you have to be brave enough to love her. Now get up, because the spell hiding me from the gray fliers could wear off any time."

"How can I love Nomadiel when she is lost to me?" Mr. Walker said.

"She can never be lost to you, any more than Feluffeen can. Plus we are going to defeat the Stormlord and free her. But your despair and guilt are just making him stronger right now. That's what his machine and his world are made from and what keeps them strong. Bad feelings. He took Nomadiel because she is brave and bright and because she loves you."

"Then . . . he did not take me because I . . ."

"Mr. Walker, there is no time for this. We can talk when we are safe." At last, Mr. Walker allowed her to help him sit up. Rage gave him another drink from the flask. She lifted him to his feet, but when she let him go, they crumpled under him.

"It's no use," he said.

"I can carry you," Rage said, trying not to think how narrow the bridge was. She braced herself and hauled him as gently as she could onto her back. He tried to help but was too weak. "The main thing is for you to keep really still," Rage told him, setting off.

Oddly, this time she found it easier on the bridge because their combined weight steadied her and the wind could not buffet her so easily. Despite the impulse to hurry, she forced herself to walk at a measured pace. Three-quarters of the way across, Mr. Walker began to cough violently. Rage stopped until the fit of coughing abated, then continued. She had just reached the end of the bridge when a chittering cry filled the air. The spell had worn off!

She heard the whirring of wings overhead and stepped with awkward haste down onto the snowy ground. She continued doggedly toward the settlement, keeping to the furrow she had made earlier. She would not have dared run even if she had the strength left for it, because Mr. Walker now flopped loosely against her and she was afraid he had fainted. If she was right, any sharp movement would topple them both.

The whirring grew louder and more menacing, and Rage remembered the sleep dust in her pocket. She pulled the pouch out with her one free hand, but the wind tugged it from her. The contents whirled away in a glittering arc.

There was no option but to keep trudging on.

"Go back over bridge," chittered the nearest of the fliers, hovering between her and the settlement. Rage noticed absently how the snowflakes beginning to spiral down melted the moment they touched the smooth surface of its armor, and dimly wondered why it didn't simply grab at her, as the other flier had done in Stormkeep.

"Let me pass or you'll be sorry!" Rage gasped, because what did it matter now?

Rage expected the creature to attack then, for more fliers were hovering about. Then all at once she heard Billy calling her name. She looked through the fliers and saw him hurtling toward her from the settlement.

"No!" she cried as several fliers turned to face him, brandishing their long lances.

Billy stopped and so did Thaddeus, who was coming along behind him. They only had knives, which would be no use against the armor of the fliers. One of the creatures threw its lance. It struck Billy a glancing blow that sent him to his knees in a flash of bluish light. Rage screamed as the other fliers lifted their lances.

At that moment, a cry rang out across the barren waste. Rage turned to see Elle racing toward them, her blond hair flying like a pale, bright flag. Behind her were dozens of young summerlanders, their faces pale and determined in the light of the torches they carried. The fliers retreated as if some unbearable ray had been turned on them. And softly as rain, it came to Rage that the fliers were retreating not from the summerlanders' makeshift weapons but from their courage and hope.

"Yes, fly away!" she shouted, exultant, understanding that this, too, was a weapon against them.

In minutes, the fliers had retreated behind the walls of Stormkeep. Elle lifted Mr. Walker gently from her back and Rage found herself crushed in Billy's arms. She turned in his embrace to look at Mr. Walker, and the little dog-man's eyes fluttered open. He smiled and then closed them again. But it was enough.

"They retreated!" called Shona, her face shining with triumph.

"They did," Elle said as they made their way back to the settlement. "I take it the wizard has recovered enough to cast a spell."

"No," Billy said softly. "Don't you see, Elle? The gray fliers retreated because you and the summerlander rebels came rushing at them so hopefully and bravely. That's what hurt the Stormlord and his world. We must prove to him that hope and bravery are stronger than despair and hopelessness."

"An interesting strategy," Elle said thoughtfully.

The wizard turned away from the sleeping form of Mr. Walker, his lined face grave. "He has pneumonia and he is suffering badly from exposure. He will probably lose two fingers and a toe, but he is clinging to life, and that gives me more hope than his condition should allow because in this world, as Billy discovered, it is hope and courage that are the strongest weapons."

"It wasn't me," Billy said. "It was our friend Logan, back at Winnoway. *He* figured most of it out. I just took the next step when I saw the way the fliers didn't grab at Rage when she was bringing Mr. Walker back. I remembered how they hadn't wanted to touch me when I was alone with them on the wall of Stormkeep. They used one of those lances to push me over the edge after the Stormlord woke. I thought I was dead when that flier threw its lance just now, but it only hit my backpack. And that was when it came to me that it had thrown the lance from so far back because it hadn't dared to come any closer."

"You were lucky the flier's aim was not better," the wizard said.

"Maybe it wasn't luck," Rage said, putting her arm through Billy's. "Maybe Billy is so brave that this world can't hurt him. Just like Elle."

"Not like Elle!" Billy laughed, but he looked pleased. "No one is like her. I think Logan is right about her causing the earthquakes here. And by bringing hope and light to the summerlanders as she has done, she is making this whole world unstable."

"Let us hope she does not shake it to pieces while we are here," Puck said darkly, slipping through the door. "Anyway, she wants you now."

The wizard nodded. "You two go. I will stay with Mr. Walker."

"So, what is your plan?" Puck demanded in his usual bumptious way. He was seated on a table a little distance from Elle. There were many sorts of creatures as well as humans, all the offspring of parents who had been drawn to Null through the gaps. A red-haired foxlike girl with red ears and a great bushy tail sat close to Elle and gazed at her in adoration.

"We can storm the place just like you suggested before," Thaddeus was saying. "Now that we know the fliers can't attack us. . . ."

"But they *can* attack, if only from a distance," Elle reminded him. "They can throw their lances or drop things on us when we are crossing the bridge. And from what Rage and Billy have said of the door, I doubt it could be opened even if we *did* get there safely."

"Can we not leave this accursed place, then?" asked one of the summerlanders. "We need no longer fear that the fliers would attack us."

"Perhaps we could leave, but would you leave behind those who would also choose the sun, but for their long, weary life in this place that has sapped their hope? Would it not be a black and cowardly victory to go into the summerlands and leave them behind? And in the end, it would only be a short retreat, for the darkness here would be flowing out into all worlds as darkness and winter and despair."

No one spoke.

"Aside from all else, *I* must remain no matter what you would choose because I have sworn to stop the deadly winter harming Valley," Elle said.

"I will stay with you," the fox-girl cried, jumping to her feet and swishing her great soft tail. The others took up the cry, and Rage saw that this adoration, too, was a power that could be wielded.

But Elle said, "I would urge you to go if I did not truly believe that this is a battle we can win, for I have also sworn that you will see the sun, all of you." A wild cheer greeted her words. And then the ground twitched so violently that two or three of the standing summer-landers were thrown to their knees. After the first shocked silence, they burst out laughing and cheered again.

"See how this world tries to shake us from its back!" one of the summerlanders shouted.

"They would die for her," Puck muttered sourly.

"I think they would, but she would not allow it," Billy said softly. "She knows that she is the greatest weapon we have, and I believe she could face the Stormlord alone and still win, but she chooses to share the victory because it will make them all stronger."

"So what *are* we to do?" Shona asked. "We can't just sit here and do nothing."

"We will not do nothing," Elle said, giving them all a grin so alight with mischief that Rage felt her own lips curl up. "We will celebrate. You will tell me all the fragments you have heard from your olders that have come together to form the great tale of the summerlanders, the making of which was the first blow you struck against the Stormlord. Then we will feast and sing—"

"What is it to *sing*?" the fox-girl demanded.

Elle smiled. "We of the summerlands will teach you how to sing and then we will make such story-songs between us as to cause the Stormlord in his icy fortress to clasp his hands to his ears."

"I hope your plan does not mean that we will destroy ourselves as well as the Stormlord," Puck said tartly.

Elle laughed, flashing strong white teeth. "You have a point, little man. But I think the Stormlord will succumb before his world falls apart."

"I hope you are right," Puck muttered.

"What do you think he will do?" Billy asked Elle a little later as the summerlanders dashed about preparing a feast. Elle had them laugh and talk loudly as they worked. Some of the summerlanders were also putting together rough drums and stringing thin lines between chairs, strumming and tapping to test their makeshift instruments.

"I think that at first the Stormlord will do nothing, because he will expect us to try to attack or leave. When he realizes that we don't intend to go and he realizes *how* we are attacking him, he will seek to parley with me. Before we will agree to that, he must release all the prisoners in his machine," Elle said. "If nothing else, that will reduce his power and the flow of winter through the door."

"Nomadiel—" Rage began.

"She and Rally and all the others will be released," Elle said.

"Then what?" Thaddeus asked.

"Then we will talk about those wanting to leave for the summerlands being permitted to do so, and then about how we might deal with the winter door."

Rage said worriedly, "If Billy is right about it being a gap that was turned into a door by the firecat, then—"

"He was right," the wizard interrupted softly, coming over to join them. "I realized the truth during my imprisonment." He looked at Billy. "You are very clever to have seen what I did not. I suppose the firecat happened on the gap, for it is ever sniffing about anything that smells of magic. It would have conjured the door because it wanted to explore the world beyond the gap in its never-ending search for a soul. But once it had magicked the door, it would have been terrified by the darkness of Null, which would have begun to leak through into Valley."

"How did the firecat reach you, once the manacles were on?" Rage asked.

"It dreamed its way to me."

"Can the winter door be closed?" Elle asked.

The wizard shook his head. "No, but it could be dismantled. However, it would take more power than the firecat possesses. We need to widen the gap. Once the door is removed, the Stormlord can close the gap quite simply."

"The Stormlord might still refuse to help," Rage said. "He could just wait us out."

"That is why we must not merely oppose him passively. We must fight with the weapons that are best for this battle," Elle said. She stood up and in a ringing voice commanded that the celebrations begin.

And so began the strangest, most wondrous war ever waged; there was no anger and no bloodshed or fear or death. There was only flavorful food, stories, songs, and dances, all of which the summerlanders excelled at, once they understood what these things were. It was Puck who taught the summerlanders to sing. He had a voice of surpassing beauty, and he sang of the witch Mother, Rue, and of Wildwood. Thaddeus sang a comical song that required hand-slapping and foot-stamping, and the summerlanders sang the nonsense chorus back at him with laughing relish.

Then Elle was begged to sing. She obeyed, but her voice was so astonishingly bad that Rage gaped to see such a sound come from such a fair face. Incredibly, the summerlanders began to sing the same dreadful croaking song. Thaddeus began to laugh because Elle had stopped singing and was staring in amazement. She hadn't known how bad her voice was. But rather than being hurt or resentful when she understood, Elle announced solemnly that having discovered that her voice was so unusual as to require listeners of an unusual degree of sensitivity, it might be better if she demonstrated dancing.

And dance she did, with such fiery grace and beauty that Rage felt she would never see anyone dance again without remembering this. Soon the summerlanders were inventing their own dances, hammering out a rough, surprisingly musical racket on their crude instruments. And throughout it all, the ground shuddered and sometimes quaked with such force that everyone stopped and looked up warily at the roof. The celebration seemed endless, and in the lulls where everyone was exhausted from reveling, there was storytelling. Afterward, Rage always said that it was the stories, most of all, that had won the battle.

Elle told of roaming in the highest hills of Valley on bright summer afternoons. She told how she had tramped over hills bare but for grass that blew and hissed and swayed over the hills like a sea, and of climbing mountains whose peaks were ever wreathed in mist.

Thaddeus told an exciting story of the days in which he had been a renegade keeper rescuing animals intended to be conserved. When he came to the part about being captured by the wicked High Keeper, Rage was taken aback to hear herself described in such flattering and flowery language that none of the summerlanders could possibly have imagined it was her.

Puck told a wicked tale of two lovers who had got muddled up with another two lovers in a forest, and of his riotous role in the confusion. Halfway through, Rage recognized the story of *A Midsummer Night's Dream.*

One of the summerlanders shyly told a modest tale of how he had heard about the summerlands from his old grandmother.

Shona rose to tell a grave tale of her first meeting with the great summerlands lady warrior, Elle. "I did not know whether the stories she told of the summerlands were true, but I desired to believe they were," she said at last. "It seemed to me that if they were not true, then I had better die fighting for them anyway, rather than accept that this blackness was all that there would ever be."

Her story proved so popular that in the hours to come, a number of other stories about meeting with Elle were told. Each teller vied to clothe their heroine in more magnificent and beautiful words, until she laughingly called a halt to it, saying she was having trouble recognizing herself under such finery. When at last the spontaneous storytellers faltered, tales were requested, and at length Rage found herself called upon.

Feeling shy, she rose and told the story of her coming to Valley and of her search for the lost wizard. When she came to the part where Bear passed through the night gate, never to return, she faltered. "I'm sorry. I shouldn't have told this story. It's sad," she said huskily.

"Sadness is not dark," the wizard said from his seat against the wall. "Or it does not need to be. Sorrow can have great beauty in it, when it is a remembering."

"Bear's story is a story of courage," Elle said. "True courage is always beautiful."

"Beauty erodes this dark world more than laughter or love or hope because, in a way, it is the opposite of all that this world represents," the wizard murmured. Rage saw how his eyes lingered on Elle when he said these words.

Prompted to finish, Rage gathered her wits and did so. She was surprised when the summerlanders applauded at the end, several of them dabbing at their eyes and blowing their noses.

"You told it well," Billy said huskily as she sat down.

Before Rage could respond, the ground trembled and shook more strongly than it had at any other moment. At the end of the long rumbling, there was a terrific *crack*. Everyone fell silent, and in the sudden absence of noise came the sound of running feet. An outer door banged opened, and a summerlander boy came running in with a swirl of snow and a chill gust of wind.

"Stormkeep's gates have opened!" he gasped, eyes wide at his own tidings.

11

It was true.

The enormous gates that had never been seen open now stood ajar. A dim, bluish light showed from within, illuminating a great domed hall. Not a single gray flier was visible within or without.

"What are we supposed to do now?" Puck asked.

Everyone looked at Elle, who wore a long, dove gray cloak that fluttered in the faint icy breath of night. Snow fell softly, wheeling through the pools of light given off by the torches carried by the summerlanders. It fell onto Elle's hair and hung like tiny seed pearls in the golden flow.

"It is an invitation and a challenge," she finally announced.

"If a few go, it will be a message to the Stormlord that we do not fear him," the wizard said. He, too, was wrapped in a thick cloak, but still he shivered.

"You ought to go inside," Thaddeus told him.

"I will go into Stormkeep and accept this invitation," he said. "I have been there before, and the fact that I am returning must make its master believe we have no fear of his power."

"No," Elle said gently. "You are ill. The machine may bind you again."

The wizard hung his head and nodded.

"I'll go," Billy said firmly. "It should rattle the Stormlord to see me alive when he thinks that I fell to my death."

"I will go, too," Rage said, and was glad that her voice did not quiver. "It should be Billy and me because in the end, no matter what he does, we will wake. But he wants to see *you* most, Elle. I think he is curious about you."

"Would that it were true," the wizard murmured. "For it would mean his heart is not dead."

"That is what I am hoping and why I have made no attempt to see him," said Elle. "But if he would meet with me, he must first release the prisoners. That is the message that you will carry to him. I will come to him only when they are free."

It was over an hour before Rage, Billy, and Thaddeus approached the bridge. It had been decided that the witch man must accompany them so that he could bring the prisoners out, in case Rage woke in her world and she and Billy vanished. There had been many volunteers, but Elle insisted that a small delegation was better, say-ing, "The Stormlord has felt our power. Now we will show him our confidence."

The stone bridge was higher and more precarious than ever. Walking across it between Billy and Thaddeus, Rage was slightly protected from the worst of the wind, and there was no need for her to look anywhere but at Billy's broad shoulders. This time she did not make the mistake of looking down. As one, they stopped at the threshold of the gates. There was no sign of life save for the light of two flickering blue candles. They stopped again before three doors, all leading away from the domed hall. Through each lay identical long, ill-lit passages whose ends were lost in shadow.

"Do you suppose we are meant to wait here?" Thaddeus asked. His voice sounded thin in the cavernous space.

"I think we are to find our own way to the lord of Stormkeep," Billy murmured.

"Very well," Thaddeus said. "But how shall we choose, for all three ways look the same to my eyes?"

"I bet it doesn't matter," Rage murmured, thinking of Fork. "All doors and paths here will lead to the Stormlord."

Without waiting for the others to respond, Rage walked through the central door and entered the long corridor beyond. Thaddeus and Billy followed. It was very cold and their breaths came out in white puffs. They had not gone more than two steps when a great *whoosh* made them all turn back. The huge front gates shut with a great, somber clang.

"Steady," Thaddeus said.

"Doors are a bit like mouths, aren't they?" Billy said thoughtfully, then he smiled wryly when he noticed their expressions. "Sorry, I didn't mean to be grim. But it's like there is a fate that will swallow you behind every door you come to."

"I know that you are fond of this gruesome philosophizing, but under the circumstances, I would think this is not the time for it," Thaddeus said.

Rage couldn't help but laugh at the pained expression on his face. "Just be glad Gilbert didn't come," she said. She was surprised how much better it made her feel to laugh, and she remembered Elle's warning not to let their spirits fall.

"I suppose we ought to go on," she said as firmly as she could.

"Yes," Billy said gaily. "For there is seldom any point in going back." He linked his arm through hers and nodded to Thaddeus to do the same. They marched forward that way, Billy and Thaddeus measuring their longer strides to Rage's. She smiled to think how silly they must look.

They continued in this way to the end of the corridor, then parted to pass through a narrow doorway that rose high above them. They were in another passage. One side consisted of long columns, and through these was a vast, snow-covered courtyard. It looked the same as the one Rage and Billy had passed through before, when they had tried to escape with the wizard. But that one had been filled with gray fliers whereas this one was empty.

"We might as well keep going." Thaddeus nodded along the corridor.

They passed through a door into another vast room. It was so silent that it took Rage a moment to realize that it was not empty. Rank upon rank of gleaming gray fliers stood silently around the walls. In their midst, on the black chair, sat the Stormlord in his heavy draperies, watching them through hooded eyes.

Rage glanced about but there was no sign of the beasts.

"Come on," Billy said. He began to walk toward the Stormlord. Thaddeus followed and Rage brought up the rear. The Stormlord's face was paler than ever, and there were dark circles under his eyes. He looked exhausted and ill, but it was impossible to pity him because of the coldness in his eyes.

Billy stopped and bowed, forcing Rage and Thaddeus awkwardly to do the same.

"What do you want?" the lord of Stormkeep asked in his flat, tired voice.

"We bring a message from our leader, the great summerlands warrior, Lady Elle," Billy said in a clear, formal voice.

"Is she afraid to come here herself?" the Stormlord asked.

"She is afraid of nothing," Billy answered proudly. "We are here to tell you that she will meet with you when you release all who are imprisoned here."

"You dare to make demands of me?" the Stormlord asked hollowly.

"Our mistress dares all things," Billy said.

"What does she want?"

"To see those who wish to leave Null go in peace, and to stop the darkness flowing through the winter door."

"It cannot be closed," the Stormlord said.

"No," Billy said. "But it can be destroyed with your help."

There was no way to tell what the Stormlord was thinking. "Why would I help your mistress?"

"To return your world to what it was meant to be," he said. "A refuge for you. Once everyone goes, there will be no one left here to disturb you. If you will not agree to her requests, my mistress and her followers will remain in Null and beat away at the despair that binds this world until it cracks open like an egg."

The Stormlord closed his eyes as if he were unutterably weary. "Perhaps I do not care if this world dies, and I with it."

"That is your decision?" Billy asked calmly.

"I will reveal my decision to your mistress. She must come here to receive it."

"You must release your prisoners before she will come."

The Stormlord regarded them impassively for a long moment, then he sat forward in his seat slowly, as if it took a great effort of will. "Tell me how you escaped death when you fell into the chasm, boy." This was to Billy. "Not knowing has caused me to feel curiosity, and this is the most irksome form of wanting."

"You will have to ask my mistress about my escape," Billy replied, cleverly implying that it was Elle's powers that had saved him.

"Very well," the Stormlord said. "You may go and tell your mistress that I will release *half* the prisoners. In return, she will meet with me, and I will give my answer to her demands."

"Why wouldn't he just tell us his answer?" Rage asked hotly. "Why does he want to meet with Elle if he doesn't mean to try to hurt her?"

Elle turned to Thaddeus.

"Freeing half the prisoners is just a way to lure you in!" the witch man told her. "He will still have a lot of power because of the other prisoners, and you can be sure he means to use it against you."

"Perhaps," Elle said almost dreamily. "What do you say to this, Billy?"

"I'm not sure," Billy admitted, pushing the soft fall of his toffee-colored hair from his eyes. "I mean, what Rage and Thaddeus said are true, but he wouldn't have opened the gates to the keep unless he was acknowledging your power. If you refuse to go, he will know that you fear to be hurt and therefore that you have less power than he has come to believe."

"That is my thought," Elle said. "I will go and meet with him. You will go and tell him so immediately, Puck. He will sense that you are created, and this will further rouse the curiosity that troubles him. Tell him that one of the prisoners must be Nomadiel."

Rage looked worriedly at the wizard, who had greeted them on their return with the news that Mr. Walker had relapsed.

"I don't trust the Stormlord or this parley," Puck protested darkly as he left.

"I have to admit that I agree with Puck," Thaddeus said to Elle. "Lady, what need is there of a meeting between you and the Stormlord when we have told him what you want? Think what will happen if he hurts you or takes you prisoner? Or—" He stopped abruptly, but everyone knew what he had meant to say.

"If anything happens to me," Elle said gently, "the force against the Stormlord is merely diminished by one."

"No!" Shona cried. "You are our leader. Without you—"

"You can still succeed. In fact, you must, because I will be relying upon you to rescue me."

This did what perhaps no other argument would have done. "We will come for you if there is any treachery," Shona vowed through gritted teeth. "If he dares to take you, we will unmake his world."

The ground trembled as if in agreement. After a startled moment, the tension in the room broke as everyone began to laugh.

It was not long before Puck returned to tell them sourly that the lord of Stormkeep had been informed that the

Lady Elle would come to the fortress.

The prisoners were already being carried from the fortress by gray fliers and laid in the snow at the other end of the bridge. The summerlanders labored for some time to lead or half-carry them inside the settlement, where healers waited to tend them. None of the ex-prisoners responded to friends or family, or to the change in their circumstances. Rage wondered how many of them would recover, for some must have been imprisoned for years.

Nomadiel was the last, and to everyone's delight and relief, she walked out on her own. Her friends were watching anxiously from the other side of the chasm when she appeared, her little form silhouetted in the blue light. She broke into a run as soon as she was out of the gates, but she fell at the start of the bridge. Everyone gasped as she clambered to her feet and crossed the narrow bridge as if demons were at her heels. In a few moments, Nomadiel was hurtling across the snow toward Elle, who had run forward to meet her. The dog-woman gathered the tiny girl into her arms and carried her to where the rest of them waited.

"Oh, Elle," Nomadiel gasped, "he let me go, but he made the gray fliers put Rally in a tiny, horrible cage right in front of my eyes. Rally is deathly afraid of cages. He couldn't even speak to me because they had tied his beak. They took him away and told me to go." She dashed away a fresh scatter of tears. "I love him so much, and he loves me. He is the only one who has loved me like that. . . ."

"Hush, child. There are many who love you," Elle said firmly. "Do not fear for Rally. He will soon be free, so dry your tears and go to your father. He is very ill and needs you. . . ."

"He does not need me," Nomadiel said sadly.

"He has thought that, but *you* have always had the courage to know better, my dear. Don't lose heart now. Trust me," Elle said.

The anguish faded a little from Nomadiel's face and she let Shona lead her away.

"We got her away from the Stormlord just in time," Thaddeus said. He glanced back at Stormkeep. "I wonder why he did that with Rally."

"I think he was trying to break Noma in those final moments as a way of showing me his power. But he has underestimated the child." Elle looked at Thaddeus and smiled. "I doubt that her father will be any match for her determination that he live." She took a deep breath. "Well, I will go now."

"We will go with you," Billy said decisively.

Elle smiled. "If you want to come, then I should be glad of it." She turned back to Lod, who hovered at her elbow with several other summerlanders. "I want the rest of you to return and celebrate the release of your companions so brightly that you will leave the Stormlord in no doubt that I am not the only one with the power to oppose him."

"We will celebrate your courage, Lady," Lod promised fiercely.

"And your own," Elle said, clapping him on the back. "Tell some good stories for me, and remember the best so that I can hear them when I return."

Thaddeus caught hold of her arm. "Be careful, Lady."

"I have learned that caution is sometimes the better part of valor," Elle said, waving a brief farewell. Catching Rage's look of surprise, she laughed.

Elle took the lead as she, Rage, and Billy walked to

the bridge. They were soon passing through the cavernous maw that was the door to Stormkeep. With Elle around, ways were always short, burdens light, and dangers less fearsome. Had Elle been so special in her old world as a dog? Rage thought not. As with Billy, her transformation as she passed through the bramble gate had continued and deepened, so that far more had changed in her than her appearance.

When they reached the Stormlord, he was still seated on his black chair, but there were no gray fliers in sight, nor any beasts. He regarded Elle for so long that Rage had to stop herself from fidgeting. Elle merely returned his dark stare with her own lively, untroubled gaze, her long, bright hair undulating in the chill breezes that played about the chamber.

"You are the one the rebels call the Lady Elle." It was a statement.

"And *you* are the fearsome Stormlord," Elle said, making it sound as if his title were a joke between them. "I have come to learn your decision about my requests."

"Requests, Lady? I would call them demands, unless your boy there misspoke."

"Billy is not my boy," Elle said. "He is my friend."

The Stormlord sat up and gave her a haughty look. "What sort of creature are you? You are no more human than this boy, and yet I sense that you are both from the human worlds."

"Once I dwelt in the world of humans as a true beast—a dog—but I was changed when I passed through a world gate to the land of Valley, that land into which your winter pours so dangerously."

"A dog?" There was the faintest suggestion of a sneer.

Elle laughed easily. "Do not imagine that I am

ashamed of my past, Lord. I loved being a dog. To run and romp and bark and think of nothing but bones and rabbit smells. Oh, the smells! My one regret is that I cannot smell as well as once I could, but still I would wager that my nose is better than yours."

The ground rumbled.

"Stop that," the Stormlord said with a touch of petulance. Then he frowned and his gaze sharpened. "I thought that you were a wizard of some unknown kind, but now that you are here before me, I see that this power is no more than that which Null was built to oppose. You have no true power."

"Then why am I here?" Elle asked. She did not wait for him to speak but supplied her own answer. "Because I *do* have power and it is the *best* kind: the kind that rises only from my decision to oppose your world and all that it stands for. And I have taught the Null-landers to do the same."

"Perhaps you do not understand your peril, Lady. I do not value my life, and it is possible that I will allow it to end simply to be rid of you."

"But . . ." Billy hesitated, and the black cold eyes turned to him. "I was just going to say that if you are a wizard, you wouldn't die, would you? Not just by your world ending."

The Stormlord's face might have been carved of ivory for its stillness. Although nothing showed in the night-dark eyes, Rage began to feel frightened for Billy.

"I think it is true that you would not fear death, but you do fear life," Elle said lightly. "And once your world was destroyed, you would be forced to face life because you would have to live in the sunlight, and deal with worlds filled with beings who yearn and sing and dance and laugh."

"There is darkness in all of those worlds that can be made to serve me," the Stormlord said, shifting his black regard to the dog-woman.

"Yes, but think what effort it would require to darken the sun and oppress the people of another world. And it would not be as easy as it is here in Null. No, I think it wiser and simpler for you to grant what we ask. Why shouldn't you, after all, if you want nothing, for that is what I am offering you? Unless you *desire* us to remain here."

The Stormlord frowned.

Rage waited with bated breath to hear what he would say. At last he rose and said in a clear, chill voice, "What you have said makes me realize that your demands sowed in me the seeds of anger. This has revealed to me that my own soul is less pure than I had believed, for if it had been pure, you would have been unable to provoke any emotion. Therefore I have decided to agree to all that you have asked. But there will be a price."

"A price?" Rage almost shouted.

The Stormlord ignored her, for all his will was bent on Elle.

"What price?" Elle asked calmly.

"You," the Stormlord said. "You must remain here in Null after the door has been dismantled. Without your friends or followers, or any route of escape to the sunlight, your brightness will fade. And as you become aligned to Null, so will my heart become pure and empty of emotion. Then will the power contained within you serve to strengthen Null and hold it against future invaders."

"No!" Rage cried. Then she felt herself being drawn back to wakefulness in her own world.

Logan was shaking her. It was pitch dark and the only light came from two candles jammed in a jar. Five other candle stumps were lying beside it.

"I'm sorry I had to wake you, but they're here," Logan was saying urgently. "The pig things. There must be ten out there. They've started bashing against the door, and I don't think the hinges will hold up for too much longer."

"Door!" Rage sat bolt upright because there was only one door to the extension. *"They're in the house?"*

"They got in an hour ago. I heard the sound of breaking glass. But they've only just started on the door." Rage went to look at the hinges and saw that he was right. They had buckled and the screws were bent. It would not take much to snap them.

"We'd better get the gun."

Logan held out his hand, and she saw that he had found it already. Logan opened his other hand, and the bullets lay gleaming in his palm. "I didn't know how to load it," he confessed. "I've never even held one before. I didn't say anything before you went to sleep because I didn't really think they'd come."

Rage took the gun and bullets from him and loaded the gun without thinking as they walked back to the bedroom. She twisted the chamber closed with a practiced flick of her wrist that made Logan gape. She sat on the bed crosslegged beside an alert Billy, telling Logan to get on the bed, too, so that she could have a clear shot. They had shifted the bed earlier, so she had a good view of the door through the study. She sighted along the short barrel of the gun, as if some other part of her mind that she had not known about had taken control.

The bed springs creaked as Logan got himself comfortable. Then he said, "Bloody hell, Rage, you did that like Annie Oakley or something. How come?"

"Mam taught me when I was six," Rage said, realizing that she had actually forgotten that until this very moment. "I've never shot anything live. Only tins and paper targets. But we lived in a pretty wild area, so we needed the gun to frighten things off. Mam said I ought to know how to shoot just in case something happened to her or . . ." She frowned. Or to whom? For a moment, she seemed to see a man's face as if through water. Then it was gone.

"You shot a gun when you were six?"

"I never liked it," Rage said. How long ago that memory of Mam teaching her to shoot was!

Suddenly Rage heard claws clicking against the floorboards outside the room. Ice water seemed to pour down her spine, but she just sat up straight and steadied her gun hand with the other.

"They'll pace like this for a bit," Logan said, nodding toward the door. "That's how it's been since they arrived. They pace, then they throw themselves at the door and bark, then they go away. Waiting for them to do something is almost harder than when they attack. Tell me what's happening in Null."

Rage told him, but it was hard to concentrate.

"I still don't see that the Stormlord sent those beasts," Logan said when she stopped.

As if they had heard, the beasts outside the door began to howl and batter at it. Billy barked in response, and this seemed to drive the creatures mad.

"I really don't want to end up as some sort of monster snack," Logan said.

Rage couldn't believe that Logan could make a joke at a time like this. Then it struck her like a bolt of lightning that if the Stormlord *had* sent the beasts, maybe the same weapons that could defeat their master could defeat them.

"Tell me a joke," Rage commanded Logan.

He gaped at her as if she had gone mad.

The door hinges creaked.

"Come on! Make me laugh!" she shouted, grabbing him by his sweater and shaking him.

"You *are* crazy," Logan said with such glum conviction that Rage did laugh.

At once, she felt stronger and braver. Then a recklessness came over her. She stood up and headed for the door, flicking the gun safety on and laying it on the desk as she passed it.

"What are you doing?" Logan hissed, catching hold of her arm. Billy had reached the door and was barking and snarling. The creatures outside responded in kind, still banging against the door. Any second the hinges would give way.

"I'm going to open the door," Rage said.

"No way!"

"Logan, everything to do with the Stormlord feeds on fear. If *we* feel afraid, it just makes those things stronger and it attracts them. We have to fight them with laughter and courage and things like that."

"You are not trying to tell me that you are going to open that door and laugh at those things!" Logan said.

"I'm not scared," Rage said, and for a wonder, it was true.

"Well, *I'm* scared enough for the both of us!" Logan said flatly. "All right, open the door, but I just hope we don't regret this." He was white as he let go of her arm, but he turned and took up the chair from behind the desk like a lion tamer.

Rage turned to face the door, holding the warmth of her feelings for Logan close, and dropped one hand to Billy's soft head.

"Stop it!" she shouted. The battering stopped. Heartened, she shouted again. "Go away and leave us alone!" Without letting herself think, she reached for the bolt, unlatched it, and dragged the door open. It moved slowly, then jammed halfway because of the bent hinges, but there were no growls and no attack. Rage put her shoulder to the door and shoved. It opened the rest of the way with a protesting screech.

The hall outside was dark, cold, and empty. There was complete silence except for something outside banging in the wind. Rage stepped out into the hallway.

"Be careful," Logan said, coming out behind her. "In the movies, the dead guy always gets up and grabs you."

Rage smiled. She looked down to where Billy stood at her side, sniffing hard. When he looked up, his brown eyes were clear.

"They've gone," Rage told Logan.

"What a sleepover!" he said.

They managed to push a cupboard and some pillows up against the broken window. While they were mopping up, the power came on, so they were able to make toast and hot cocoa, even though it was four in the morning.

"You really think they were sent by the Stormlord?" Logan asked a while later, licking cocoa from his top lip.

"Who else?" Rage said. "We couldn't have got rid of them the way we did otherwise."

"Yeah, but it doesn't really make sense. I mean, why send them after you when it sounds like it was Elle that he wanted?"

Rage frowned, remembering the last thing that the Stormlord had said. She hadn't told that part to Logan earlier, but she did so now.

"What do you think she'll do?" he asked.

The toast Rage was eating turned to sawdust in her mouth. Because she knew what Elle would do. The Stormlord had known, too. She would agree to remain in Null. Rage looked at Billy and found him watching her with sorrowful brown eyes. She thought there was nothing designed to express sadness more perfectly than the eyes of a dog.

"I mean, keeping Elle there will only weaken his world," Logan was saying.

"He wants to crush Elle as a way of proving to himself that hope and love and courage and all those things she used against him don't mean anything when you are alone in the dark."

"Maybe you're right, but you know what?" Logan said. "If it's a one-on-one competition the Stormlord is after, I'd bet on the Lady Elle anytime," Logan said. "You know, of all the people you talk about from your dream-travels, it's her I most want to meet. She sounds . . . special."

"She is," Rage said huskily. She looked down at Billy resting his head in her cupped palm, his forlorn expression perfectly reflecting the ache in her own heart.

12

"So you're going to try to sleep again?"

Rage nodded. They were back in the extension, having decided that they did not want to bother moving to her bedroom. "I have to find out what happened. I wish I could take you, Logan."

"Don't worry about it," he said. "But maybe you should will yourself to Valley. I mean, if a couple of days have passed, the winter door might already be gone."

"I think I'm supposed to be there when it happens," Rage said. She lay down on the bed and Billy stretched out beside her. Logan switched the overhead light out. The only light came from the desk lantern.

"I'm going to leave it on," he said. "I was thinking that I might have a look at your uncle's notebooks. I mean, if you don't think he'd mind."

"I don't think he'll be back for them anytime soon," Rage said sadly.

She relaxed, feeling tired but peaceful despite her fears for Elle. Forgiving the wizard had done that. Mam had often told her that she had a good rage inside her, but now she understood that there had been the potential for destructive anger as well. Anger, Mam always said, made people stupid.

Rage's eyes drooped, and she tried to picture herself and Billy standing with Mr. Walker. In her vision, Billy had an arm around her shoulders. Whether he was a dog or human shaped, they belonged together, she thought. Then she tumbled into a dream of walking through snow falling on a snowy plain. There was nothing to indicate where she was, nor any sign of Billy or Mr. Walker. But she heard the same voice that she had heard calling her before.

"This is a dream," she muttered. "I must have gotten sidetracked."

She was about to close her eyes and try another dream leap when she heard the voice quite clearly.

"Help me!" It was weaker than it had been, and she had the feeling she knew the voice.

"Who are you?" she shouted on impulse.

"Who are you?" the voice responded. Rage gave a snort of disgust, realizing it must merely be a distorted echo of her own words. She closed her eyes and willed herself and Billy to Mr. Walker.

This time when she opened her eyes, she and Billy were standing on a snowy plain surrounded by jagged mountains. There was no snow falling and it was night. Before her stood a great crowd facing what could only be the Null side of the winter door: an enormous, pale arch of glowing ice with a fringe of icicles that glimmered white in the light of the torches carried by many of those assembled. Humans and other beings were passing through the door, one by one, and vanishing.

"Look!" Billy cried, pointing. "It's *her*! Elle!"

Rage scanned the crowd until she saw Elle standing to one side, talking with the wizard, Mr. Walker, Nomadiel, and the rebel leader, Shona.

"Maybe she said no," Rage murmured hopefully.

Billy shook his head. "Just before I woke, I heard her agree. She would never go back on her word."

They made their way over the slippery ice. They skirted the gathering until they came to where Mr. Walker was speaking with Elle. Rage was touched to see that he was holding his daughter's hand.

"This is not fair," Mr. Walker was saying hotly.

Elle laughed. "Dear Prince Walker, you know that the real stories do not always end with everyone getting what they want. But do not think you have seen the last of me, for I intend to torment the Stormlord with my endless desire for the summerlands, until he begs me to leave Null and him in peace."

"What of Fork?" Mr. Walker asked.

Elle sighed and a shadow crossed her face. "Part of Fork's grief is caused by what flows through the winter door. But the city will grieve for me, I know. Upon your return, someone must go there and make it understand that there was no other way. Tell Fork that I send it a world full of lost souls to fill its empty streets, and charge it to produce beauty enough to open their withered hearts and help them grow. Tell Fork not to fail me."

She caught sight of Rage and Billy and stepped forward to clasp them close. "I am glad to see you to say goodbye."

"You *are* staying," Rage said, unable to believe that it would come to this.

Elle smiled. "Do not be downcast for me, darling

heart. The master of this place and I are about to enter upon a contest. He will seek to dull me and I will strive to brighten him. If I succeed, gaps will open again and again, and one day he will weary of the battle and I will be coming home to Valley."

Such was the power of her personality that Rage could almost believe her.

"But to choose darkness and winter," Shona wept. "How can this be a good ending for the story of our journey to the summerlands? That we sacrificed the golden lady who was our champion in order to gain the sun?"

"I am no sacrifice," Elle said firmly. "You mustn't think it, any of you."

"Oh, Elle," Nomadiel cried. She let go of her father's hand and flung herself into Elle's arms.

"Do not weep, little one. Grow well and expect me to come to visit you one day. But mind, I will expect a royal feast and many fine songs and stories."

"You shall have them," Nomadiel whispered.

Elle straightened. "You had better go now before the master of this place discovers what a bad bargain he has made. He will arrive soon with the last prisoners, and you must be ready to tend them on the other side of the door."

Rage could see nothing through the door, but she hoped that the summerlanders would be stepping into a blaze of sunlight. The crowd diminished as more and more streamed through the door.

"Maybe Rage can dream us to visit you," Billy said.

"I am afraid that cannot be," the wizard said. "You see, the magic that Rage is using to dream-travel is not hers but a magic the firecat stole from me in its desire to bring me aid, though I did not want it. The dream-traveling spell will wear off before long. Indeed, it is a wonder to me that it has not done so sooner. No doubt the firecat meddled with it."

"Where is the firecat?" Mr. Walker asked. "Didn't you say that you would need it to help you close the door?"

"I will force it to come to me when the time is right, but being here in a land steeped in despair will torment it because of its own hungers. I do not wish it to suffer more than it needs to," the wizard answered.

At last, it was their turn to pass through the door. Before any of them could speak, there was a blinding flash of bluish light, and the Stormlord, clad in his heavy gray robes, stood in front of them.

"Now he will betray us," Puck muttered.

The Stormlord ignored him. "I have listened to your words, Lady, and I find myself . . . troubled. You spoke of a challenge, and it comes to me that my decision to keep you here was a challenge. Perhaps I do need a real contest to remind me of what I meant to do with this world. Things became confused once I began to put Null-landers into my machine. Since it has fallen silent, my mind is clearer. I still believe that conquering what you represent, Lady, will cleanse me and purify my world. But I desire the challenge to be more honorable."

"What do you mean?" Elle asked.

"You will remain here, as we have agreed, for six months. In this time, we will contest. But if at the end of that time you retain the will and desire to leave Null, I will open a true gateway to your land, and you will pass through it. There you will remain for six months so that we can gather our strength, and then you will come again. So it will continue until I do not desire you to come to Null, which means that you will have won, or when you lack the will to leave Null, and you will have lost."

"Six months here and six months there?" Elle asked. The Stormlord inclined his dark head. "Very well, I accept your renewed terms, my Lord. Gladly."

The Stormlord bowed to her and then lifted a long, thin hand toward the winter door. There was a flash of light, and suddenly a line of people was shuffling toward the door. The remaining prisoners. Most did not even look to see where they were walking.

"Where is the creature who created the false door?" the Stormlord asked.

The wizard lifted his hands into the air and made a twisting motion with his fingers. There was a hissing burst of light, like that of a rocket that had not been released. The firecat appeared, a spitting, screeching brightness hurtling through the winter door.

"No! Not coming. Hateful place. Hurting!"

"Firecat! Hear your master. I have told you that you must help us to dismantle the door you created."

"Letting go! Must going! Hurting!" it shrieked.

"Be calm. The sooner you help, the sooner we can leave this place," the wizard said firmly.

"Wizard not leaving firecat?" Rage saw its red, slanted eyes clearly for a moment, beseeching but filled with fury.

"Of course not," the wizard said gently. "Now will you help us willingly, or must I cast a spell to make you obedient?"

"No! Not making ssspell. Firecat doing what isss wanted. Nice wizard." It began to snarl and weep.

The wizard gave a sigh and turned to the Stormlord. "We are ready."

"Are *you* ready, Lady?" the Stormlord asked Elle.

"I am ready," Elle said. She crossed the little space between them to stand beside the Stormlord, bright flame alongside dark flame.

The wizard lifted his hand and nodded gravely to Elle.

"Farewell, my friends." She gave a flashing smile. "Look for me in six months!"

"Goodbye," Thaddeus called.

The others did the same, then they turned to pass one by one through the door: Thaddeus, Mr. Walker, Nomadiel with Rally on her shoulder. Billy passed through the gate before Rage. She turned to look one last time at Elle, who smiled.

Weeping, Rage stepped through the winter door. There was a moment of extreme coldness, then she was stepping onto the hillside in Valley.

It was dark and raining heavily. The snow underfoot was a muddy slush, and Rage slipped. Billy caught her arm and held her steady. He shouted over the rain that the others had gone up to the wizard's castle. Then the wizard stepped through the door, the firecat struggling in his arms. Its heat did not seem to trouble the wizard, and he seemed not to notice the rain as he turned to face the winter door.

At that moment, Gilbert came dashing out of the darkness with an armful of umbrellas that he promptly dropped in the mud. He fell to his knees to gather them up. The wizard helped him up and said a little water never hurt anyone.

The wizard turned back to the door. "Now, to

complete the spell, firecat, you must desire the door to be gone. I will send the power through you to make it so."

"Door gone!" the firecat shrieked.

There was a flare of light. For one moment, Rage saw them through a slit-shaped hole: Elle with her bright golden hair, and the tall, pale-faced Stormlord as he held out a formal hand, and Rage saw Elle look at him and then lay her own hand in it.

Then the Stormlord lifted his free hand and pointed toward the slit.

The door vanished.

"Wetnesss! Horrible cruel wetnesss and coldnesss!" the firecat hissed.

"Go and find a fire to curl up by," the wizard said wearily, and he released it. The firecat vanished in a fizzing flash of light. "I shall have to do something about that firecat," he murmured, "else I will spend the rest of my days being enmeshed in its mischief."

"Come out of the rain," Gilbert said. "There is hot soup and fresh-baked bread and warm fires back at the castle. I'm afraid I didn't know so many would be coming, and I was so upset about Elle not coming back that when I tried to create enough food for them all, I misspoke, and the castle is full of purple chickens. I can't seem to remember how to make them go away. I am sorry, master."

"Dear Gilbert, how I have missed you!" the wizard laughed, and threw a long arm around the bedraggled faun's shoulders.

"I am glad to see you, too, master," Gilbert said. He looked at Billy. "You have grown so much," he marveled, then his pale eyes watered. "Was there really no other way but to leave her?"

"I don't know if there was another way, but Elle chose this way," Billy said. "But Gilbert, maybe no one has thought to tell you that the Stormlord of Null changed his mind. Elle will not remain there forever now, but only for six months at a time."

"You mean that she will come back here . . ."

"For six months. But then she must return to Null for the next six months. This will go on until the Stormlord desires her not to return to Null, or she desires not to return here," the wizard said. "Well, we seem to be wet enough that we might have gone bathing in our clothes. Let us go and try your soup and deal with these chickens." He turned to Rage. "Will you remain awhile with us? I can ensure that you do not wake until you desire."

"Just for a little while," Rage said, torn between knowing Logan was waiting anxiously and knowing this might be the last time she could be in Valley. "Until day comes."

"Day . . ." The wizard's face was transformed by longing. "Oh, to see day again, even if it is a day full of gray skies and rain."

"Maybe it won't rain," Gilbert said.

The castle was now an enormous mansion with dozens of bedrooms, which was lucky, given how many guests had arrived through the winter door. Most of those from Null were eating in a great dining hall, for the wizard had conjured a feast tempting enough to dazzle the most numbed senses. Rage, Billy, their companions from Valley, and a few of the summerlanders were sitting in the library by the fire, drinking soup out of big mugs. As they ate, they took turns telling Gilbert and the witch Mother all that had happened. The silver streaks in Rue's hair shone in the firelight, but despite this, she seemed younger when Thaddeus sat very close to her.

Then they moved on to plans for the future.

"There will be a lot of cleaning up because there will be flooding now that so much snow has begun to melt," Thaddeus said. "But as the sun is shining and the flowers blooming about us, I won't mind how hard I work. I have never longed more for the smell and sounds of spring."

"I, too," Mr. Walker said. "I will plant a honeysuckle on Feluffeen's grave. She always liked honeysuckle."

"Did she?" Nomadiel asked him shyly.

"She did," Mr. Walker said, reaching out to touch his daughter's cheek. "And violets, too, but only wild ones. I will show you where she used to pick them."

"I shall be glad to get back to my little tree house in Wildwood," Puck said grumpily. "Goodness knows what a mess her squirrels have made in my absence." He was sitting on the arm of the witch Mother's chair. She reached out a long hand and patted him like a cat. He cast Thaddeus a sly look of triumph that made the witch man laugh and tweak his ear.

"I will go and tell Fork what happened to Elle," Nomadiel said softly. "I will sing to it of Elle and her great quest through the winter door into the land of darkness. I will help Fork to win its battle against despair just as Elle helped the Null-landers."

"I will come with you," said Shona, her eyes shining. "The Lady Elle told us of this magical city and of her great affection for it. She said there were many empty streets and houses. I should like to live in such a place, if it will have me."

"I will go to the mountains she spoke of, and run with bears and wolves and foxes," said the boy Lod.

"There will be a place for all of you here," the wizard

said. Then his eyes turned to Rage and Billy. "For you two also, if you wish to remain, but do not decide now, nor even think of it. Gilbert, why don't you conjure up some more food? Some good honey mead and a very rich chocolate cake would do nicely."

"Chocolate?" Nomadiel murmured, then her eyes widened as she remembered that this was what she had drunk from Rage's flask. "Oh yes, a cake of chocolate would be lovely."

"I will try," Gilbert said nervously. He stood up. "All right." He squeezed his eyes shut and lifted both hands and twisted his fingers in a peculiar fluid way. Then he opened his eyes and stared in wonder at the enormous confection he had created. The smell of chocolate rising from the cake made Rage's mouth water.

"Is it meant to be purple?" Puck demanded.

"Oh yes," Billy said quickly. "Why, the very best chocolate is that color."

"It smells heavenly," the witch Mother pronounced.

"Well done, my boy," the wizard said.

Gilbert blushed with pleasure.

At last the wizard rose and suggested that they all go out to watch the sun rise.

It had stopped raining outside and the ground was wet and boggy. Great patches of bare ground showed through the snow, and a mist hazed the air. Rage hoped the Null-landers would not be disappointed, but she need not have worried. When a seam of light opened up on the horizon, they began to cheer wildly.

"Oh," Shona murmured as the mist thinned and grew pink, "I cannot believe that we are here in the summer-lands at last."

Humans and creatures emerged from the castle, and

others came out of Deepwood. Then a bird began to sing, and in a moment others joined in. The Null-landers' faces were entranced. The sun rose at last, a burnished disk of molten orange, saturating the skeins of cloud in red-gold, pink, mauve, lavender, and peach. Then it rose higher, and grew as radiant as Elle's hair while the sky turned the brightest and clearest of blues.

Rage marveled herself, for it had been so long since she had seen a sky so blue.

"You do not need to go back," the wizard said softly. "If your mother is too ill to care for you and Samuel has gone away, I can create a door and bring you through to Valley in reality. It will take time and a good deal of magic, but I will do it. You can wait here until your mother recovers enough to take responsibility for you again. I can enable you to visit her in her dreams."

Rage shook her head. "I am needed back in my own world," she said at last.

"You have great courage, Rage, and honor, too. Rare things in the human world," the wizard said.

"Maybe not so rare," Rage answered, thinking of Logan. "Goodbye, Great-Uncle Peter."

He blinked and then smiled. "Goodbye for now, Great-Niece Rage Winnoway."

Rage nodded. Then she turned to Billy. "You could stay here and be human shaped and . . ."

He shook his head. "Like Elle, I have made my choice. I will stay with you."

Rage nodded and turned to the wizard. "I would like to go home now."

The wizard lifted his hand.

The sun-drenched hillside fell away.

Rage did not wake at once. She passed into the dream of snow falling and falling. The landscape seemed vaguely familiar this time. Then she heard the voice calling out for help again. This time she recognized it.

It was the voice of her uncle.

"Help!"

Rage woke to Billy licking her face.

She sat up, and Logan sat up, too, his hair sticking up wildly, making him look like an astonished owl. "What happened?"

"It's all right. The winter door has been dismantled and most of the Null-landers went to Valley. Elle stayed." Rage told him briefly what had happened, but she kept thinking of the voice in her dream. Finally, she interrupted herself to say, "You know, what if there was an accident but no one knows about it yet?"

Logan blinked at her in confusion. "What do you mean?"

"My uncle," Rage said. "What if he had an accident, but no one saw it? That would explain the police saying there hadn't been any accidents. Maybe he didn't just leave."

Logan gave an exclamation. "Come and have a look at this."

Rage climbed out of her blankets. The room was freezing, which meant the power was out again, or maybe it hadn't come on. Logan went to the little desk, where two notebooks had been laid out side by side, both open. One was the older stained notebook. The other was the new notebook with the writing ending in the middle of a sentence.

"I'm not much of a reader, Rage, but look. This is the

notebook you read, right?" He was touching the new notebook, and Rage nodded. "Well, the words on this page are the same as the words on this page." He tapped the older notebook. "So here's the thing. I think the stuff in this new notebook is just a copy of what's in the other one. So it can't be about leaving you. It just looked that way."

"But . . ." Rage stopped. If her uncle *had* come home when she had been in the hikers' hut with Billy, he would have gone looking for her. He would have driven round the back of the dam because it would be a lot quicker than walking there. There was an access road that he could have used, and as soon as she pictured it, she was certain that was where she had been walking in her dream. She told Logan what she thought.

"We can't call anyone since the phone is out, so we'd better go and look, just in case he has had an accident. If he is hurt, there's no time to lose," Logan said. Billy gave a bark of agreement. They dressed warmly and ran out into the darkness. It was early morning, but it might as well have been the middle of the night. But one thing had changed.

"Logan, have you noticed?" Rage asked.

"Noticed what?"

"The weather! The air is milder—almost warm. And look how slushy the snow is."

"It's like in Narnia after the witch was defeated." Logan sounded delighted.

The ground was treacherously slippery, but they struggled along as best they could.

"You said he called out for help in the dreams?" Logan panted as they turned off the main road and onto the access road.

Rage nodded, but she thought uneasily how weak the last cry had been.

"If he came back when you were gone, that means he came on Saturday or maybe earlier on Sunday. He would have read your note and come to look for you. That means he might have been hurt for more than a day. . . ." His voice trailed off as he saw Rage's face.

Rage was thinking that if not for Billy, she would have died unconscious in the snow after her fall. She could only pray that her uncle had stayed in his car. If so, there was hope for him.

After following the access road for some time, Logan suggested they split up. He would continue along the road. She should cut across the hills to the hut and come along the access road from the other direction. "We can cover the ground twice as fast that way. Yell or get Billy to bark if you see anything."

Rage set off with renewed energy, but she remembered there was a steep gorge in the hills somewhere near. She slowed, hoping it wasn't snowed over. If so, she might fall into it. Then she spotted it, a dark slit against the snow. Billy looked at her.

"Can you smell for me?"

He flapped his tail, sniffed, then barked excitedly and ran toward the gorge. Rage floundered after him. She stopped well back, knowing that the snow might give the gorge a false and fragile edge. She couldn't see anything below because of how narrow and steep it was. If not for Billy barking wildly and pawing at the ground, she would have turned back. Instead, she took a deep breath, unbuttoned her coat, and put it on the ground. Then she lay on it and slithered forward until she could see over the edge. Her breath caught in her throat because about ten feet down a man lay spread-eagled near the edge of a wide ledge.

"Uncle Samuel," Rage whispered.

Billy barked and the figure on the ledge moved. The movement made him slip a little, and she realized that the ledge must slope downward. Beneath him lay a sheer drop to hard rock. If he fell, he would die.

"Uncle Samuel! Don't move!" Rage shouted. "I'll go and get help." But before she could turn away, she saw the figure move and slip again. Now one foot hung over the drop.

She did not dare leave him. "I have to get down there," she told Billy as she crawled back from the edge of the gorge and stood.

Billy barked frantically at her.

"I've climbed down here before with Mam," she said fiercely, ignoring the fact that it had been a clear and perfect summer afternoon when they had scaled the rocky wall. She found the place where there were rough handholds and brushed the snow away. "There's a ledge down at his level. I'm going to climb to it now and see if I can reach Uncle Samuel from there. You go and get—"

Billy growled.

"All right," said Rage, "then bark until Logan hears, but go away a bit, because I'm afraid you'll make Uncle Samuel move and slip again."

Billy gave a soft bark and pawed at her leg. She held his eyes for a moment, reading the desperation in them. She knew he would take her place if he could, instead of simply barking for Logan.

"It will be all right," Rage said firmly. She eased herself over the edge.

Rage had just reached the ledge when a warm rain began to fall. It washed the snow off the handholds, making them easier to see but slick and treacherous. She edged sideways carefully, feeling the ledge beneath her feet grow more and more narrow. She could see her uncle's face now and bit her lip in alarm at the splash of red on his temple. She reminded herself that he had moved, so he was alive. The main thing was to get to him and stop him from moving any closer to the edge.

"Rage!" Logan cried in horror from above.

She didn't dare look up, sprawled as she was against the face of the rock and reaching with one leg across the gap from her ledge to the one where her uncle lay.

"Rage, come back! I'll go and get help!"

She ignored him, concentrating on stretching the little more that was needed. At last, she felt the tip of the other ledge beneath her toe. Logan had fallen silent. She leaned farther over until she felt that her foot was secure; then, very carefully, she transferred her weight to it.

Slowly—for the ledge that her uncle lay on was both sloped and crumbling in places—Rage straightened her body, bringing her other foot over the gap. Now she was standing directly above her uncle. He was frighteningly still, and she prayed that he would stay that way for both their sakes. She stepped over him and put her foot onto the flat, wide place by his outstretched arm. The strange angle of the limb suggested it was broken. Again she transferred her weight, and finally, trembling with strain, she lowered herself carefully into the space between her uncle's sprawled body and the wall of the gorge. Pressing her back to the stone, she placed her feet carefully on rocky juts to give herself leverage and reached forward to wrap her arms around her uncle. His skin felt cold to the touch.

Rage looked up, blinking against the diminishing

rain. Logan's head was outlined against the gray sky. The edges of the clouds glowed, and Rage knew there was sunlight somewhere behind them.

"Logan, his car must be somewhere. There will be rope in the back!"

Logan shouted something in response that she couldn't hear, then he was gone. Billy barked once: his way of telling her that he was still there.

Rage settled herself more comfortably, knowing that they would probably have to wait for some time. She had been hot from the climb, but now that she was still, a chill settled on her. She regretted leaving her coat behind in the snow.

Her uncle moved again, and as Rage gripped him, he slid a bit farther down the ledge. Now both his feet were hanging over the drop. She knew that if she had not been hanging on to him, he might well have slid the rest of the way.

"Please don't move again, Uncle Samuel," she whispered. "I'm sorry I didn't come sooner. I'm sorry I thought you would go away and leave me like you left Mam. Please lie still or we'll both fall."

Her uncle muttered something and then, opening his eyes, turned his head to look at her. One of his eyes was swollen and blackened, and the whole of that side of his face was abraded and bloody.

"Rage . . . ," he mumbled.

"Shh. You have to keep still. Logan's gone for a rope. But we shouldn't move because this ledge is crumbling."

His eyes widened with realization. "Rage . . . why did you climb down? . . . Should have gone for help. . . ."

"You were slipping off the edge."

"It doesn't matter if I fall," her uncle said wearily.

"It *does* matter!" Rage said. "It matters to me and it would matter to Mam. She's been waiting her whole life for you to come back."

"Mary . . ." Her uncle said the name with a tenderness that bordered on sorrow.

"She loves you and she needs you to help her be brave enough to live," Rage whispered. "She needs both of us."

Her uncle did not answer, and she worried that he had lapsed into unconsciousness again. But at least he was still.

Rage's arms began to ache and then they grew numb. Where on earth was Logan? For a while, her mind wandered. She thought of the Stormlord offering his hand to Elle.

"Rage!"

It was Logan, and there was a note of panic in his voice. Rage was stunned to realize that she had almost fallen asleep. She sat up and, to her horror, she felt the whole ledge give slightly. Only then did she realize that this was not a ledge of rock as she had thought, but a clump of earth dangerously weighed down by rock, by snow, and now by them.

Rage looked up and called, "Logan, did you get the rope?"

"I did," he called, and she saw it snake down. "But there's nothing to tie it on to."

"Just hold it. I'll tie it around my uncle. You pull it taut and take his weight so I can climb up. Then we'll pull him up together."

"All right," Logan said.

Rage looped the rope about her uncle, but as carefully as she moved, pieces of the ledge kept breaking away. She was almost crying with frustration by the time she had managed to knot it under his arms. Now she could only hope that the knot was strong enough—not to mention the rope—and that the two of them would be capable of pulling up an unconscious man. Logan was strong, certainly, but her uncle was a tall man for all his thinness, and there would be little purchase on the snowy ground.

Rain was falling again, and her hair was plastered to her cheeks. Her clothes were wet through.

"Take his weight!" Rage called up. Logan shouted something. She could not make it out, but the rope grew taut. Slowly she released her uncle and rose carefully to step over him.

In one terrible instant, the ledge was crumbling and pulling away. Rage screamed and grabbed the rope just as the whole ledge fell away.

There was a cry overhead as Logan took their full weight. Dangling helplessly in midair, Rage's heart beat like a maddened bird against her chest.

". . . can't hold you both!" Logan yelled. Rage heard the strain in his voice. The rope slipped, and Rage bit off a cry, desperately scanning the sheer rock face, searching for the slightest handhold.

"Rage!" Logan screamed.

They slipped another few inches.

"In my pocket . . . knife . . ." Rage stared into her uncle's face. "Climb over me and cut me loose."

"No!" Rage said. "No. I won't let you die."

Then, miraculously, they were being pulled upward. In lurching increments, they rose toward the rim of the gorge. Then hands were reaching down to haul them up. Two sets of hands.

Rage gaped in bewilderment to find that it was Billy dragging her up and into his arms.

Billy in his human shape.

"How can you be . . . ?"

"Later," Billy said. "We need to get the two of you back to the farm."

They used Logan's coat as a stretcher and dragged Uncle Samuel to the car. To Rage's relief, Logan could drive. It was a difficult, slippery trip through the continuing drizzle, but Logan managed to get them right up the hill road and into the drive of Winnoway. The power was still off inside, but they stoked the fire and wrapped her uncle in blankets.

"It's better to let him get warm slowly," Rage said when Logan suggested they put him in a hot bath.

"He has really good snow gear but it's still a miracle that he survived that many days lying on a ledge," Logan said, staring down at her uncle as he rested peacefully in the makeshift bed. "It looks like he only got a few cuts and bruises and that broken arm."

"We were lucky you were here," Rage said.

"I would never have managed to pull the both of you up without Billy," Logan said. "And I'm glad my fingers were so stiff, or else I might have let go of the rope altogether when he just appeared like that. I nearly died. One minute he's a dog going crazy barking and howling and the next minute he's helping me with the rope."

"I don't know how it happened," Billy said. "I just wanted so desperately to be able to help. To have the hands I needed. And when the rope slipped, it was like something in me burst and . . . well, I was the way I am now."

"Maybe *that* was what Bear meant about you being

able to change if you wanted to badly enough. Maybe she didn't just mean that you had to want it as you came through the night gate, but anytime. Do you think you can change back to a dog again?"

Billy nodded, a dreamy look on his face. "I think I can. It's like finding out how to make something work. I feel as though I only have to want to do something dog-gish badly enough and it'll happen."

"So I guess you're like a weredog," Logan said. Rage stared at him. "I mean, he can change shape, so he's like a werewolf, only he's a dog."

Rage started to laugh. It was a good laugh that filled her with warmth and relief. She was glad to be alive and safe and even happier to know that Billy would be able to talk to her anytime now.

She leaned back in her seat and stretched. "Now all I have to do is convince Uncle Samuel to see Mam."

"In a proper fairy tale, it would be worth a wish," Logan said.

They all laughed as, outside, the steady rain melted away the snow.

"So, are they still moving Mary to Leary?" Mrs. Johnson asked. She was slicing scones while Rage buttered them. Billy sat below the table watching them determinedly.

Rage smiled to see her uncle take a scone and pass it furtively under the table to Billy, who wolfed it down happily before reassuming his famished expression.

"They have to eventually because of the operations," Uncle Samuel said, "but given that she's turned the cor-ner, they're not going to do it until summer now. They say there's no need because she can improve here as well as there." He poured himself a cup of tea.

"That's wonderful news," Mrs. Johnson said. "I'm sure it did her a world of good to see you. I never did think those doctors were right in keeping you two apart."

"It was Rage who made the doctors change their minds," Uncle Samuel said. The look he gave Rage was so warm that she felt the blood rush to her cheeks. "She insisted I go, and she bullied those doctors so much that she cowed them into obedience."

"I didn't!" Rage gasped, laughing.

Her uncle chuckled. "Well, something like that. It's funny, though. The doctor might have been harder to convince, but it seems as if Mary had been dreaming about me. She was tossing and turning and calling my name in her sleep. I suppose seeing the real me was a bit of an anticlimax."

"Silly man," Mrs. Johnson chided. "There's such a difference in Mary since you've been visiting. It did my heart good to see her last weekend sitting up in her bed and smiling in her pretty pink nightie. And after such a bleak and awful winter! How lovely that the weather changed just as she was feeling better. As I said to Henry, there's something to be said for the healing power of sunshine and fresh air."

"How is he, anyway?" Uncle Samuel asked, sipping at his mug. He was holding it in his left hand because of his broken arm. Fortunately, the arm was on the mend, and his black eye and grazed cheek were barely noticeable now. Both Rage and Logan had made light of their rescue of him, and he had gone along with it. Privately, though, he had told them both that he knew they had saved his life, embarrassing all three of them dreadfully. Now they didn't mention it at all, but it was a lovely warmth among them.

"You know him," Mrs. Johnson said. "Grumbling and grouchy as a bear with a thorn in its paw because the doctors insist he's to stay in bed for another week. But we've decided to sell the farm come autumn. We'll stay on through the spring and summer and tidy the place up a bit for the sale. But it's more that we don't want our last memories here to be so dreary. And it's not just Mary who seems revitalized by the nice weather, is it?"

Rage and her uncle exchanged a grin.

"I do like that friend of yours, Rage. Logan, is it? He seems a nice young man."

"He's a good lad," Uncle Samuel said. "His parents are moving to Leary come the end of the school year, but in the meantime, Logan'll be up here a bit, doing some work about the place on weekends and school holidays."

"I heard he's involved with that acting troupe down at the school," Mrs. Johnson said.

"He's very good," Uncle Samuel said.

"And what about that other lad? You've hired him, too?"

Uncle Samuel was midway through a sip of tea. Rage held her breath as she waited for his answer.

"What other lad?" he asked at last, taking another scone and biting into it.

"You must have seen him on your land. A bit older than Logan. A handsome lad. Strong-looking, with a nice, sweet smile. Always goes about with bare feet, though," Mrs. Johnson said with faint concern. "Someone should warn him about snakes."

"I think a boy such as the one you describe would probably know what dangers there were, and how to deal with them," Uncle Samuel said. He was so casual that Rage studied him discreetly, wondering for the hundredth time if he remembered being rescued from the gorge by *two* boys.

"As for who he is, I couldn't say," her uncle continued. "But there are a lot of new families around here since the winter. I don't mind having a neighbor wander about on Winnoway. I never did much take to fences myself."

"Well, it is good to see new faces, and so many of them young," Mrs. Johnson said. "Oh, just look at that poor dog. He looks so hungry. Rage, give dear Billy a scone. One won't hurt."

Rage obeyed, trying not to laugh as Billy gulped down the scone. She looked up and caught her uncle suppressing a grin, and they both burst out laughing.

"Land sakes!" Mrs. Johnson said, putting her hands on her hips and looking from one of them to the other. "If you two aren't a pair!" She smiled. "It's about time there was laughter on Winnoway again."

Join Rage, Billy Thunder, and their

companions in the exciting conclusion

to the Gateway Trilogy:

THE FIRECAT

Also by Isobelle Carmody

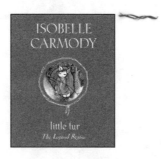

Discover the magic of Little Fur. She's
half elf, half troll, and about to embark
on a dangerous quest—into the world
of humans!

Coming October 2006
from Random House
Children's Books

ISOBELLE CARMODY

is the eldest of eight children. Her father died in a car crash when she was young, and she grew up telling stories to her seven brothers and sisters while her mother worked at night. She began the first book in the award-winning Obernewtyn Chronicles when she was fourteen, and won both the prestigious Children's Book Council of Australia Book of the Year Award and the coveted Children's Peace Literature Award for her fourth novel, *The Gathering*. She has also won numerous awards for her short stories. *Winter Door*, the sequel to *Night Gate*, is her sixteenth book, and the first installment of her highly anticipated Little Fur series hits U.S. shores in the fall of 2006. Isobelle lives with her daughter, Adelaide, and partner, Jan, a Czech poet and musician. They divide their time between homes on the Great Ocean Road in Australia and in Prague, Czech Republic.

ACKNOWLEDGMENTS

I would like to thank the two loves of my life, Jan and Adelaide, for forcing me to live outside of my head at least some of the time.

Thanks also to my editor, Mallory Loehr, who again reminds me that what is left unsaid is sometimes more powerful and beautiful than that which is said.